BLACK AUGUST

BLACK AUGUST

William Harrison

Texas Review Press
Huntsville, Texas

Copyright © 2011 by William Harrison
All rights reserved
Printed in the United States of America

FIRST EDITION, 2011
Requests for permission to reproduce material from this work should be sent to:

Permissions
Texas Review Press
English Department
Sam Houston State University
Huntsville, TX 77341-2146

This is a work of fiction and the characters bear no relationship to friends or casual associates of the author. Really. Honest. —William Harrison

Author painting by Merlee Harrison

Cover design by Nancy Parsons/Graphic Design Group

Library of Congress Cataloging-in-Publication Data

Harrison, William, 1933-
  Black August / William Harrison. -- 1st ed.
    p. cm.
  ISBN 978-1-933896-75-5 (pbk. : alk. paper)
  1. Family vacations--Italy--Como, Lake--Fiction. 2. Missing persons--Investigation--Italy--Como, Lake--Fiction. 3. Murder--Fiction. 4. Interpersonal relations--Fiction. 5. Americans--Italy--Como, Lake--Fiction. I. Title.
  PS3558.A672B57 2011
  813'.54--dc22
                                    2011023290

to MERLEE again, the lifelong partner

BLACK AUGUST

The Friends at the Lake

HARRY *the photographer and his wife* ZETA

LEO *the businessman and his wife* JACKIE

ROPER *the lawyer and his girlfriend* APRIL

WADE *the doctor and his wife* VAL *the novelist*

OLAN *the psychologist and his wife* ROBIN

KELTON *the journalist and his wife* ISABELLA *(deceased)*

ONE

*Here a new season is born. Here a new country
Is found deep in the soul of that Rome we loved
of old. We must welcome the new and live in
its joy and be gay; soon will the night come on.*
—attributed to Ovid

He and his friends were on Lake Como again.

They had been coming to the Villa Cappaletti for seven years. A few spats had occurred, but the six men remained compatible—five of the six played golf together—and they were all resilient, good humored, and with considerable energies as they drifted into their middle years.

Yet they really didn't know one another.

That summer Harry took an interest in their relationships as he hadn't done before. It was as if he waked up from a long sleep to study them. Men, he usually supposed, thought in terms of projects—with a few impersonal stories told to one another along the way—while women were more often the ones who analyzed interactions and fretted over who thought what about whom. But then Harry began to think about them, the men and women alike. Among other revelations he found that he didn't completely know his own wife.

All of this because of the August murders.

Each August for years and years, he learned during this visit, some child went missing around the lake. Sometimes the body was quickly discovered, sometimes not. These were little girls around eight or nine years old.

This was the summer Harry began to suspect that one of his own group might be responsible.

Although the great Hotel Villa d'Este remained one of Europe's exclusive retreats Lake Como was no longer particularly fashionable with the rich. An American actor bought a villa, yes, and the German industrialist still had a place, but in recent years visitors tended to be the newly wealthy Russians, a few Japanese, Brits or American tourists—solidly middle class with homes, cars, stock accounts and the common luxuries back home—who came for a week or so then drifted away. Harry's group spent a month at the villa near Lenno, a residence situated directly on the water. For all of them the lake kept its old world charm and although Leo Jones was renovating a stone ruin nearby—work on his villa dragged on and on—they continued to like the Villa Cappaletti well enough. The days there were interrupted by brief showers and afterward sunlight played on the cliffs opposite the villa—they loved the changing colors—and illumined the Alpine peaks to the north.
 Along a private footpath not far from the villa stood a ferry station where one could catch a water taxi or the public ferry over to Bellagio or travel up or down the elongated glacial lake to other small towns. While the wives usually shopped around the shore the men played golf or hiked. Each couple usually rented a car. Leo sometimes bought a used van and left it behind in September.
 Everybody took breakfast together on the open porch of the villa then came back each day to dress for dinner at the local restaurants. They sometimes split into smaller groups for the evening meal and during the days they drifted away for their private time. They observed an unspoken agreement that wives and husbands needed to be apart, that couples had to free themselves from other couples, and that they rhythms of separation had to be observed.

They came together originally because of Leo Jones and his money.

Some fifteen years ago in Texas he hit a winning streak that never stopped. Until then he had worked for a number of companies, but then his luck started: successful gambles, options that paid off, and the ride in tech stocks that took him into the hundred millions. His climb was so fast—and Leo never went to college—that he soon dropped all his barroom pals and looked for brighter ones: the psychologist, Olan, who helped him with the stress of it all; the photographer, Harry, who produced an especially flattering portrait; Kelton, the journalist who ran with the Texas Monthly crowd; his doctor, Wade, whose wife was a romance novelist and local celebrity; and Roper his lawyer. The men and their wives became his new intellectual guides.

Leo demanded conversations with real topics, information, good gossip, and entertainment value. He wanted wit, if possible, or lacking that at least some crude humor close to his own. Consciously or not, each member of the group competed to give him what he wanted.

In turn, they enjoyed the perks he provided.

His private jet took them to New York each year where he sometimes upgraded their commercial airline tickets. He rented the limos that delivered them from the Milan airport to the courtyard of Villa Cappaletti. He paid for the better wines at dinner. There were yachting excursions up to Gravedona at the north end of the lake and shopping safaris over to Lugano. He spoiled them with mud baths, massages, dozens of small gifts—matching umbrellas, bits of jewelry—and insisted that all of them were special and talented.

They accepted the perks and allowed themselves to fall under his spell, feeling that they were part of his run of luck and that he certainly deserved to have such friends. None of them—and they conceded this—could resist the flattery that such a wealthy man wanted them in his life.

"What's the specialty here?" someone asked when they visited a new restaurant one evening.

"I think the Heimlich Maneuver," answered Zeta, Harry's wife.

It became Leo's favorite line that season, often repeated.

He was a small man, paunchy, with tiny hands, yet one of the better golfers. He had an abundant mane of grey hair, always coiffed, and insisted on being tanned—dark and shiny, if possible—so that his hair and toothy smile showed up well in contrast.

Along his temples and at the top of his cheekbones the small red veins of a hard drinking man also announced themselves. His standard was Bushmill's Irish whisky, but he also ordered quantities of champagne—which he only sipped during the occasional toasts—and lots of red wine for the group, both French and the Lombard vintages, so that cases accumulated in everyone's room as the holiday went along.

Leo specialized in the inappropriate. Jackie, his wife, called him pottymouth and tried to ignore him when he called attention to some woman's cleavage, usually some stranger's at a nearby restaurant table. He also told too many anecdotes about a high school majorette or a secretary or some whore in his past, revealing more about his own embarrassing tastes than anyone in the group bothered to acknowledge. Yet he was never discourteous to wives in the group; he seemed to remain true to the sacraments of friendship.

As his success grew he moved upscale in wives. At first there was an Austin bargirl, then, briefly, a hairdresser who might have run a few hookers on the side. His third wife had divorced a Texas legislator and had turned to Leo in an act of vengeance, but she had a cocaine problem, so Leo became immune to criticism when he left her and also managed to emerge from the marriage with new political contacts.

Jackie, his current wife and the only one known to those who went to Italy in the late summers, was an amateur painter and a widow with money of her own. In her fifties she possessed a regal look and somehow gave Leo a more substantial bearing too.

A few years ago Leo became annoyed with Jackie when she set up her easel and watercolors on the cliffside near Bellagio, selling her works in competition with the artists across the lake before the *polizia* shut her down. She paid a modest fine for operating without a license, but told Leo that she sold three of her works and broke even on the money.

"You didn't need the money!" Leo pointed out.

"But I wanted to see if I could compete. And I sold three little paintings in less than four hours, so I found out!"

"You should've asked me about it!" he protested.

"Why? You would've said no."

"What was your big sale?"

"I sold one for a hundred dollars."

"That's not bad," he admitted, and the crisis passed.

Zeta, Harry's wife, tended to analyze Leo, observing that he made inappropriate sexual remarks because he felt inferior. "He might not even be sexual at all," she remarked. "All this Texas macho male bullshit. I've heard all of you indulge yourselves in it. Maybe Leo's really shy. I think Jackie just lets him carry on, but I believe she knows the truth about him: that he's really not a bit like that."

At his best Leo was entertaining, especially about his family and its physical characteristics. "Put bluntly," he announced, "we specialize in ugly. We're short legged, pot bellied, little red people with nice hair. Maybe too much hair. Our eyebrows get bushy and we have great clumps on our backs—even the women. None of my brothers can walk across a room without belching or farting. They even have ugly nicknames: Cooter, Horse, Nobby and Doodah. I've set them up in business dozens of times but they lose every penny. Doodah lives in four double-wide trailers lashed together out south of Lubbock and he's got a goddamned ocelot as a pet. Cooter spends all his time parachuting outta airplanes in Oklahoma. Owns airplanes, but just so he can jump outta the windows. Horse resides in a turf house—sorta dug out of this hill near Fort Stockton. Mama moves from one house to another and says she likes Horse's place best. Says it's cool as a root cellar."

Leo especially picked on his mother. She abused all her boys, he observed, for which she gained their curious devotion, and Leo's complaint with Olan, his therapist, was that Olan wouldn't listen to the entire list of offenses Leo wanted to recite regarding her.

Although he scarcely looked it Leo was light on his feet and liked to dance. He preferred Zeta—Harry's wife and by anyone's measure the best looking of the women—unless Roper brought along a particularly hot date as he liked to do. Leo's golf swing was oddly classic and sure: the slow backstroke, then the sharp forward lunge during which his paunch somehow got out of the way. His tee shots were around two hundred yards in length, but his play around the greens and his putting were solid. Harry once witnessed a drunken footrace between Leo and Roper, the much younger lawyer, and although Roper won—the distance seemed about sixty yards—it was only by a step. Afterward, too, Roper threw up while Leo, red in the face, had another Bushmill's.

As the group continued to travel together in August and to see each other occasionally in Austin—always at one of Leo's occasions—Olan began to annoy Leo more and more. The portly psychologist spoke slowly with a trace of a British accent and a slight lisp. It was part of an effort, Roper once noted, to somehow increase his authority. Olan also slapped his palms on tabletops by way of punctuating his speeches. At the end of his jokes he always slapped the table, rattling the silverware, as he led the laughter to his own punchlines.

His style and authority got Olan rough treatment within the group, but Olan knew it and often turned neatly on himself.

"Knowing nothing about human nature I became a psychologist!" he boomed out from time to time, always slapping the table when he said it.

But Leo increasingly didn't like the way Olan played golf—too slow—or how he gobbled his food—

too fast—or how his lectures and jokes went on and on.

"If he hits a ball in the woods he goes in there and kicks it around," Leo complained to Harry. "I'm gonna follow him in there someday and beat him to death with an eight iron."

"Yeah, choose the proper club, that's important," Harry managed.

Everyone tried for a merciless conversational style.

They valued wisecracks, put-downs, self-effacements, good gossip or any anecdote—brief, please—with a stinger at the end. The style wasn't always achieved, but it was Texas hardball: okay, talk on, but up yours if you expose any piety or earnestness.

As they sharpened their wits on each other somebody invariably got cut, but recovery was part of the game—all good comebacks had special merit—and they liked to imagine that nobody really kept score.

Val, their romance novelist, was the occasional mistress of the malapropism who, describing the group, once, to some fellow Texans, said, "We're a talking and thinking group of friends, you see. We talk together, then we go back to our separate rooms and try to think what we might've said."

She was also their mystic, prone to accept the fashions of the New Age, everything from crystals to the Tarot, so often stepped into their line of fire. "My visions," she once explained, "aren't exactly seen with my eyes." To which Olan replied, "Would those be visions you see with your ears, Val dear?" She was always ready to cast horoscopes, give palm readings or dabble in numerology.

During one of the group's first years at the lake Val had an affair with a local Italian, a minor bureaucrat who owned a rickety sailboat. Wade, her husband, wandered back to the hotel room unexpectedly to catch them in the act. After a shouting match in the corridor and on the carpeted stairwell during which many threats were exchanged,

Wade took her home. But they were back the next year with everything forgiven.

"Dalliance is just research," she explained to Kelton upon their return. "Everything I do, you realize, is for my art."

If Val took the greatest number of barbs from the group, she seemed to float above them, taking no offense, perhaps not detecting any.

"You're looking pale," Olan once said to her. "Is your mysticism getting worse?"

Val gave him only a smile. Meanwhile, her books—given loyal support by both Robin and Jackie—were considered unreadable by Zeta and the men. Zeta observed that Val started writing without knowing what she wanted to say and ended without knowing what she had written. The remark was occasionally repeated, but Val discounted Zeta.

"Zeta could possibly recognize a good book," Val countered, "but in my opinion she couldn't even write a bad one if she tried."

Val's mystic optimism sometimes gave the group a kindly view of her. Down at Bruno's restaurant one evening when everyone had moved beyond wine to cognac she stood at the stone wall above the lake with the spangled canopy of stars above her and said, "It's a benevolent universe, you know! Just look at this sky! The great wheel of the cosmos! You don't see the stars and planets bumping into each other out there, do you? No, everything is held in a beautiful balance by gravity and motion! Everything wants to survive—as we do, dear hearts—and to spin around in this wonderful dance! The universe wants us to thrive and receive its benevolence! And our molecules never die, not ever, just think! We are cosmic dust and our smallest particles live forever!"

"Personally," said Leo, "when I think about my smallest particle it depresses me."

The counterpunch got Leo a score and a few inebriated smiles.

Roper, Leo's energetic lawyer, brought his newest

girlfriend, April, that year. April was not yet forty. She had been an exotic dancer at the Yellow Rose in Austin, then met Roper at his health club where she currently worked as a trainer. She still had her figure and wore a bikini to sunbathe that first afternoon at the villa, giving the men an expectant throb.

She also had two children back in Austin and didn't understand why no one else in the group had any.

"Because we're selfish as hell," explained Jackie, waving a martini their first evening together in the lounge. "I explained to my first husband that I wanted to do my watercolors and travel around. No kids. Of course Leo and I married late, so it isn't an issue. But I think everyone here's the same without many regrets."

"None here," Val agreed.

"Zeta might have a few," Robin observed.

"Maybe I used to," Zeta said. "But now I'm in my forties and that's that."

Harry reached over and touched her hand.

It took a few weeks for them to tell April that they all supported charities, gave to universities, served on civic committees and considered themselves good people. Also, although no one said so, they assumed that April had lived an unplanned existence: a good body, strip clubs, cigarettes, the wrong men, kids, a trailer park world, and luck that would soon probably run out entirely. Roper, they knew well enough, would love her and leave her, for he was already a man of two divorces and numerous girlfriends—many of whom had accompanied him to the lake in the last years. April wasn't even the youngest or prettiest, but she did possess that body—long-legged, long-waisted with large round breasts, undoubtedly enhanced—that turned heads, male and female alike, in every room she entered.

That evening as they undressed for bed Zeta sat at the dressing table removing her makeup. Harry strolled around the room, enjoying the moonlit lake from the open doors to the balcony, and speculating about Leo's project, the Villa Franscesca.

"I'll bet it doesn't have six bedrooms," he said.

"But it's huge. It must have a dozen."

"I guess we'll know soon enough. Did you hear Leo invite us for another look?"

"I'm tired of walking around on loose boards telling Leo it's going to be wonderful, aren't you?"

"Yeah, but I'm curious. At least the roof's finished and they're at work on the interior. But, seriously, I'll bet there are only four or five bedrooms."

"Why do you think so?"

"Because of Olan. My hunch is that Leo wants to leave him out."

"Olan and Robin? Leo likes them, doesn't he? Besides, he's still seeing Olan for counseling. For that matter you're not doing more photography for Leo, so maybe he intends to leave us out. Do you think this lipstick is too red?"

"I don't discuss cosmetics. But I do think Leo wants to end it with Olan. And I'm sure he doesn't do therapy with him anymore."

"If you don't discuss lipstick, then you don't get to taste it."

"I will say that sitting there in your panties you look very tasty."

"Is my shape as good as April's?"

"You have a perfectly wonderful shape for a woman of your advanced years."

"Bastard," she said, and she rubbed off the lipstick that she knew was far too red.

Roper, their tireless athlete, usually jogged uphill into the center of Lenno to pick up the *Herald Tribune*s every morning before breakfast, but he and April had gone to a disco and planned to sleep late, so he asked Harry to do the morning errand. Harry didn't mind an early walk, so that's how he found the doll on the private path. It lay just beside the path in the damp grass. He saw it on his way up to the newsstand, but didn't pick it up until he came back with the papers.

The private path from the villa kept to the

lakeshore, passing the ferry station. It was neatly laid out with crushed rock and planted with lilac and roses along its edges until one crossed a small iron bridge and climbed above the lakeside promenade and entered a canopy of candelabra trees. Harry enjoyed the views at the top of the path: boats pulled up into the shale, stone walls covered with bougainvillea, the ochre house out there on the promontory.

The final uphill walk took Harry into the town square where a monument to those who had fallen in two world wars occupied its place in the center of the cobblestones. He bought six newspapers in an awkward flurry of bad Italian, paying in Euros.

On the way back he stepped off the path and scooped up the cloth doll.

He arrived on the terrace as Olan and Kelton came down for coffee, then went to the office where he presented the doll to Madame Cappeletti. Seeing it, she registered some mild alarm, but he didn't ask why. The madame was always slightly theatrical and his mission was to get the newspapers into the hands of his friends, so he placed the doll on the counter, turned, and left.

Val and Jackie now appeared on the terrace, placing their chairs at their respective tables to give themselves the best views of the placid lake. Everyone eagerly took a newspaper—one copy for each married couple—and began reading. Kelton, their news junkie, began scanning headlines in his personal copy without so much as a good morning Harry or thanks for the delivery.

Back home in Austin Kelton and Harry were best friends, closer to one another than any other combination of acquaintances in the group. Kelton's wife, Isabella, had died of breast cancer just after the last visit to Lake Como. On the night she died Zeta had held her hand at the bedside. As couples they had enjoyed years together at movies, usually stopping for dinner afterwards at Jeffrey's or Sullivan's or some barbeque shanty. Like Harry, Kelton was a bogey golfer—usually at some public course—and they drank beer regularly at The Dog and Duck, their favorite tavern.

Isabella's death had sent Zeta into introspection and depression. "When she died she let out this long sigh," Zeta later told Harry. "It went on and on as the breath left her body, as if she took a long time to expel herself from that little creature she had become." In the weeks following the death Zeta once again fretted that she had no children, that she had no real professional identity, and that she and Harry weren't doing so well. He tried to cheer and understand her. Kelton often visited in the evenings and Harry felt like a discussion leader, guiding them through topics as they drank too much. After the funeral they saw little of the others in the group: one dinner at Olan's and Robin's house, a book signing party for Val, a day on the lake with Leo and fifty others, nothing from Roper. They were a morbid trio and knew it. But as summer arrived Kelton said, yes, he figured he'd definitely go back to Italy with everybody, and the slow healing started. Although part of Leo's group—whatever its energies and definitions—Harry, Zeta, Kelton and Isabella had always defined themselves as separate from the others. They didn't bother to examine it, yet they knew it to be true. By way of a small example, like Harry and Zeta, Kelton and Isabella often touched or nuzzled each other. The others in the group never indulged except for Roper and his girlfriends—and this often seemed like public foreplay, a vulgar activity aimed at Leo's amusement.

Kelton, his reading glasses on his nose that morning, studied his copy of *The Herald Tribune*, going over the agate print in the box scores and stock quotes.

Harry temporarily sat with Jackie and Val, leaving Olan with his own headlines. Once again Olan had shaved himself badly, leaving patches of beard on his neck and chin and giving himself a cut that required tissue paper.

"Remember when we used to jump in the hot tubs?" said Jackie to Harry. "Why don't we strip down and go for it these days? Remember how much fun it was?"

"We're all getting fat," Val answered.

"We shouldn't become ashamed of our figures," Jackie protested. "I'm not. I'd still like to pose for you, Harry, and you used to say you wanted me to, but we never actually got around to it."

"I could set up the camera in the garden this afternoon," he agreed.

"You don't mean it. But, really, just because we're all into middle age shouldn't keep us from getting naked."

"Only Zeta still has a great figure," Val put in, folding her newspaper and peering at an inside page.

"There's April," Jackie said. "Every man here'd like to get a look at the full April. I know Leo would. He almost fell off our balcony yesterday afternoon when she stretched out in her bikini."

"She left very little to the imagination," said Val from behind her newsprint.

Olan grunted his approval of April from six feet away.

"Well, aren't you old eagle ears?" Val asked him, and for a moment nobody commented or laughed. "What?" Val wanted to know, suspecting a blunder.

"Eagle ears?" Kelton called to her, smiling. She didn't respond, concentrating instead on a movie review.

When Zeta joined them nudity was still the topic.

"Tell them what you packed for the trip," she urged Harry, taking a seat.

"Oh, what?" Jackie guessed. "Special body oils?"

"No, a dozen of those little pencil flashlights. Tell them, Harry, what you mean to do with them."

"It's an artistic secret," he replied.

"He wants me to pose for him," Zeta revealed. "I suppose with little flashlights dangling off me. Tell them what else you packed."

"You tell them."

"Talcum powder."

Everybody groaned with derision except for Kelton, lost in the news, and Olan especially perked up as April arrived with Roper. She wore a white sundress cut low. Roper gave the morning sunlight a series of painful blinks. Leo, already dressed and ready in a golden golf shirt, and a crumpled Wade, looking less like a doctor than an aging invalid in his worn running suit, soon arrived, too, so everyone started on the fruit as it was served. Yet the topic remained.

"What about you, April?" Zeta asked. "You wouldn't mind posing for Harry wearing a few flashlights, would you?"

"April only stripped for a coupla years," Roper put in, defensively. "And all that's well in the past."

"I modeled at the university once," April admitted brightly. "You know, figure drawing. Very professional. The students were so polite they wouldn't make eye contact. But the pay was miserable. I wanted to take a couple of classes, but the modeling fees wouldn't cover tuition."

Her good natured frankness made Harry feel that she wouldn't mind modeling, but he didn't care to follow his wife's offhand suggestion. Better not touch that, he warned himself, and he turned to the sports page. By this time everyone began pairing off as couples: Olan with his shy Robin, Val with Wade, Roper with April, Leo with Jackie, Harry with Zeta, and Kelton alone, the morning ritual, spouses aligned, for the benefit of the two maids who spoke no English, didn't know who went with whom, and had been ordered by Madame Cappeletti to keep the checks separated.

Leo soon demanded an agenda: golf arranged, an evening restaurant confirmed, and a visit scheduled for his villa-in-progress. As breakfast went on he pointed out that the tee time for golf approached.

"I'm off to Bellagio!" Val announced, and Robin quickly asked permission to go with her. Val liked sitting in some restaurant overlooking the lake with an unlit cigarillo in her teeth, sipping a glass of wine and composing with her fat Mont Blanc pen. Robin liked to sit across the table working crossword puzzles, reading, or jotting down entries in her own thin journal. She was Val's loyal reader and often defended the genre of the romance novel against the somewhat sly attacks of Zeta who preferred mainstream literary authors. Robin, who always seemed to wear something trimmed in lace as she did this morning, also needed Olan's permission to go off with Val. When he played golf or went on another of his solo hikes he wanted her back at the villa drawing his bath at his return, but today he grunted, yes, okay.

Kelton again found something to read aloud from the newspaper. A boy in California had found a cloth bag filled with money that had fallen out of an armored truck. Sometimes the group talked over Kelton when he read aloud, but since Isabella's death they smiled and indulged him.

Meanwhile, Wade went into his familiar arguments against golf: boring, too many rules, a combination of light exercise and an Easter egg hunt. Once again he announced that he meant to keep his daily regimen hiking the trails around the lake—with or without Olan, Roper, or others who sometimes joined him. He went on. Golf doesn't provide the body a sustained workout, he lectured, but Zeta interrupted him.

"When you speak as a doctor, Wade, your voice tends to get deeper."

"In fact, you sound like Olan," Leo added, and these lines got the morning laugh.

The men played at the course above Menaggio that day: each fairway a curved bowl of bright grass between hilly slopes with heavy brush that claimed a number of errant golf balls. The par threes, oddly, all required uphill shots and only the last hole –a short par four—encouraged players to return to the course again. They sat in the clubhouse afterward drinking too much and observing that the building—lots of glass and stone—would look at home in the Texas hill country.

Leo commented on the falling market and mentioned his villa—they all hoped he'd say what the renovation had cost so far—then he began to repeat his familiar distaste for Wall Street. Harry felt uncomfortable talking about money because he and Zeta had so little. At such times—Leo idly talking, Harry keeping silent—he knew that he was an outsider and wondered how Leo even thought to include him in the group. After all, he owned a storefront camera shop just off a main thoroughfare in Austin, a business that could be sized up at a single glance: middlebrow, nothing fancy. Zeta wore her outfits longer than the other wives and sported gold, not diamonds. Did Leo like Harry precisely because Harry had never been a success? No, it was Zeta, not himself. Much more than the golf, a bit of humor, and all the rounds of drinks between Harry and Leo it was Zeta who kept his wealthy friend interested and in his gut Harry knew this well enough.

Before they finished their drinks in the clubhouse Leo presented each of them with customized bank cards.

"Bank of Milan," he told them proudly. "This'll get you some ATM privileges and some Italian ID. Put 'em in your wallets."

"So now we're officially on your company payroll?" Olan asked with a laugh.

"Hell no, it don't mean that. You can open your own damn accounts if you want to, but I'm not takin' you to raise. There, Harry, you may never use it, but it might come in handy."

Everybody remarked on this new generosity, then drove down from the golf course in the big rented sports vehicle with Harry sitting up front with Leo. With two beers and a whiskey inside him Harry fixed his eyes on the melancholy lake as they descended. A fading light gave the scene a soft blue glow and he thought how this place like Italy itself resisted all invaders by seducing them, lulling them with food and drink and good weather. The invaders always charged in, Harry reflected, Visigoths then, tourists now, and succumbed to a land that melted their aggressions, drugged them with warmth and pulled them under.

"Maybe I'll buy this machine for the villa when we go home this year," Leo said in his loudest voice.

"The Cappeletti folks'll go crazy if I do. Roper, you think it'd be too big a splurge?"

"God knows, don't ask me," his lawyer replied.

In the past, Harry knew, Leo had donated older used vans to a convent school, to a local soccer team, and to the fire brigade.

"That'd be a nice gesture!" Olan shouted from the back seat. His generosity with Leo's money got a chuckle from Kelton who otherwise kept silent.

Back at the villa Madame Cappeletti came out of her office and called Harry aside as the men trudged in.

The *Investigatore*," she said in a hoarse whisper, drawing him into a corner beside a potted plant. "For you."

"Who?" Harry asked, and he saw, standing just inside the office door, a small man smoking a cigarette and littering himself with its ashes. As Madame Cappeletti ushered Harry in, the man turned.

"*Investigatore*," the old woman repeated. "Police."

On the counter, now sealed in a plastic bag, was the rag doll Harry had found on the path.

Terminella and Harry went into the empty library.

"If you don't mind," the detective began, "I would like you to show me exactly on the path where you found the doll, but first, please, I am having one or two questions."

"Sure," Harry said, puzzled. "What's the matter?"

"Perhaps you are not knowing about our murders of little girls?"

"No," Harry said, then caught himself. "Wait, I remember Madame Cappeletti telling me about such a murder, but that was—what?—maybe two years ago. I'm sorry to hear all this. Awful. Little girls, you say?"

"How many years are you and your friends coming to the lake?"

"Hm, seven years."

"And each year you and all of these same friends come together?"

"Every August. We stay here at the villa and occasionally a few of us stay into September. And there have been several murders?"

"You don't read our newspapers?"

"Actually, no. None of us read or speak your language. We just read the American and European papers in English."

"And so you don't know Italian? None of you?"

"It's embarrassing," Harry admitted. "We read the menus in restaurants and know a few phrases."

The little detective strolled around the study while lighting another cigarette. He was an uncommonly careless smoker, dropping ashes everywhere. An odd thought crossed Harry's mind: like an animal leaving a trail or marking its territory. The detective's grey suit wore a sprinkle of white ash as he paused at the big reading table and placed his burnt-out match on its edge. The bookshelves contained used volumes left by former residents, mostly American bestsellers, a few recognizable as some of Zeta's, and a complete set of Val's romance novels, still new and probably unopened. One couldn't see the lake from this room—just a narrow walled garden—and the old books gave off a musty odor.

Terminella blew a perfect smoke ring and admired it.

"If you do not know the language of a place it must be—how do you say?"

"Limiting," said Harry, helping out.

"Yes, such a disadvantage. Do you even know about the history of the lake?"

"Some of us have read histories written in English."

"Ah, yes, and you play golf?"

"We played today," said Harry, and in his embarrassment he felt the detective's dislike of the group and seemed to hear it clearly in his questions.

"We are having eleven little girls missing or found murdered in these last seven years," said the detective. "Our newspapers call this *Agosto Nero*. Black August. Such a shameful thing. It happens this month only. We are thinking, very well, this is perhaps some tourist who comes on holiday. A demon who comes only in this season. And the doll you found this morning belongs to a little girl gone missing. When Madame Cappaletti phones I hurry here to pick up the doll. The parents see it at noon, then I come back to see you now."

"This is terrible," Harry said. "I'm so sorry. I didn't know. Would you like me to show you exactly where I found it?"

His sincere anguish obviously softened the detective, who nodded and said gently, "Please, yes, we can go now."

They walked beyond the villa's terrace and down the path of crushed rock curving through the garden, passing beneath a stone archway and continuing toward the ferry station. Terminella lit another cigarette on the way.

"How many in your group at the villa?" he asked.

"Six couples. Except this last year my friend's wife died, so now there's eleven of us. Are we suspects?"

"Not so much, I think, but I would like you to tell me about your friends. Each one. You are all wealthy Americans?"

"Only one could be called really wealthy. We're all okay financially."

"And you come here for what reason? Just the holiday?"

"We all know each other in Texas. And, yeah, we come here for the restaurants and the beauty of the lake and—well, the solitude."

"And every day the men play golf and the women visit the shops?"

"About that, yes. We usually have several cars. Some of my friends go hiking instead of playing golf. The friend whose wife died rents a Vespa every year. You're suspicious of us, aren't you?"

"Not so much because in all these years we are having no clue like this doll. It is very peculiar, so I am thinking, no, this demon would not leave such a doll near his villa. Understand?"

"Yeah, I follow. Here's the spot. There, just off the path."

"This was early morning, correct?"

"The newsstand in Lenno opens just before seven. My friend Roper usually jogs into town for the American papers, but I agreed to go today. I saw it, oh, around half past six this morning and picked it up on my way back."

"Last night comes the heavy dew," said the detective, inhaling his cigarette with great satisfaction as ashes fell on his shoes. "The doll, it was wet only on the bottom side, so I believe it was placed here this morning. Which is curious also."

"Why is that?"

"Because the first ferry arrives at seven."

"Yes, and so?"

"You are walking to Lenno before the first ferry. Did you see someone waiting at the shelter?"

"I didn't look. There could've been one or more persons waiting for the ferry, but the shelter is some distance away. I really didn't pay attention."

"Because you are walking and thinking of newspapers?"

"Yeah, and just enjoying the morning."

"Suppose my demon this morning comes to the ferry," the detective speculated. "Yet he goes up the pathway toward the villa and leaves the doll. Why leave such a clue? *Eccezionale*. Remarkable."

Harry experienced a bump of pride that Detective Terminella shared all this with him, a tingle. He had secret information to share, but also a stirring of his own suspicions and curiosities. Terminella stepped away from the path and stood on the spot where Harry had found the doll, keeping his silence and thinking. Then he flipped his cigarette butt into the lake.

They strolled back toward the villa.

"If my demon stays at your villa," said the detective, "he would not make such a blunder. Unless he desires to be caught. But I don't think so. This person we seek is a secret hunter. This man—and, yes, certainly a man—can look at a group of children on a playground and will know the one child who is weak or susceptible. He will see that one child like the lion who sees the wounded calf in the herd. He will know. His hunting skills are very great and as the years pass, I believe, he becomes an even better hunter, very clever."

"In the month of August there is no school," said Harry, thinking of playgrounds.

"Yes, true, you are intelligent to think this. But there are places children go. A little park in the mountains on the way to Lugano. Many children once went there to play, but no more. The parents are now careful and watching. Two girls in different years go missing from this same little park."

They stood for a moment beside a stone bench while Terminella lit yet another cigarette. Harry felt both flattered and excited. *Intelligent to think this.* The detective had said that.

"Eleven children," said Harry with a sigh. "All of them local girls?"

"Oh no, three were tourist children. And they have disappeared from Como, from Erba, and from the hills around Porlezza. Let me think. One from Menaggio. Everywhere around the lake. This killer is very mobile. I could tell you many strange things."

"And you believe it's some outsider?"

"My theory, not everyone's. Otherwise I am thinking why does this madness come only in this one month? Does some local man have his appetite only in *Agosto*?

Mothers now send their children away. Some fathers—we have very much trouble in this way—stand watch with their weapons. They send their daughters outside to play and hold the rifle. Very desperate and crazy, this whole region. Big headlines in the newspapers, but you say you have never seen them?"

"No, and I feel stupid."

The detective's cell phone rang and he answered it while Harry listened, understanding nothing. A word stood out: *omocidio.* Was that possibly the word for homicide? When he finished the phone conversation Terminella crushed out his cigarette in the gravel.

"My wife," he explained, smiling. "I should tell you I have two daughters—eleven and nine years of age. So these killings—well, I have been angry for many years. Frightened and angry, do you understand?"

"Absolutely. Hearing about all this makes me angry, too."

"Good. You should be. Everyone should be. Do you know why I am seeing the doll today? I am one of many on this case, but my English is better than others. But, also, I am the angry cop. I will go anywhere quickly. I have seen the bodies of the children and I have imagination: those could have been the bodies of my girls."

They walked to the villa. On the balcony of the second floor Zeta stood watching their approach.

"Up there," Harry said. "That's my wife." He raised his chin toward her and she smiled down at them.

"Ah, a beautiful woman. You have no children?"

"No children, but a long marriage. By the way, just a thought: couldn't you take DNA samples from all of us at the villa? Surely you have a DNA profile of your murderer?"

"Perhaps we could borrow the technology, but we don't have it. I could argue that we should test everyone at the villa and everyone in Lenno, but it is expensive and many of my colleagues would argue against it. And we don't have a suspect, do we? The doll was found here, but this is also at the ferry station. No, the DNA test, perhaps, is for absolute confirmation when we have this demon."

"One more thing," Harry said. "What do I tell my friends about this conversation we're having?"

"What you wish. Everyone should know about these crimes. And I'm sure your friends are innocent, but this doll—as I say, a curious surprise."

They climbed the stone stairway onto the empty terrace. The group would show up later for cocktails before dinner.

"I was wondering what is your business in Texas," the detective asked.

"I'm a photographer. I'm happy to tell you about

the others, too, but I'm sure they'll agree to tell you themselves."

"A photographer? Portraits?"

"I wanted to be an artist, but, yes, portraits. Children and families, that sort of thing."

"Would anyone in your group be a *dottore*?"

"A doctor? Yeah, that would be Wade. Why do you ask?"

"So many doctors travel here. Many nationalities. Many doctors. You will tell me a little more about your friends another time, I hope, but for now *buona sera*. And, please, don't trouble yourself too much or do anything extraordinary. You have been very helpful."

"What sort of extraordinary thing would I do?"

"Like the fathers standing guard over their daughters with rifles. They could shoot someone innocent, yes? This is a distressing business and we should all remain calm and rational. So please."

They shook hands and Harry went upstairs.

"Who was that?" Zeta wanted to know.

He told Zeta about the doll and about all the horrible murders he had learned about, leaving out some of the detective's questions and his own wild conjectures. As he related all this he felt excited to have more information than any of their friends and a somewhat special role. Perhaps fate had given him an insider's destiny. He resisted saying as much to Zeta, yet the thought tugged at him.

She recalled seeing the big tabloid headlines, photos of the children, and the news stories they couldn't read.

"How stupid of us," she said, and Harry agreed. They owned a big study guide of the Italian language complete with cassettes—and had meant to study—but actually just carried little phrase books in their luggage.

That night they went to La Valuu, their favorite restaurant, and sat in candlelight with the group beneath wide stone arches overlooking the lake. Lights came on slowly from both shores to accent the beauty of the evening. Harry and Zeta shared a serving of fresh asparagus covered with newly grated parmesan. The two brothers who served them—one with a bad leg and limp—presented everyone with the favored local wine. The men wore blazers and the women looked radiant.

Harry told about his interview with the *investigatore,* leaving out this or that, and then murder became a topic rather than a matter of concern.

Wade told about their cruise out of Barbados and his conversation with the ship's captain. "Three years ago in the spring, wasn't it? Val went to our stateroom, but I strolled up to the bridge with my cigar and found the captain smoking his pipe at the rail. Not a moon in sight. We talked about navigating by the stars—which he claimed he could easily do—and I asked if he'd ever had a passenger fall overboard. He said no, never happened, but damned bad luck if it did. They had themselves a drill, he told me, and rigged up a huge floating dummy that they tossed over the side in broad daylight. Took them twenty minutes to come about, and they had tenders in the water long before that, but they never saw the dummy again. So they painted an eleven foot door. Painted it orange and tossed it over for another daylight drill, but never saw the door again, either. At night, the captain said, forget it. A man could commit the perfect murder: toss his wife over the side, say, then go have a nightcap and a good night's sleep. The propellers would probably pull her under and chew her up or the sharks would get her. Along about lunchtime the next day the man tells the crew he can't find his wife anywhere."

They talked about serial killers, real and fictional. Bundy. Hannibal Lecter. That Russian. Gacy in Chicago.

Kelton and Isabella lived in Spain for more than a year early in their marriage and he remembered the perfect crime there. "Poisoning," he said. "Because of the Catholic burial laws. No embalming, you know, so a body had to be in the ground in twenty-four hours. An autopsy was also forbidden by law. The

Catholic thing again: desecration of the corpse and all that. So you simply dose up your enemy or your business partner or your annoying neighbor. Give them something that doesn't turn them a suspicious purple, naturally, and there is never a police follow up."

"Pass the arsenic," said Roper, and that got a laugh, yet everyone agreed that murder was really in bad taste and rude.

"Is that still the law in Spain?" Jackie wanted to know.

"Don't even think about it," Leo snapped, and his retort received by far the biggest laughter so he was obviously pleased with himself.

They talked about Agatha Christie, Sherlock Holmes, and Harry's favorite detective writer Robert B. Parker. Robin ventured that she liked Mary Higgins Clark, but glanced at both Val and Zeta hoping they'd approve.

They wondered aloud if anyone at the table had ever considered murder.

"Only second degree," Olan boomed out. "I always want to get the guy who cuts me off on the freeway!" He slapped the table and laughed at his contribution.

"I had this geek uncle who beat his wife and children," Roper admitted. "Broke the kid's arm. A bad drunk. Borrowed money from my dad and never paid it back. He asked me to keep him out of jail, once, and I told him I didn't practice that kind of law. I wanted 'em to put him away for good, but he got off. Also, he swiped an antique paperweight off my desk that time he came to see me. So I wanted to hire somebody to make him disappear and I asked Leo what the job might cost. Remember, Leo?"

Leo nodded. "Sure. This was four or five years ago, right?"

"Correct. I was serious enough to be thinking how much it might cost me. The figure I had in mind was maybe ten thousand dollars, something like that, and I was also worrying about blackmail if I did find some goon to do the dirty work. Anyway, I figured Leo might know somebody."

"Recall what I told you?" Leo put in.

"You told me five hundred bucks cash."

"That's what I said," Leo confirmed. "I told you I know two guys in Oklahoma who enjoy their work. Oil rig roughnecks in the daytime and nobody wants to think about how they dispose of a body."

"Five hundred dollars," said Roper, smiling. "I had that much in my wallet."

"Whatever happened to this uncle?" Kelton wanted to know.

"Heart attack got him. He was a big boozer and smoker, so I didn't have to put out a contract on him after all."

They soon moved back to the somber subject of the little girls at the lake. The topic became homicide and sexual pathology. All serial killers, Wade noted, seem to have twisted sexual proclivities.

"True," Olan agreed. "Sex is the terrible wild card. The brain is sometimes a rational instrument, but it can't deal with a powerful sexual urge."

"That's your professional opinion, is it?" Leo asked, and the question had some bite to it.

Val's opinion was that testerone was a lethal poison.

"That's testosterone," Jackie corrected her with a sympathetic smile.

As he continued to listen to the banter Harry tried to account for everyone's whereabouts in these first days. The missing girl had been gone three days. Where were we that first day? The men—except for Wade who didn't play—had been to the golf course twice, yet each one had later gone his separate way. Kelton had quickly rented a Vespa and tooled off somewhere. Wade went hiking, driving out to some of his favorite trails. Olan also said he had gone hiking. Wasn't Robin going with him? Roper had gone jogging one afternoon—yes, that first full day—but had spent the rest of his time with April or playing golf. Leo had driven to Lugano, placing him near the playground in the mountains mentioned by Terminella. But wait. Was the missing girl with the cloth doll from that area or not?

They finally rose from the table. Several from the group wandered across the lawn to gaze at the lake surrounded by lights, yet Harry's thoughts continued to ambush him. How could it possibly be someone from our group, he asked himself, when a little girl had gone missing on the day of our arrival? We were checking in at the villa, getting our bags unpacked. Didn't a killer have to stalk his victims? How could one of us strike so quickly without the slightest preparation? Or perhaps somebody knew exactly where the little victim would be.

Terminella had also asked as casually as possible if there was a doctor in the group, so Harry began to think about Wade. Not a golfer, hiking every day, out and about.

When he arrived at the edge of the lawn Zeta and Kelton stood close together at the low stone wall. For a moment Harry thought they might be at pause before a kiss: their faces close, Zeta's head slightly tilted, Kelton whispering something.

"Hello," he said, breaking their spell.

Zeta reached out for his hand and brought him in close.

"How drunk are you, sweetheart?" she asked. "We're tipsy. Can you drive us back to the villa?"

"No problem," he said, wanting to know what they whispered about.

"Maybe you could bring the car up?" she asked. "I don't want to stagger down those uneven steps in the dark."

"Sure," he agreed. "I'll get our van now."

He somehow didn't want to leave them together, but committed himself. Now they can finish their whispering, he told himself, turning. He had never felt jealous of Zeta—especially with his old friend Kelton—but now he experienced a stab of uncertainty.

She smiled and gave his fingers a reassuring squeeze, dismissing him.

He crossed the lawn, said good night to the brothers who served them dinner, then started downhill toward the parking spaces. Others went before him—he could hear Leo's big vehicle starting up—as April fell in beside him, taking his arm to steady herself.

"Lemme hold on," she said. "It's these damn high heels."

She seemed to be wearing cleavage surrounded by a black sheath and her perfume filled the night air.

"Be my guest," Harry managed as she gripped his arm with both hands.

"You're really upset by the little girls who've disappeared," she said.

"Isn't everyone?"

"I guess so, but you really care. It showed."

They made three or four steps in silence.

"If you want me to pose for you," she said suddenly, "then I will."

"That would be great," he allowed, and struggled for something more to add.

"Your wife suggested it, you know. That I pose for you? But Roper, bless him, does want to watch if we do it. So do you set up at the villa?"

"No, I'll have to make arrangements."

"Strictly professional," she made clear.

"Absolutely."

They went down to the car park and waited for Roper. Wade and Val stood beneath a gnarled pine tree as the conversation about sex and violence obviously resumed. Wade was talking about Hitler and the biography he had recently finished.

Sexless, you know, or almost so. Some reports say he never actually slept with Eva Braun. He might've actually murdered another mistress of his, that young woman who came before Eva Braun—what's her name? Anyway, he was probably a sexual psychopath and definitely a monster."

As Wade talked a fine mist descended, then turned into a drizzle. Everyone took refuge underneath the pine branches as Harry made his excuses, left April, and slid into his rented van. He drove slowly back uphill, backed into the narrow turnaround at the front door, then waited. Zeta and Kelton didn't arrive, so he sat there trying to sort things out.

Maybe Zeta is still trying to console Kelton, he decided, but how much consolation is she offering? She'll probably tell me tonight at bedtime what they've been talking about. And what was that perfume April wore? Was it Chanel?

Kelton took pride in his humility—a bit of a contradiction, Harry always thought—and regarded himself as a listener, an intimate, a reporter, and never truly a principal player.

When everyone else tired of a topic Kelton always asked one more question, requesting an expansion of some thought, wanting another detail, extending the subject. He was also the group stoic: detached and cautious.

He played chess with Harry, always winning.

He often spoke with his hand over his mouth, mumbling.

He loved gossip and considered it one of the better sources in all stories. "As they say in Hollywood," he often remarked, "all rumors are true."

Although he was only an average golfer—a fourteen handicap—he was a stickler for the rules.

He tended toward hypochondria and suffered fashionable ailments. Sometimes he wore light cotton gloves—no, not arthritic fingers, he explained, just poor circulation. A patron's at Bruno's one evening took him for a waiter because of those gloves. Although allergic to almost everything in the Italian countryside he insisted on renting a Vespa every year and put-putting around the lake in open air.

He was also the dear friend who phoned to ask about one's work, about health and welfare, and about promising movies in town or items in the morning news.

When Kelton told stories they were usually about Africa where he spent twenty years as a reporter before moving to London. In his quiet way he once confided, "Harry, I get terribly skeptical of my skepticism. At heart I want to believe everything no matter how outlandish. In Africa, once, I might've seen a man raised from the dead, but I couldn't allow myself to believe it. I rejected it and told myself, no, he just sobered up quickly. But who knows? Maybe he was actually dead and I witnessed a miracle, but I couldn't accept it."

Kelton also had a talent for listening to women. He seemed to love the cadences of their voices as if he heard a secret language beyond whatever they talked about. He always leaned in close, nodding as they spoke.

"Most men can only listen to a woman for thirty seconds at best," he claimed. "After thirty seconds a man's eyes tend to wander. He peeks at his watch or glances at nearby television screens or gazes out the window. Women don't get a man's full attention all that much, Harry, and they appreciate it when they do. Hear what I'm saying? At the moment, Harry, I get the feeling you're really not listening to me."

"I must've had a whole bottle of wine myself," Zeta said that evening, and she turned over in bed, pulling the covers over her head in a way that made clear no more talking was in order.

"Good night, honey," said Harry, and no answer came back.

So he didn't know what she was whispering about to Kelton. As a result a bothersome insomnia set in. After an hour he stood on the balcony outside their room, a blanket pulled around him, gazing at the low clouds moving over the lake. The rain had settled into an evening mist and the scene before him was a beatitude of nature unlike the harsh Texas landscapes that had been his life and curse. He began thinking of the girls of Texas—both Zeta and April pulsed in his head—and all the exciting summers long ago: nights when he tried to get his eager hands into the peninsulas, the forbidden straits, the deepest valleys of their bodies. A young sexual explorer in those days: there, let me in, I'm a ship at full sail, my rigging is on fire, show me all your latitudes.

At the University he fell in with the arty

crowd. His photos were always of girls and his most pretentious pals called them nudes, wanting to see what he had in his darkroom, and he moved around the campus like a celebrity. His names were Harry, Hap, Cocky, darling, honey, and the photographs went on and on: girls whose gazes were as pensive as poets and others, wide open and brazen, and some that might have resulted in his arrest.

For a short while he had mobility and a career filled with assignments. A small publishing house in Houston brought out a fancy volume and he went to New York where he told an interviewer, wisecracking, "Lyric tits and butts, that's the message," and later he regretted saying it. He was part of a group of young Texas cockbirds who with their girlfriends gave their inebriated grins to Lincoln Center, the bistros in the Village and the midtown gallery scene. He had fun, made very little money, and his artistic reputation, never all that substantial, swirled high for a year, then quickly spiraled down into portrait work. One girlfriend, a model, introduced him to a covey of clients who paid high prices. Soon the arty stuff faded away. Women, though, remained a kind of currency. He picked them up with practiced ease—the camera, at least for a session or two came between them—then he discharged them when the cycle ended, seeing to it that his moves were quicker. If they hated him afterward, okay, it was his ruthlessness winning out, not theirs.

He moved back to Austin where life became linear, a series of projects, temporary alignments, free lance portraits, and always copulation or one of the several good substitutes. There was nothing pathological to it, he insisted, no, none of that, it was comedy, it was bachelorhood.

As Harry drew the blanket around himself to keep the night's chill away a phantom fog brought in the old memories. His photos even now adorned the walls of bars and boutiques around the University. He remembered the dance instructor and the car dealer's daughter.

And Zeta arrived, asking, please, can I pose for you, too?

She had seen his nude studies at a popular used bookshop near the campus. The girls who approached Harry in those days usually had naked rutting on their minds as much as he did, but Zeta had a line: you're an artist, you are, she insisted, and it would be my privilege.

"Sure, let's go down to Galveston this weekend. I wanta do a series of pictures on the dunes. Can you get away?"

Zeta studied his face, deciding.

She later told him that he had no talent whatsoever for deception.

On a low, weathered, littered dune beyond the boardwalk, a curve of sand ruined by garbage and gnarled stumps of low bushes, Harry shot a sequence of photos with Zeta, covering her in sand and rock until her nakedness looked part of the blighted landscape. He added debris to several shots: a broken pop bottle, a shapeless piece of plastic, an old sock. Excited over the shoot he found a camera shop and rented its darkroom that afternoon, developing the film with Zeta standing beside him in the soft red glow of the workspace until she said, "Do I get lunch?"

They went to Guido's, sitting at a table by the window as clouds turned the day to iron. They ate chowder and studied each other. She had an unexpected beauty: high cheekbones, a delicacy.

She had finished her master's in English literature and wanted to write, but couldn't just yet. "You have to go for it," Harry advised her at lunch.

"I'm not ready," she told him, smiling. "I haven't even seen Europe yet. And a couple of guys have disappointed me, you know, but maybe I'm looking for something really major and tragic. Or maybe I need to betray somebody myself. And the act of writing, well, I'd have to sit down and just do it, but I'm far too restless. I'm also practical and want money. But more than money I want love, a great love. It'll take time. I have to fill myself up before I can pour out anything on paper."

As she talked more clouds rolled in and the rain started.

"Okay, that's it for today," he said. "No more pictures. I guess we're weathered in, so what do we do?"

"We can stay right here and talk. In three hours or so we could order more food. The chowder was good, but I wouldn't mind a huge supper. A fried fish platter with beer. Can you afford me?"

"I can, sure."

"I don't know why I'm starving. And I wouldn't mind getting drunk."

"Then what?"

"Maybe you're the great love of my life."

A short laugh of surprise came out of him, then just as quickly a fateful seriousness came over him. Zeta had touched something deep inside him and he knew she was reading him completely.

"We don't have to stay here," she told him, and they both got up from the table. He fumbled out a pile of cash to pay the bill, then as they turned to leave—in a sudden hurry now—Zeta scooped up a five dollar bill and stuffed it into her jeans. "Don't tip so much," she said, and her lifelong practicality revealed itself.

Thirty minutes later they fell onto a chenille bedspread at a pastel colored motel in Galveston's back streets.

The book of photographs, titled *Zeta,* although published by a solid New York house, made no money and gave him only modest reviews, but it was soon praised by a much more famous photographer and the director of a sci-fi movie copied its techniques: the curves of a naked woman blent into a slope of sand dunes, a breast or pubis sometimes exposed, eyes closed, hand slightly raised, a shoulder turned, skin and earth in clever accord and then—in the movie— sand and figure blown away in a gale.

They came back to Austin and married and for years Zeta stayed angry that he wasn't properly appreciated. Later, together, they photographed Padre Island for a conservation group and he published his third and last book.

Their house sat atop a limestone cliff in the western hills: cypress wood, lots of glass, a darkroom, thousands of Zeta's books. He opened the camera shop and portrait studio in an Austin strip mall. They drove two Toyotas. In time, they met Leo Jones.

Apart from doing Leo's portrait—flattering in an almost mystical way—Harry presented him, framed, one of those photographs of Zeta in the dunes. Leo gave it a crude remark, yet valued it more than he could admit and perhaps saw in it something of Harry's best. After that they were invited to parties. Exactly how they moved into Leo's newly invented circle Harry wasn't sure. Zeta, of course: maybe Leo felt a healthy lust for her having looked at those Galveston photos. Maybe more: the arty thing—Harry's past work, her bookishness—and possibly their independence, too, for everyone else in the group worked for Leo in one way or another. Roper the lawyer, Wade the physician, like that: Leo might have instinctively wanted a couple of objective acquaintances who might tell him the raw truth and Zeta, always candid, fit that part if not Harry himself.

Harry drew the blanket tighter and watched a thick fog move across the lake. Zeta, he realized, never became the writer she wanted to be, and her remark at Guido's that rainy afternoon long ago in Galveston came back clearly: *Maybe I'm looking for something really major and tragic or maybe I need to betray someone myself.*

He hoped not.

In any case he decided not to worry about Zeta and Kelton and whatever secrets and consolations they shared.

Instead, he considered Wade.

A *dottore,* Terminella had said. Harry wondered if the little victims had possibly been surgically cut or drugged or dealt with as a physician might do it. He also decided to ask Roper about Wade because Roper always knew everybody's financial business and often talked too much. Yet be careful, Harry warned himself: Roper had his own ways of disappearing from the group, after all, and maybe had his own mischief.

* * *

Of everyone in the group Wade seemed overworked. His clinic often phoned to interrupt his holiday with some crisis at the workplace and he fretted over the health of patients back in Texas as well the health of everyone in Leo's group: Roper's occasional pipe or cigar, Kelton's assorted complaints, Olan's obesity, and all the headaches and heartaches among the women. He was always the doctor, reminding others of it, and giving elaborate attention to sore backs, sprains, prescriptions, hangnails or unruly bowels. Kelton regarded him as the court physician and asked daily questions, using him without mercy.

With his wife, Wade was even more dutiful. He overlooked Val's more hysterical moments, honored her writing—although without an exalted notion of its profundity—and respected her mysticism. From time to time he even repeated one of her many malapropisms. When Val told Zeta to please pay for some of her shopping items and that she would be "re-embraced later" Wade regarded it as slightly endearing.

Wade thought of golf as silly and his own daily regimen of brutal hikes as manly, healthy, and somewhat heroic. They certainly served his appetite for food. He was clearly the group's big eater—Olan a close second—and Harry had more than once witnessed Wade devouring two restaurant entrees.

The doctor's frustrations with money were well known. He was once sued for malpractice by a Muslim family who claimed that he improperly touched their child—a seven year old daughter—although the child's mother was in attendance when he examined her. He hired an inept lawyer, then decided to take the annual trip to Italy with Leo instead of remaining in Austin to appear at the trial. When he lost—the jury thought him arrogant in his absence if not guilty—he asked Roper to take over the appeal and managed to get the award for damages reduced. It was typical of

Wade that he expected fortune to smile on him, but it seldom did.

Roper, furious at him for hiring that bumbling lawyer, summed it up by saying, "It matters not if you win or lose until you lose."

As the years passed Leo stopped seeing Wade except occasionally and instead went to Mayo Clinic for an annual checkup. Wade became the guy married to the romance novelist, his influence in the group diminished.

On one of the rare occasions Wade played golf with Harry and Kelton at an Austin country club, he said to Harry, "Tell me the truth. Do you think I'd look better if I grew a beard?"

"My suggestion," said Harry, "is that you should shave off your face and go for plastic surgery."

"Bastard. I'm being serious. I used to be damned handsome, you know."

"So did everybody with the possible exception of Leo Jones."

Harry and Wade shared the laugh and enjoyed the golf that day, but never really grew close.

They toured Villa Franscesca with Leo's architect, a thin man of indeterminate European stock who wore an ascot. The house was grey stone with sweeping arches, bright windows with lead panes, loggias, hidden gardens, a Palladian pavilion, three sitting rooms, a library, a bar, a greenhouse, breakfast and dining rooms, a putting green near the swimming pool, winding rock paths, a boathouse, and only four bedrooms including the master suite.

"Told you," Harry whispered to Zeta. "Somebody's definitely left out."

The house stood three floors tall on a rocky point of land. The path down to the boathouse was already trimmed with rosemary and nicely planted with flowers. Above a rock seawall and dock stood a single Ionic column, white, with a brass eagle on top that announced the villa to those passing by on the lake. Zeta noted that the bird was a little tilted, a bit out of kilter.

Leo's architect, moving like an actor on his stage, made a short speech in a somewhat French accent. "Places are stronger than people," he intoned. "People come and go in the passing events of the centuries, but the mountains remain, the lake endures, and the stones live on. Places have ghosts. They are the timeless receptacles of the past."

"Hear that, honey?" Harry asked under his breath.

"The man enunciates well," Zeta commented.

Leo constantly asked Zeta about furnishings, but she was hesitant to offer opinions since Jackie had announced that an interior designer from Houston would be employed. Yet Leo kept pressing Zeta for ideas.

"Maybe tapestries," she offered.

"I can procure for you some very fine antique tapestries," the architect quickly put in, undoubtedly thinking of himself as the timeless receptacle of future commissions.

"I love Zeta's beautiful little house on the cliff back in Austin," Leo told everyone. "All those bookshelves. With books. I'm thinking of matching leather bound books for the library here. All the classics. I want your help with that, too, okay, Zeta?"

Jackie became sullen with all this and Leo, taking notice, quickly added that his wife would of course fill the rooms with her paintings. The Lugano architect kept a poker face.

As the garden and boathouse tour began Harry stopped with Roper. He mentioned the small number of bedrooms in the villa and learned more than he anticipated.

"You know about Leo's loan to Wade, I suppose?" Roper asked.

"No, what loan?"

"Lent him half a million against his clinic. This was, oh, two years ago, and if you ask me Leo intends to foreclose."

"Nah, c'mon."

"That land where the doc's clinic is? I tell ya, Harry, Leo wants it. Maybe that's why there's only four bedrooms in this place. I figure Doc's out. I'll lay you odds that Olan won't be with us, either."

"Maybe we're out," Harry suggested.

"No, believe me, you and me and Kelton we're the mainstays."

"Maybe. But, listen, I want to hear more about Wade."

"Sure, we'll talk. And, hey, are you gonna do some nude shots of April?"

"I'm thinking about it."

"I wanta watch that. And she seems ready to go with it."

"Why did Wade need such a big loan?"

"Don't know, but I hear Wade spent it all. So I figure his clinic's gone and he is, too."

As April joined them Harry followed the others down the path to the boathouse.

Harry went looking for a studio and darkroom he might rent. He started in Menaggio, a crowded tourist town near Lenno with a busy waterfront and worn backstreets. At lakeside everything was beautiful: an abundance of flowers, brightly painted boats, lapping waves on the stone embankments, and musty hotels with striped umbrellas along their terraces. As in the other towns around the lake the backstreets offered an everyday life of stray cats, garlic smells, bicycle parts, and dozens of loud children and babies. For a hunter of little girls, Harry realized, this was a world teeming with prey.

He rode the ferry over to Bellagio. Great pavilions of cloud rose over the Alps reflecting the day's sunlight. At a sidewalk café in the famous little town he sipped a Coke and ate a salami sandwich while watching shoppers with their Gucci and Armani bags.

He found a camera shop where a young man without much English—his neck in a brace—finally drew back a curtain to interrupt his father's lunch. The old man emerged like a mafia don: wide red suspenders, a bushy white mustache, clever eyes and an air of arrogant fatigue. After a lengthy effort at interpretation Harry was made to understand that a British photographer had a studio—yes, for rent, possibly, *affitto, si,* in Bellano.

Once again Harry went down to the ferry station where he ran into Jackie, Val and Robin. They had bought shoes and purses.

"Will you see that detective again?" Val wanted to know.

"Maybe," he told them.

Jackie had had too much wine with lunch.

"We want to make a donation to the family that lost the little girl," said Robin, and she seemed near tears. Perhaps they were all tipsy, Harry decided.

"It's the least we can do," said Jackie, and they wanted Harry's opinion on what would be an appropriate sum.

"I don't have the faintest idea," he told them, and he somehow felt this wasn't a particularly good idea, yet didn't know why.

Until the ferry arrived they chatted about Bellagio. The women had seen a marble plaque noting that Franz Liszt had lived and worked here. Stendahl had also stopped in the town, Harry informed them— remembering that Zeta had once told him this—and they all gave one another weak smiles, trying, he supposed, to think of a piece of Liszt's music or exactly what Stendahl had written.

Val introduced another dimension. "I expected to see those Italians with cameras riding around on their motorbikes," she said. "You know, the pepperoni."

After a moment of consternation, Zeta—wishing she hadn't barged in—corrected her. "Pepperoni is the sausage," she said. "The guys with cameras are the *paparazzi.*"

Jackie and Robin looked on confounded.

Harry turned away to smile as the women picked up their conversation without losing a beat.

At last his ferry arrived and he made his getaway.

By the time he reached Bellano, the next stop

to the north, the afternoon had turned hot. He stood in the shade of a narrow side street across from a statue of a citizen who had served the little town as mayor, doctor and poet.

In a nearby jewelry shop he asked a pretty clerk about a photographer's studio and she smiled and denied that such a place existed. Her English was slow and perfect as if she were reading it.

Half an hour later he found a kiosk where a little woman, perhaps a dwarf, sat on a high stool selling film and disposable cameras through a narrow window. She gave him general directions: climb there in that street, then go higher, cross a bridge, *si, ponte,* then take the trail uphill, keep going, to the great building with the *lucernario, si,* the skylight.

Beyond the cliffs on which Bellano was built the trail led to a high meadow. At the end of the climb Harry was covered with sweat.

He found an old abandoned factory with a series of elongated windows and a large domed skylight. Out front sat an old Fiat truck. He banged on the greenish brass knocker on the double oaken doors, but nobody responded. After that he walked around shouting hello, then gave up. The surrounding field, overgrown, was littered with old wooden frames. Silk frames, he decided. An old silk factory.

Across a culvert he saw a curious row of boulders, a circle of stone, and he strolled toward it, again with slow recognition. He gazed at the boulders and how they were laid out until he detected a pattern. Megaliths. Dolmens. He tried to think of the correct term and wanted his camera. A strange place.

Turning back downhill he felt thirsty and exhausted.

Then he smiled to himself.

Val's question about pepperoni.

Some years ago Robin had gone to work for Olan as his nurse, office manager, assistant or secretary— her skills, when described, remained vague—and had become in time his second or third wife.

Her frame was small and breastless and she ducked her head when she smiled as if to hide any real mirth. This timidity extended to opinions: she had them, but they weren't for display. Ideas and judgments were for others to explore, for the men, especially, or for the more outspoken women like Val or Zeta. Harry often wondered if Olan dominated her, keeping her down, but her reticence seemed natural and her girlish ways, he finally decided, were deeply ingrained.

In the hot tub days, though, she used to strip off her clothes willingly and step daintily into the foaming water, covering herself with her small hands, giggling, and obeying the unspoken rules: get naked, get in, and get social. Olan might have demanded it of her as his ticket to get a look at Roper's current girlfriend or Zeta's well proportioned body or Val's buxom assault, but Robin went along with it. When Val in all her sagging splendor stood at the edge of the tub, raised her arms and stuck out her bush, stretching for everyone to see and admire, Robin ducked her head, giggled, and seemed to enjoy it. Those were the early days of the group—the Capelletti villa had the tub—and there was no groping, no trading of partners, certainly, and no vulgarities except for Leo's.

Robin loved sitting on the terrace with her little diary or a book of crossword puzzles. She wore her lace and sensible black shoes. And although she never added to the repartee she had a way of looking up—a startled, smiling glance—that showed her appreciation of a good comeback, especially if someone put down one of her husband's pomposities.

Harry had few conversations with her one-on-one, but in the most memorable she asked him if he ever considered disappearing.

"You know, just vanishing," she said wistfully.

"Sounds suicidal," he ventured.

"No, not that. Just getting a new set of ID papers, another self. I'll bet Leo or Roper know somebody who can arrange that sort of thing. I've thought about it.

Getting the proper papers then going someplace far away."

She sounded unhappy in a hopeful sort of way. Life after Olan, Harry assumed: that was clearly what she wanted.

Harry told Zeta about the pepperoni remark as they dressed for dinner, but she only smiled and went back to being out of sorts.

"Didn't you have a good day?" he asked.

"It was all right."

"What did you do?"

"Read a bit. Went to lunch. Waited around for you."

He told her about the old factory and the circle of stones. Like a little Stonehenge, he said, but she wasn't listening.

"What's upsetting you?"

"Harry, it's nothing. I live in my head and it's not always wonderful in there."

"We're all like that."

"Not you. You're much more simple. You see the surface of things and take pictures."

"So that means what? I'm superficial?"

"I didn't say that. But Kelton, for instance, has a keen sense of the world. He knows quite a lot about Africa. He thinks about politics. He's engaged in a way you're just not. And you know it. You're proud of your simplicity and I've heard you say so. But not all of us are so uncomplicated, that's all I'm saying."

"I went out looking for a proper studio. Are you upset about April posing for me? Roper's going to be with us. I told you that."

"It's not April. Just leave it alone."

"So you and Kelton are highly evolved and I'm superficial, that's it?"

Zeta didn't reply.

They went down for drinks where Val, Jackie and Robin showed off their new shoes. Leo was explaining his new phone system to the men. He had all the newest equipment and a couple of military items that weren't even on the market. Two years back he had a new satellite system, but it had failed during a visit to Kilimanjaro and embarrassed him. He could phone and e-mail all over the world, he said.

They drank vodkas and tonic and talked about where they wanted to eat dinner. Bruno's Ristorante was the pick, but Kelton seemed exercised over the choice.

"I'm tired of that asinine fascist," he declared.

"We haven't been there this year and Bruno's the second best chef at the lake," Roper countered.

"Besides," said Jackie, "he'll remember how everybody argued about Mussolini and he won't bring up the subject again."

"Sure he will," Kelton argued. "He'll get drunk and have a fit of nostalgia for *Il Duce*. Let's go somewhere else."

"Take a vote," Olan suggested.

"I'm going to Bruno's," Harry said flatly. "I want some of his seafood pasta." He surprised himself, realizing belatedly that Kelton had annoyed him.

In the end, under protest, Kelton agreed and went along.

Riding in the van to the restaurant Harry, Zeta, Val, Wade and Kelton went over the Mussolini confrontation of the previous year. The dictator and his mistress, Claretta Petacci, had been discovered trying to flee the country in 1945. Partisans had found them in the back of an old truck near Lenno and took them to a villa above Tremezzo where they were shot. The bodies were later taken to Milan and hung upside down. A plaque at the Tremezzo villa now carried only the name of the mistress, but admirers of the dictator came every year to leave flowers at the gate. Bruno always had words of praise for *Il Duce* at the restaurant and this infuriated Kelton who noted that a number of American soldiers had died in Italy fighting the tyrant.

"Bruno's still a hell of a cook," Harry said in the van.

"Sure, take the long view," Wade advised. "The war was fifty years ago. C'mon, Kelton, lighten up."

"Screw that," Kelton snapped back, and the dinner hour was off to a rocky start.

Harry went to dinner irritated and matters got worse. Bruno, whose red veined face grew crimson with his nightly wine consumption, was already tipsy when everyone arrived. As usual he recited the evening specialties himself while a dutiful waiter stood at his side to write down orders, then Bruno stayed on to chat—and to flatter Leo, if possible—before retiring to the kitchen.

This evening he shook a finger at Zeta who sat beside Kelton.

"Ah, you again, my best customer!" Bruno said, then he turned to everyone else and noted, "These two are coming here for lunch today! Now back for dinner! Such a compliment to me!"

He meant Zeta and Kelton, unmistakably.

Kelton stared into his wine glass as both Zeta and Harry managed to concoct smiles.

The dinner went well after this uneasiness. Everyone discussed the harrowing drive on the narrow lakeside roads. Olan quoted a verse of scripture that got him high marks for the meal. "If a man looketh upon a woman," he announced, "he loseth a fender."

The drive back to the villa was less talkative, then Harry and Zeta were alone in their room.

"Well, we know why Kelton didn't want to go back to Bruno's," Harry opened. "And I don't know why you told me a lie."

"I'd never lie to you and didn't today."

"Oh? You said you had lunch alone. Then you compared me to Kelton—unfairly. Then this little embarrassment at dinner."

"I told you I had lunch and I didn't say who with."

Harry spent time in the bathroom pondering all this, cutting hairs out of his nose with Zeta's little rounded scissors and looking across the rooftop toward the lake. He washed his hands, then washed them again. Zeta had called him, he knew, simple and superficial.

When he returned to the bedroom she was reading in bed.

"You told me you had lunch by yourself," he began again. "After that you said some flattering things about Kelton and let me know how superficial I am."

Zeta lowered her book and raised her eyebrows. "That wasn't how it went," she replied evenly and she started reading again.

Harry decided all the wives were stressed out. Zeta had this troubling new intimacy with Kelton. Poor Robin, always mousey and quiet, had almost grown catatonic with Olan's loud authority driving her into her private little cave. Jackie was obviously fighting with Leo; her eyes were so red that she wouldn't take off her sunglasses that night at Bruno's. Whatever Wade was doing he didn't want Val with him, so her feelings were hurt and she told everyone at breakfast that she supposed he'd found Sophia Loren to walk the trails with him.

Only April seemed content among the women. She had settled into flirting with the men and ignoring the wives, but at times her eyes narrowed in recognition as she watched everyone and Harry began to suspect that she might be street wise and clever in ways others weren't—and seeing a reality no one else detected.

The men soon played a round at the Villa d'Este course and Kelton rode in the cart with Harry. They laughed and talked in the old way without any mention of Zeta.

Afterward at lunch in a small trattoria Leo suddenly said, "I noticed this thing in one of Val's books I was trying to read. When her main character gets a little emotional her breasts heave."

"It's a requirement in romance novels," Kelton responded. "For the book cover. Always. Heaving breasts."

"Is that right?" Leo said, believing it, and everybody grinned over his pasta.

As lunch ended Harry asked Roper about Wade again and this opened up a brief discussion of the doctor. They agreed he was a man who believed in his own skills, so that's why he wouldn't play golf: he was terrible at it. His surgery was unquestioned and the operating room was his true arena, but he was pathetic in all his business schemes: a tanning salon in a Texas town of relentless sunshine, worthless acres out in the hill country, cockeyed stocks, and a couple of screwy inventions. He invested in molded plastic dog houses, scented, but dogs, Leo revealed, wouldn't go inside the things. He also put money into a dripless paintbrush and ended up with thousands of them in his basement. The physician's curse, Roper observed: an expert in his profession with a knack for wild amateurism in everything else.

"It's Val's novels that makes them money," Olan said, guessing. "And she writes one of those things every year or so."

"She makes forty thousand a book," Leo said with certainty.

"That's all?" Harry responded, and he decided that Leo—heaving breasts aside—knew everyone's net worth.

Leo added more. "She puts out books, but no sex. That's my information. In fact, Wade says it takes a lot more than Val to get him started these days."

"If you want to know about love and marriage," said Olan, "you have to buy two separate manuals." Proud of this entry, he slapped the table and laughed.

Later, Roper took Harry aside. "I guess you get Leo's drift. Wade's out." He let his tone drop into intimate confidentiality.

"Think so? I didn't really hear that."

"Believe me. He doesn't trust Wade anymore. Maybe because Wade's so stupid in financial affairs, but Leo pretty much thinks he's a fool. And Val's a liability. Leo used to think, hey, an author, big deal, but she writes shit and we all know it—and subverts herself saying all those goofy things."

"I thought Olan was the one out of favor."

"Olan, too. With his goddamned accent and patrician manners. Leo used to do therapy with Olan, but now he thinks that psychiatry and psychologists are bullshit."

"I guess you're in a position to know."

"You and Zeta, as I see it, are Leo's new cultural advisors. Along with Kelton. I mean, shit, Zeta and Kelton either know it or can find it out. And you're a real artist—not like Val—and Leo likes nudes and likes you. And I'm the man he depends on most. Money, litigation, business advice. Did I tell you that I don't even have another client? Leo's the man."

"Congratulations."

"So, yeah, I am in a position to know. And when Leo's villa is finished Wade's out and so is Olan. It'll be you, Zeta, me and Kelton."

"I guess I'm learning a lot."

"Tell you one more thing. Just a hunch. I shouldn't say anything, but Jackie may be on her way out, too."

"You're kidding. Divorce?"

"I just read the vibes. Leo's got a new program for himself: more upscale and more cultural. Like, he looked up the Lombards on a website recently and now he wants a detailed history of Lake Como. He doesn't want to be embarrassed anymore. We had a long conversation about skiing. He wasn't sure where—if he took up skiing—he should go to be cool, like Aspen or someplace in the Alps. And what sort of lodge would he rent, all that. I'm not sure of this either, but maybe he wants to live in Europe permanently like a duke or Count Leo or something."

Roper detected the look of skepticism on Harry's face.

"I know, sounds wild, but just wait. Maybe it's a passing fad, but I'm the Leo expert and I don't think so."

"Back to Jackie," Harry said. "Why would he want to dump her? She's pretty classy."

"Maybe in Austin, but not everywhere. And maybe she knows too much. Hey, this is just conjecture. I read the indicators, but it's just an informed guess. By the way, when are you doin' those photos of April?"

"Soon. I'm looking for a studio and I'll let you know."

Roper had his headlong passions: sports, women, and Leo Jones. He was also a party animal who liked his picture in the society pages: functions at country clubs, on the university campus, out on Lake Travis or wherever Leo popped the champagne. Kelton once speculated that Roper had a press agent and noted that he courted a few local reporters so that when the group made its annual sojourn over to Como the society pages or the columnists would hear about it. Ditto for fancy dress balls or charity softball games. Or one of Leo's expensive weekends.

Harry and Zeta accepted some of Leo's many invitations although they rarely spoke to him at the events. They often darted in for the drinks and food, looking for Kelton or other friends, then made a quick getaway. Sometimes they found themselves in the backgrounds of grainy newspaper photos of Leo at the book fair or cinema festival. Unlike Roper, they clearly knew Leo in a second hand way except for the weeks and golf games at the Villa Capelletti.

Roper on the other hand filled his days and nights with Leo and it came as no surprise that he had achieved the status of personal lawyer. If he prayed, it was to the Dow Jones or Leo Jones. If he spent money on flash—cars, trips, gifts—it was actually a business expense.

He was five foot nine inches of good muscle and he ran hard every day, even after golf. Like Leo, he worked on his tan.

At golf and in the courtrooms he always improved his lies.

That night Zeta went upstairs to her book and her bed without so much as a goodnight touch for Harry. He went to the lounge to find Kelton and Leo talking about the blue lotus.

"We don't know a lot, but Egyptian hieroglyphics tell us they valued the flower and ate it—maybe even an extract of it. Traces of it have been found in the DNA of mummies."

"What was so special about it?" Leo asked as Harry sat down and ordered a drink.

"Oh, it was about the same medicinal properties as our herb Ginkgo Biloba—which is popular—but the lotus also might've been their Viagra. A general health herb, you know, but also maybe a sexual stimulant."

Leo liked that.

"So how'd you come to know this?" Harry asked.

"Television. Either the Discovery Channel or PBS. And this had to be in the last month or so—or I'd have forgotten it already."

They shared a smile. Kelton was always self-effacing, up on things, and a good guy, Harry reflected, but what was going on with Zeta?

Leo ordered another round, keen to discuss sexual stimulants.

"Olan uses Viagra," he divulged. "Says it makes him really nuts, but works. Now, me, I've tried everything. Pussy on the side is the best aphrodisiac. At our age we have to pay, of course, but we always pay. Wife or strange, we pay."

They had lurched into Leo's favorite topic, but Harry saw an opening so asked for a bit more about Olan. "He gets crazy on Viagra? I wonder how crazy," Harry ventured.

"Says he blanks out," Leo offered.

"Like unconscious?"

"Says he gets into a dream state. I think Robin encourages it. Ever see how she decorates their hotel room? Brocades, silks, flowers, candles: a goddamn Turkish harem. I think she must dress up and play concubine."

"A dream state?" Harry persisted.

"It's nice to imagine our shy little Robin in that particular theatrical," Kelton added, grinning.

"Remember Robin in the hot tubs?" Leo asked. "Damn, those were good times. Jackie and Val weren't so fat. And little Robin: no tits at all, like a thin little boy with that big bush of hers. Remember, Kelton?"

"I'm trying not to remember."

"Like a little girl," Harry said, his suspicions aroused.

"Know what Olan's favorite movie is?" Leo asked. "The fucking *Sound of Music*. Daddy and the children."

"And a mere wisp of a girl from the convent wins the baron," Kelton put in.

"Maybe you don't know this," Leo said. "But our Olan flunked outta medical school. He was gonna be a psychiatrist, see, but he flunked so he went to some little college out in West Texas and got his doctorate. After that he had a good internship in Houston, but he was never a goddamned genius."

"He studied to be a doctor?" Harry asked to make sure.

"And I'll tell you for sure he never did me a lick of good as a psychologist."

Harry had a thought: he'd like to peek into Robin's little diary and find out just how crazy her husband is.

When their drinks arrived they finished them quickly and headed upstairs. At the elevator Harry knew that Kelton wanted to speak privately to him, but Leo went back to the topic of sexual aids and wouldn't leave them. They dropped Kelton off at his floor, so Leo was the one left to speak to Harry.

"Look, Harry," Leo began, screwing up his face. "I don't wanta get on your wrong side, not ever. So did Zeta tell you about what I said to her?"

"No, she hasn't said anything."

"The other night at La Valuu I drank a hell of lot of wine. Maybe I had a couple of Irish shooters beforehand. Anyway, I got crude with Zeta. You know me. She handled it, but I apologize, okay? Nothin' should ever come between us 'cause I have a lotta respect for you two. You just don't know. I tried to apologize to her, too, but I don't think she wanted to listen."

"She's not talking to me, either," Harry admitted.

"It was outta line, what I said. But you two've got taste, you know, and real class. I'd never hurt you on purpose, but it was the fuckin' liquor, I swear."

"You don't ever have to apologize to me," said Harry, wishing instantly that he had been less forgiving. "That said, I'm off to bed. Goo'night, buddy."

"Goodnight, Leo."

Harry went into his room quietly, trying to sort out his thoughts. Tomorrow, he decided, I'll go back over to Bellano and try to find that Brit photographer. Keep busy. Keep the mind occupied. Keep all suspicions at bay.

As Harry lay in bed, though, thoughts on Olan remained.

The big guy styled himself as an authority and spiked his conversation with researched and memorized information. Kelton once told Harry that when he went to dinner at Olan's and Robin's house he had discovered a shelf of special books: quotations, jokes, anecdotes, one-liners, and even a large yellow book of witty insults. Olan had marked dozens of entries in each volume, Kelton said, and most of them had been doled out to the group at one occasion or another. So Olan had a reference library of his off-the-cuff asides and waited to slip them in when the appropriate topics appeared.

In conversation Olan gave way to Leo, especially in money matters, and conceded art to Jackie and literature to Zeta, but he wouldn't give an inch to Wade in medicine or to Roper in legal matters or to Kelton and Harry in anything. Kelton, he asserted, like all journalists, had only eclectic and general knowledge and no real expertise.

He was self-effacing only on his own terms. "Yes, all right, I'm a windbag," he once offered. "But, dear hearts, I'm your windbag." More often he reminded them that he knew the facts: politics, history, religion, all and anything.

He was six feet tall and weighed above 260 pounds, so sat like a Buddha and assumed a god-like attitude. In Italy he often said, yes, Julius Caesar gave the residents around Like Como their Roman citizenship. Or, the Como cathedral was started in

1000 AD, but changed with every century. Or, Virgil sang the beauties of Lari Maxime, the lake. Items from the guide books, often repeated.

Zeta once suggested that Olan loved information only to bully others. "After all," she said, "authority is just a form of violence."

"Damn, honey, that's profound," Harry responded at the time.

"It's just that Olan's sources are all so transparent and obvious," she said. "When he has a literary opinion it comes out of some current book review. He studies from year to year so he can berate us. Poor Robin. For that matter, poor all of us."

Olan also peppered his monologues with doubtful claims, among them: he played college baseball, he won and lost fortunes at poker, he could pilot a light plane, he could cure almost any disease through biofeedback, he had once been an excellent violinist.

"Olan, goddamn, you are so full of shit," Leo would tell him, but Olan would only laugh and slap the table in agreement, then start over again.

He was an expert on snake venoms, he insisted. Also on rugby, the ancient slave trade, the Confederate army, gunsmithing, precious stones, the gypsies of Europe, witchcraft, aerodynamics, hypnosis, and as he would say himself, much much more.

Harry crossed on the early morning ferry, ate bread, jam and coffee at a quayside trattoria, then started back uphill toward the old silk factory in Bellano.

Halfway along the climb he had the distinct feeling that someone followed him. His impression was so clear that he stepped into a grove of saplings and waited, hoping that, if true, he could get a glimpse of who it was. But no one appeared. Later on the graveled path he thought he heard footsteps—the crush of rock underfoot seemed clear—but he turned sharply to find nobody there.

At a high vista he stopped to catch his breath and

to gaze at the morning mist over the lake, a soft white. The early sunlight gave the northern mountain range a tinge of sepia. Far below he watched cargo boats, the *comballi* with their high gunwales, gliding over the deep grey water. The towns across the lake stood like histories written in stone, making him aware of the transient world of neon and asphalt he came from, and he felt like a plastic toy set down in a cathedral of nature. The old villas, ancient church spires, and terraced vineyards spoke of a lost civilization and time with some nobility of purpose and he felt outside that history: it lay back there long ago in the catacomb maze of time, a somehow richer age.

He looked back down the path again, but although someone felt near he saw nothing.

When he reached the factory he found its oaken doors wide open, so stepped inside before calling out. The lower floor spread out in dusty confusion: old silk frames, rusted machinery, discarded crates, cobwebs, motes of thick dust floating in the morning slant of sunlight. As he touched the camera bag on his shoulder he thought of a photo: the industrial revolution in shambles.

Outside: a deck with lounge chairs, a hammock, a brazier and a dining table.

A voice called from above: "Hullo! Come up, whoever you are!"

A spiral staircase, brass, curled up to the next level. The wood everywhere was grooved oak. Finally, another great cavern: sitting room and studio furnished in low couches, pillows, bright rugs and an abundance of candlesticks, trays, bowls and vases. Three corners of the vast room were hung with backdrops and strewn with tripods, spotlights, reflectors, cables, filters and an assortment of good cameras. The door was open into a tiny darkroom papered with foil. A toilet and bathtub sat out in plain sight with the screen moved aside so the occupant might view the television set on a marble table. The kitchen, also exposed, offered a chopping block with stools and a variety of tan colored Sears appliances.

The little man at the center wore a drooping mustache, green pajamas, and a pair of work gloves. He twitched before speaking, screwing up his mouth then delivering his words in a single rush of breath.

"You had yourself a long climb to see me," he said, smiling. "When you called out I made you out to be an American, correct?"

Harry confirmed it and they exchanged introductions. The little man was Bernard and Harry presented him with a gift, a box of Twining's tea that he produced from his camera bag.

"Look at this! Twining's! Let's just do the English bit and brew up a pot to start things off!"

They stood at the butcher block table while the tea steeped and instantly started talking photography.

"Had myself an early fling with photography as art," said Bernard. "It was rather like Witkin, not so gross. Anyway, one has to give up art. My commercial enterprise has been simple and easier: landscapes of Lake Como. Brilliantly original, I'm sure you're thinking, but I sell quite a few in the galleries down in Lecco and Como."

Harry told him about his own retreat to the camera and portrait shop in Austin.

"Failure, you know, doesn't matter," Bernard said with a sigh. "One can live in a state of gentle ecstasy, art or no art."

When Bernard learned that Harry wanted a studio he said that could easily be worked out. They toured the room looking at backdrops, agreed on a modest payment, and the little Brit seemed happy for company—even April's and Roper's.

After tea they went outdoors to look at the arrangement of stones and before long the murders were mentioned. "Oh yes, some rough peasants around the lake," Bernard commented. "Farmers, fishermen and bandits, that's our professional classes. All of them superstitious and worried about the evil eye. The old women wear strings of garlic. Long before the murders they worried over their children and who might give them the evil eye. These are Lombards and Franks who came over the mountains to this lake in the Dark Ages with all kinds of tortures and strange fears. Maybe they put up these stones, but they might date back to prehistoric times, god knows, when mammoths still roamed these valleys. These stones might go back before Stonehenge and hardly anyone knows they're here."

Harry took photos of the stones and listened to his host as a figure came from the house. The *investigatore*. He approached with his hands in his pockets, leaving a wisp of white smoke from the stub of a cigarette in the side of his mouth. As he drew near he raised the cigarette in greeting.

"Hey, were you following me?" Harry asked warmly.

Detective Terminella shrugged and smiled.

After introductions Bernard soon learned how Harry found the doll. "Ah, we were just talking about the local barbarians," Bernard said. "One of them is undoubtedly your killer of little girls."

"Perhaps," said Terminella without conviction.

"Many of them are demented," Bernard went on. "And sexually repressed. They touch iron for luck. They prong their fingers at gypsies or cripples or anyone who might have the evil eye. They spit three times when they grow anxious and hang the goat's horn over the doors to their houses. And the Catholic religion: it's insane, you know."

"Everybody around the lake gives us plenty to think about," said the *investigatore* with a grin.

"So you followed me to see if I was looking for little victims?" Harry asked, also smiling.

"No, and now I see: one photographer visits another, yes? And you are not my killer of little children, I know this, because the human face is a lie detector. Not all people can read the facial expressions, but I am good at this, Harry, and you would never be the good liar."

"My wife tells me the same thing," Harry admitted.

Bernard asked the detective if he had ever visited the circle of stones in the field.

"Years ago," Terminella told him.

"In the cliffs below this high meadow people lived in the caves many years before Jesus and his church came with all their love and madonnas. Other gods were here, I think: savage gods. Sometimes with the full moon I feel them—especially if I drink a bit too much wine. *Che ne pensa, investigatore?*"

"*E une giallo,*" Terminella replied. It's a mystery.

As they strolled back toward the factory Bernard invited them for wine and cheese, but they both made their excuses. Harry and Bernard concluded arrangements for the first session with April.

"You'll like her," Harry promised. "But I hope it's okay that her boyfriend comes with her."

"Perhaps I am a man who will like the boyfriend even more," said Bernard, twitching his face into a sudden laugh. "And the two of us can talk about our craft. You know, *Investigatore*, that only the very best photographers and painters can actually *see* light."

"You'll have to explain that another time," Terminella replied, fumbling in his clothes for a match and not finding one.

"Light is a presence, like darkness," Bernard said simply, and found a book of matches beside a candle at the doorway.

In a short time Harry and Terminella started back down the path. With clouds gathering overhead the lake became the color of nickel.

"I know of this photographer," the detective said. "He had a friend, his companion of many years, who died. Now do you see it? A great loneliness in his eyes. Anyway, I know about him because an acquaintance of mine bought one of his photographs in an antique frame. I believe he threw away the photo and kept the frame."

"When we talked at the villa you asked if anybody in our group was a doctor," Harry said.

"Hm, perhaps. I don't know."

"You definitely asked about it. I wouldn't forget."

They made their way down the path in momentary silence.

"I learned something," Harry began again. "There

are actually two physicians in our group. One of them studied medicine, failed, and became a psychologist. The other's a practicing surgeon. You did ask."

"Yes, I remember."

"Is there something I should know?"

"Nothing I can confide. But one thing I will share. The man who kills these children, he is a magician. The Pied Piper, this man. You know the fairy tale of the Pied Piper?"

"Yes, who called the children of Hamelin."

"*Esattamente.* Exactly."

They made their way slowly listening to the birds in the trees.

"This monster finds them alone. As if he knows. Twice in their own houses. In one house, Harry, there is a long—hm, how to say it?—driveway. It leads to a nice villa in private grounds. The mother goes away for less than one hour and the girl who stays she is, ah, eleven years old. And this man drives all the way up the driveway to find her. He could have been trapped, you see, but he is fearless, like he knows. Another girl stands in a grove of cedar trees. She loves her father and watches him on his tractor as he works. They wave to each other. She is no more than twenty meters from her father when she disappears. Always alone, these girls. Sometimes for just a moment. How does this happen?"

Harry shook his head. He didn't know.

"This photographer at the old factory: what he says is true. All around are brutal men and perhaps this is inbred, an ancient thing. In the twelfth century the German emperor Barbarossa comes across the Alps and sacks Milan. Kills everyone in his way and burns the city, then he brings all the gold and fine treasures this way. He comes north to Lake Como in the year 1178. Do you know this story?"

"No, please, go on."

"He packs the gold and treasure on a flotilla of ships. They will sail up the lake and take it back across the mountains, but at the north end of the lake at Gravedona there are our rough peasant fishermen. In Barbarossa's army they are hardened warriors who have slaughtered an army in Milan, but these sailors of Gravedona take the treasure from them. They kill and drown Barbarossa's men in these waters. At his death the emperor is still cursing the peasant fishermen of Gravedona who took his spoils. So, yes, around this serene lake we have thieves, murderers, many hard men. But this matter of the little girls, I think, ah, this is an outsider. I believe this."

"Would you like to speak with my other friends?"

The question lingered, unanswered. They reached the paved road that curled down into the town and Harry thought to ask again, but didn't.

"Yes," the detective finally responded. "I would like to look into the faces of your friends. I am good at reading faces, as I boasted to you. But suppose I see what I am looking for—without proof—what then? This magician, I am thinking, might also see my recognition. He might have this cunning."

"You believe it's someone in my group, don't you?"

"No, not at all, probably not, you must not assume I am thinking this. Yet pretend it is so. When I face this man I will want to gain the advantage in such a meeting. And let me confess something: I am quite alone in my thinking. There are many good officers at work on this case, but perhaps because of my own daughters—other factors, perhaps, as well—I have been far too troubled. Angry. Somewhat obsessive. My superior—he is named Benzetti—is often annoyed with me. With him and others I have to justify myself. My wife is distressed. My daughters want horses, but I can give them only bicycles. Everyone wishes me to sleep more, to fill out the proper papers, to stay home, to let others—ah well, I am talking too much."

The streets where they now walked had houses at the curbs and the voices of others echoed around them.

"Did I say to you that this monster of ours is a fine hunter?" Terminella went on. "He leaves us very little evidence—or nothing at all. And I think he now requires two victims in the month he does his mischief. When he began, only one. But now he is getting better and better at his sport."

At the little waterfront piazza Terminella lit a cigarette. Fat pigeons waddled around their feet as they stood looking out beyond the quay.

"You and your friends are happy? No one badly disturbed? No one who seems too angry or believes himself to be hurt?"

"Not really," Harry admitted.

"A man in my family had close friends, a group like yours. Two women in the group had an argument, though, and now no one speaks. Their children grew up together. But one woman had anger in her heart. One must always think hard about his angry friends."

"Maybe it's something else, not anger."

"Yes, and what?"

"I don't know," Harry said. "Some other deep thing."

"Again, I go back to the doll. Why would such a careful magician discard the doll on the pathway? All killers make mistakes, yes, but not such as that. Unless he wants to be found out. Or because of special circumstances we are yet to discover."

In their silence the detective finished his cigarette, then snapped it away. "I must go," he finally said. "I saw you on the ferry and decided to think about you this morning, but I have other duties. Can you imagine having other duties when such a thing is happening?"

They shook hands and said goodbye.

The news back at the villa was that Jackie and Leo had argued—over Leo's villa-in-progress, Zeta told Harry—and that Jackie had packed up and returned to Texas.

"A big stretch limo waited in the parking lot for more than an hour," Zeta told Harry while he was shaving. "Leo and Jackie were yelling at each other on the landing, then she went off to the airport in Milan."

"Roper predicted as much."

"Oh? Did he know something was brewing?"

"He hinted that Leo might be thinking of

dumping her. I figured he was talking about money and investments. Wives are more expensive than mistresses, that sort of thing." Harry raised his chin and let the razor glide over the foam. "We haven't had this sort of excitement since Val had her fling with the local bureaucrat," he continued, yet the remark was more lighthearted than he felt. Jackie, after all, was a balance wheel. Except for some compulsive shopping she usually showed good sense and softened Leo, reminding him of his manners.

"Apart from the money," Harry asked, "what do you suppose Jackie ever saw in Leo?"

"I'd say the money and nothing else," said Zeta, standing in the doorway and zipping up her slacks. "How does this look?"

"Beautiful," he replied absently, and he toweled off his chin and moved toward her, but she avoided an embrace, turning back to the bedroom. He found himself wondering if she had been with Kelton again.

That evening they went to a new bar, but found it falsely rustic—with two television sets going strong—so had their drinks quickly then went off to one of their favorite restaurants, La Fugaride, a big farmhouse on the mountainside with thick walls, rough tables, a few chickens pecking around underfoot, and family wines. They emptied three bottles before the first course so the men were tipsy and Leo became the braying Texan nobody enjoyed.

"Do I make demands of Jackie?" he wanted to know.

"Not at all," Roper assured him, being equally loud.

"You don't even have a trapeze in your room, do you?" Wade asked, laughing by himself.

April sat next to Harry, leaned over, and quietly announced that Roper had an unnatural sexual appetite. In spite of himself and knowing better Harry asked for specifics.

"He wants me to wear knee stockings," she said with a pout.

"What's wrong with that?"

"Knee stockings? He likes to play head master at the girls' school."

"Ah, what else?" Harry managed, turning to her. Immediately his suspicions bubbled up at this kinkiness.

"Nurse and doctor. White stockings and a white garter belt."

Harry found himself grinning. He also saw Zeta watching, arching an eyebrow, and suspected that one of April's suggestive words had skimmed across the table in his wife's direction. He had the impulse to ask after even more lurid details, but since April had been a stripper devoted to the business of fantasy Roper's imagination seemed well within reason.

Before the entrees arrived everybody started giving Kelton a hard time as the group's established hypochondriac. He often took abuse for his head colds, asthma, blisters, insect bites, and minor afflictions.

"I think he rides that Vespa around the lake looking for some new illness that he particularly likes," Roper put in.

"Quit worrying about your health," Wade added. "It'll go away." Everybody laughed and Olan slapped the table. Kelton, who often managed a blush, obliged them once more.

After this the topic quickly became diseases. Wade explained myacea-gravis until groans of boredom stopped him, then Olan held forth on fatal insomnia that in its last stages produced sensational visions and hallucinations before the final coma. Kelton launched into African fevers, all of them produced by lack of hygiene, he speculated. Green Monkey Fever, he noted, probably came from consuming monkey meat, especially the brains, and perhaps the AIDs epidemic could be traced there. Wade then started on Creutzfeldt-Jakob, the cousin to mad cow disease in humans: depression at the beginning, then a few memory problems as spongy holes appeared in the brain, then dementia, then the uncontrollable jerking of the limbs and muscles until death.

"Takes about six months," he added cheerily.

"Ghastly," Zeta said, and her shoulders went into an involuntary shudder that brought a few smiles.

Kelton reached over and patted her wrist.

At this point a fire broke out in the kitchen. The group passed the wine bottles around and paid little attention until smoke crept across the ceiling. Shouts, curses, and the rattle of pots and pans signaled the kitchen's distress. Then the owner's wife, wringing her hands, smoke billowing above her grey hair, came out to say there wouldn't be any further service this evening.

Leo wanted to know about the main course.

"Not having!" the signora shouted at him.

Leo stood up to make his speech. "All these years we've come here and tipped big! Chickens under the tables! Homemade wine! Thin soups—and don't think we haven't noticed! And now this! Where do you expect us to find a full meal at this time of night? Goddammit, woman, put out the stupid fire and feed us our dinner!"

The owner's wife fled back to the disaster.

Zeta led the laughter, but Leo remained furious and others decided to take their cues from him. Leo's face contorted with anger. The control freak, Harry thought, out of control.

Olan scooped up two bottles of wine and headed for the yard, so others followed. Chickens flapped around and barking dogs appeared. Two young waiters pulled a garden hose into the kitchen as the air filled with the odors of burnt meat, scorched feathers, and charcoal. Val spoke of the loves of bygone summer nights. Roper and Wade raised a toast to the white moon.

Harry moved beside Zeta. "I saw Kelton touch your arm," he said.

"So what?"

"When you were upset he touched your wrist."

"Have you gone crazy?" she asked, and turned away, joining Olan and Robin who sat on the tailgate of a rusted pickup as they finished a bottle of wine.

"We'll never come here again!" Leo shouted at the smoke rising from the kitchen.

In minutes the fire was extinguished and the waiters cheered.

"Okay, what's going on with you and Zeta?"

"Nothing. What do you mean?" Kelton asked.

"You're cozy like I've never seen you. Private conversations and touches. I'm not jealous exactly, but we've been friends for a long time, so just tell me straight."

Under Harry's gaze Kelton fidgeted and occasionally pawed at the ground with his shoe. His Gary Cooper act. Or the reticent Tom Hanks.

Harry insisted on a private lunch with Kelton while Olan, Leo, and Roper played golf. Now they waited on the street outside a busy café in Tremezzo while motorbikes and speeding cars filled the air with exhaust fumes. Across the way at dockside a guy in a turban sold Chinese knock-offs of Rolex watches. A scrawny Brit dressed in baggy shorts, brown shoes, green socks, blue tee shirt, and an ill-fitting hairpiece lent the scene his wide-eyed presence. Two Japanese tourists also stared at the noon crowd, one aiming a camera and the other carrying what appeared to be his laundry in a plastic basket.

"Zeta has a problem she can't discuss with you, so she confided in me," Kelton disclosed. He wouldn't look directly at Harry.

"So she has a problem only you can solve?"

"No. But it concerns you and she can't talk about it."

"Okay, I give up. What the hell is it?"

"Leo made her an offer. He wants her to work for him and travel with him."

"Work and travel? Permanently?"

"Sort of. He probably thinks he's in love with her."

"So that's why Jackie got mad and went home?"

"Nobody's sure about that."

"You and Zeta aren't sure," Harry repeated evenly. "And Leo just wants my wife."

"The thing is," Kelton said, shuffling his feet again. "The thing is, she's considering the offer."

"What?"

At that moment the maitre'd stepped outside, his bald head catching the sunlight, and summoned them to a table. Kelton, relieved for a break in this difficult conversation, quickly walked off leaving Harry to catch up.

They ordered beers at a table indoors while Harry assembled his thoughts.

"Okay, slow down. Zeta says she's actually considering this offer from Leo?"

"He mentioned a sum of money. Lots."

"Zeta must've laughed at him."

"No, I'm telling you: lots of money."

"Zeta's not interested in money," Harry said, and his own words sounded foolish. Kelton rolled his eyes.

"Maybe Leo told Jackie about his offer to Zeta, but we don't know that," Kelton said after a deep breath. "I heard them arguing about the new villa and Jackie was really mad about something, but maybe it was just the way Leo kept asking Zeta's opinion on the décor. If it had just been a fuss about interior decoration, though, I can't imagine Jackie going back to Austin."

Harry's thoughts spun away. "Can you imagine Zeta having sex with Leo?"

"Maybe she'll bargain to see you," Kelton suggested, his face straight. "You know, conjugal visits."

This coaxed a smile out of Harry and he suddenly felt a deep satisfaction that Kelton hadn't betrayed him. Leo was just in a trading mood, too, Harry decided: negotiating a deal for a new partner. Harry didn't even take it personally.

Their beers arrived and they agreed to split a pizza. The guy in the turban and fake Rolex watches sat nearby, his knife and fork raised in anticipation as he waited for food.

"If Zeta's really considering this offer," Harry said with slow realization, "then she must be damned unhappy with me."

"Some," Kelton conceded.
"In what way? The two of you talked about this?"
"Look, the two of you are my dearest and best. Zeta says things I know she doesn't mean because she's restless."
"My wife's damned good looking. She could have a lot of guys with money."
"It's something else. Freedom, maybe. She fantasizes about leaving Austin."
"So she's that disappointed in me?"
"You're not the promising artist she married. But, hell, I really don't have a clue about what she wants. She says she has this wild yearning. Those were her exact words."
"A wild yearning? She said that?"
Kelton nodded yes.
"That's an extravagant damned phrase," said Harry, and Kelton agreed.
They drank off their beers and looked at each other, perplexed.
"Seen anymore of that detective?" Kelton finally asked.
"Just talked to him. He told me how this killer seems to find his little victims by magic. There's something else I haven't told you. When we first talked he implied that the killer might be a doctor."
"If you're thinking about Wade, no way."
"Who knows? And we have two pals who went to medical school. Remember, we heard that Olan flunked out."
"C'mon, Wade and Olan are two old farts."
"Maybe. But I think the detective suspects our little group at Villa Cappeletti."
"You're kidding."
"He says he wants to meet with us. He can't figure the doll on the pathway."
"God, I hope it doesn't come to a meeting. Or any sort of real investigation involving us."
"Why would that bother you?"
"Maybe I have something to hide."
"It would have to be some little girl in your past for it to make any difference."

"She wasn't all that young."

"Christ almighty, Kelton."

"It's getting so crowded in here we'll never get another beer."

"We'll order another with the pizza. Tell me. What's bothering you about all this?"

"Harry, it was years before Isabella. In Kenya. And in Africa, hell, who cares? It wasn't like I was arrested or anything."

"All these years and you've never mentioned this."

"It was something I wanted to forget."

"Sounds awful."

"I had this housekeeper in Nairobi and she had a daughter. Fully developed. Hell, I didn't know how old she was. Anyway, I took up with the daughter and the mother—well, she stepped aside so the daughter actually became the housekeeper."

"But something happened?"

"Yeah, and, damn, I need another beer. Maybe something stronger if I'm going to tell this."

The guy in the turban twisted spaghetti on his fork. The two Japanese tourists also came in, one carrying the laundry basket. Harry tried to calm himself as Kelton waved at a waiter. He wanted to think about Zeta and Leo, but Kelton and a nameless young girl in Africa crowded in. When a waiter finally arrived and more beers were ordered Kelton propped his elbows on the table and popped his knuckles.

"For Christ's sake," Harry urged him.

"She was this gorgeous black girl. I made a point of being seen with her she was so damned good looking. Took her to the Muthiaga Club once. Of course we sat on the verandah, not in the lounge. Anyway, I guess I was trying to make a statement because, hell, I was young. And one hell of a reporter who wasn't going to get fired. When you're young, Harry, you begin to reek with confidence."

"Nobody around here could possibly find out about some girl in Kenya thirty or forty years ago," Harry assured him.

"She got killed," said Kelton in a hoarse whisper. "I took her with me to cover a story up in the Sudan. Never should've done it. I was covering a little war at the time. She drank too much and wandered out in the street in front of this stinking hotel where we stayed. There were maybe a total of fifty vehicles in all of Juba at the time, but one of them hit her. She turned out to be fourteen years old. At least that's what her mother said."

"And you got into trouble?"

"Officially, no. But my newspaper moved me out of the assignment to avoid it. Sent me back to the States where my editor said he considered me on probation. Said he didn't want to hear about my taste for little girls ever again."

Beer and pizza arrived and they drank slowly, ignoring the pizza.

"Anyway, I feel guilty as hell. And it's on my record someplace. Or at least I feel like it is. If anybody ever wants to check up on me."

"Nobody's going to check up on you," Harry maintained.

"I was happily married to Isabella for more than twenty years," Kelton said as if pleading his case. "It was Africa."

"Forget it," said Harry.

"I can't. I'm Southern Baptist. I've been all over the world and I know better, but I can't shake off this old Calvinist shit. I'll make a confession, too: I still like young girls. I shouldn't breathe a word of it, but Lolita, for me, is still a fascinating little wench."

"I didn't hear that. And for god's sake, Kelton, don't ever say it to anybody else."

"It maybe makes me a pervert, but I feel guilty about it. And young girls are attractive, but I'm already sorry I told you about what happened in the Sudan."

"You needed to tell me, buddy, but now that I've heard it I'm going to put it out of my head."

"You won't be able to."

"Yeah, Kelton, I will. Anyway, this conversation isn't about you, is it? It was about Zeta. It blows my mind that she'd actually consider going off with Leo."

"She's still very much attached to you, Harry."
"Oh, thanks."

Kelton picked at a piece of sausage on the pizza and absently began to nibble on it. As he chewed he said, "You know who interests me?"

"Let me guess. April."

"Right, Roper's girlfriend. Wanta know my opinion? She has children at home, a job, and she's a sane working girl. She knows exactly who she is. You see it in her eyes. I think she's a person with substance."

"A look in her eyes? You're daffy about that body of hers."

"Sure, that too. But she's definitely not crazy like a few others I could name."

"Like Zeta, you mean?"

"I didn't say Zeta."

"A wild yearning," Harry said, smirking. "Christ, she's never used an idiotic phrase like that."

They returned to the villa feeling—because of Kelton's confession and their mutual dismay over Zeta—somehow closer than usual. Madame Cappeletti and her son waited for them as they entered. She said that the detective had requested an audience with every guest and staff member at six o'clock.

"So embarrassing, sorry," she said, and she lifted her chin to give her head an elegant shake. "We will serve free—no charge—aperitifs. And if you are having trouble for dinner plans we are also serving the special roast beef here this evening. Also fish."

Harry watched the son as Madame Cappeletti spoke. A brute of a boy: thick eyebrows that joined on his forehead, big hands, the smile of an ape. A possible suspect, Harry found himself thinking.

"Oh god," Kelton moaned as they went up in the tiny elevator. "I'm going to be investigated, I know it. I have a real headache coming on, too."

"May I say that my colleagues and I are having many such meetings as this one," the *investigatore* began. "No one here is a suspect in these terrible crimes. I am here to review just how Harry found the doll on the path and to see if anyone else perhaps saw something curious. Anything. Many times you will see something significant and not know it. I will finish with you well before the dinner hour, so, please, if you will."

Zeta, arriving late, moved beside Harry and whispered, "What a beautiful man! Very courtly. You didn't tell me."

The group sat in a semi-circle of armchairs in the main room while the staff of maids, waiters and cooks lined up around the walls. Madame Cappeletti and her son stood in the doorway within reach of the office phone. He wore a thick sweater and a sullen face.

Terminella's double-breasted blue jacket was trimmed with brass buttons and he wore a dark tie, grey slacks and shiny black shoes. Except for the cigarette ash on his lapel he looked dapper and energetic. Searching for a match and not finding one he was handed a matchbook by one of the maids—it contained only a single match—then fired up and blew a perfect smoke ring toward the crystal chandelier.

"Your friend Harry, he finds a doll before seven o'clock in the morning when the first ferry makes its stop near this villa," he began, indicating Harry who stood with Zeta beside Val's club chair. "Who else comes along this same path? Someone from the staff?"

This started an exchange in Italian with a maid and a kitchen worker who came to work along that same route, but who had seen nothing. As they chatted another maid, Gladyce, arrived with sherry and tiny snacks, but Terminella waved her out.

"Please," he said. "Later a tea party. Just questions for now."

Madame Cappeletti, embarrassed, ushered Gladyce into the corridor, and the detective, annoyed, paid elaborate attention to his cigarette until he returned to his conversation. The staff version remained: no one had seen the doll along the path before Harry found it.

Madame Cappeletti's son was then questioned

at some length. He kept his head down, looking up through his bushy eyebrows, so the detective moved in, finding his gaze as they talked together. As their discussion went on, Val came to tears.

"Are you okay?" Harry asked, passing her a handkerchief.

"The poor, poor little children," she managed, and because of her dramatics some attention was turned to her.

Leo's cell phone rang and he answered it.

"Sweetheart, we're sorta in a meeting," he explained loudly. "Can't talk just now." His twang was both bass and nasal, filling the room so that Terminella winced and turned. Meanwhile, Jackie obviously had a lot to say at the other end.

"A meeting!" Leo explained again, his voice gaining strength. "Ever'body in the whole damn villa! I'll call you back!"

Jackie's long agenda clearly continued because Leo kept the phone to his ear.

Harry became fascinated with Terminella's technique: drawing close and boring in so that his quarry couldn't avert his eyes even for a moment. Harry became especially intrigued when Terminella drew a bead on Olan.

"And in America you are what, a doctor?"

"Psychologist," Olan responded, not without some familiar puffing up.

"Ah, psychology. And we have at this lake eleven little girls missing or known to be murdered. What sort of monster does such a thing to little girls? In your professional opinion?"

"I don't know," Olan admitted. "Evil exists."

"So it does, truly. I know this. Would you say that evil has ever been done to you?"

"I'm not sure I understand."

"You say you believe evil exists. Has anyone ever done evil to you personally?"

Olan hesitated, then replied, "Perhaps."

"Many of us can claim this. Let me ask you another question. Have you ever done evil to anyone else?"

"I hope not," said Olan.

For a moment Terminella held his gaze before moving on.

During this time Leo tried to get Jackie off the phone, but she obviously wanted to speak with Val or Robin. "They're in this damn meeting, too!" he shouted. "We're all here! I'm hangin' up now and I'll call back in an hour, okay? Yes, I promise!"

The detective produced another cigarette and once more fumbled for matches. This time Leo, closing his phone, provided the *investigatore* with a cheap Bic lighter and with a wave of the hand made clear it was a gift.

"You are talking to America on the cell phone?" Terminella asked, lighting his cigarette.

"My wife," said Leo with an apologetic grin.

"Everything is now high tech, yes? I have such a phone. My signal bounces off a satellite, but here in the mountains not always so good. We are also using DNA. You know, of course, DNA?"

"Sure," said Leo.

"Would you agree to take our DNA test if I asked you?"

"I'd be happy to." Leo wore a sincere and earnest expression.

Terminella turned to his audience. "In Rome and Milan we have the DNA experts, but not yet here. We have thought of using it—your Harry and I we are speaking of this strategy—but many visitors come to the lake—and, well, it would be difficult or impossible. But is there anyone here who would not take this test at our request?"

No one responded.

"It is argued that such a test would compromise a person's freedom. Some say, who knows how the police might use such a test against me? And such a test could possibly be inaccurate, yes, I understand anyone's reluctance. But, also, there are dead children, so I ask the question of you."

He moved to Roper.

"I'm a lawyer," Roper began, taking the lead. "If there's anything we can do for the investigation just ask."

"Thank you," Terminella said slowly, and he drew deeply at his cigarette as he studied Roper's face.

"You might want to fill us in," Roper said. "I assume a great deal is being done to solve this case."

"Yes, many rewards are offered. From Milan this summer we have a special squad to help us. I am one of three local detectives. There are psychologists—one of whom works with your FBI to profile this killer. There are counselors for the families of the little victims. Many reporters from newspapers. In Rome this is very much a big story. Yet many tourists who come here are not aware. I am hearing that you and your group read no Italian newspaper stories even though you come here for many years."

"I'm ashamed to say that's so."

"This is not so unusual. For centuries others come to Italy. The climate, very nice. Good wine and food. You know us as waiters and servants and you are aristocrats taking the holiday. You are leaving behind the business of your own lives and not so much caring about local problems. Not so unusual, not at all."

Harry detected the bite in Terminella's little speech and wondered if others did, too.

As the *investigatore* turned away from Roper he dropped a rope of cigarette ash on Robin's skirt. She sat prim and stiff at the edge of her armchair, her skirt pulled tightly across her knees, and the wad of ash lay there for an instant before Terminella apologized and moved to brush it off. Before he could act, though, Wade reached over and brushed it away and the two men bumped heads.

"And you are?" Terminella asked.

Wade promptly introduced himself and objected to something the detective had said.

"Ah, and what is this?"

"That we consider all Italians merely waiters and servants."

"I don't think I said exactly this. But you are offended, are you, doctor?"

"Some of us could be," Wade responded, and Harry saw that Terminella had correctly identified their physician. "We are very aware of local situations," Wade went on. "Perhaps you don't know it, but we've donated cars and vans to local groups—including the fire brigade. We know the mayor of Lenno and other officials. We've bought property here and hired local attorneys and construction companies."

Harry also noted that Wade spoke proudly of Leo's activities, not his own, and that the only local official actually known to the group had enjoyed a fling with Wade's wife.

"So, good," Terminella conceded. "And tell me this, please, doctor: are you one of the golfers?"

"No, I dislike the game."

"Ah, so perhaps you take long walks?"

"Every day. I've hiked most of the trails around the lake."

"Our killer of children does this as well, we believe."

The two men stared evenly at one another.

"Have you visited the botanical gardens and the famous villa of Carlotta?" the detective quickly asked as if he were a tour guide. Wade managed to nod and make an affirmative sound. "Cupid and Psyche," Terminella said. "Very famous, this sculpture by Canova. In all the towns of the lake there is not such an art object as this one."

He turned quickly to Kelton.

"I'm not feeling well," the journalist told him. "I'm afraid I have to go to my room."

"Yes, in a moment," said Terminella holding up a hand. "But tell me, please, are you the friend of Harry's who runs?"

"No, I just play a bit of golf."

"Then perhaps you rent the Vespa?"

"That's me, yes, and I also tour around the lake. All of us do."

"I think you are also a solitary man," said Terminella, peering into Kelton's eyes.

"I suppose so."

"So am I." The detective stubbed out his

cigarette in the room's only ashtray and smiled. "It is often difficult being solitary." He made a graceful turn, not unlike a dancer's, and said to everyone in the room, "Good, thank you. I hope you have a pleasant stay and that our terrible business doesn't inconvenience you so much."

With that the interviews closed and a number of conversations commenced. Olan announced loudly that he was hungry and intended to remain at the villa for dinner and this pleased the Cappelettis who moved their staff toward the kitchen and dining room.

"It's early yet," Leo countered. "Let's have a ton of drinks, then decide. How about you, honey?" He gave April's midsection a pinch.

Zeta moved to the detective's side, offering her hand. She regarded him, Harry decided, as a visiting prince.

Robin stood at the window fingering her lace collar and listening to Val's ongoing chatter.

Roper found Harry. "Leo suggests we stroll up to the piazza in Lenno. Dinner at Stephano's. What do you think?"

"Maybe," Harry replied, watching Zeta. He hoped to get her alone for a talk. As she spoke with Madame Cappeletti and Terminella she threw back her head in laughter, tossing her hair. Harry recognized it, painfully, as the false laughter she sometimes employed when she became solicitous.

Instead of going anywhere for dinner Zeta and Harry argued.

"Kelton told you about Leo's offer?"

"Yes, and by god he's a good friend for letting me know."

"I'll never trust him again! All reporters are gossips and he's the worst! I can't believe he told you!"

"It's because I accused him of carrying on with you."

"Carrying on with me? Kelton?"

"You're indifferent to sex. How the hell should I know what's going on in your head?"

"You're the one indifferent to sex."

"The hell I am!" Harry shouted, and he pulled all the covers off the bed and marched them out to the balcony. Zeta came out, too, hissing at his back.

"Leo offered me a job! It wasn't a proposition!"

"Don't kid yourself! He's trying to buy you and you're trying to decide if you're for sale!"

"For your information it was a hell of a big offer! More'n you'll ever see!"

"Big news! Leo has more money than I do."

"It's not just the money, but you're content to run a camera shop! You used to be a hell of a lot more, you know, but now you're a shopkeeper!"

"I'm making a living!" he said, turning on her and following her back into the bedroom. "And I haven't given up anything! I'm still what I was. But original ideas are trouble! Millions of goddamned photographers shoot up miles of film trying to get something different, trying to see something nobody else sees!"

"I know it, but you're not looking anymore! I won't say I'm not disappointed in you!"

"I've been disappointed in myself!"

"And you're getting as fat as Olan and Wade!"

"Goddammit, I'm not! And I'll go on a diet!"

"Why'd you pull off all the covers?"

"I don't know!"

They sat on opposite sides of the bed, exhausted.

"Leo wants me to think about the décor in his villa," she began more calmly. "He's going to buy some art so he can impress people. I feel sorry for him. Money and bad taste always seem to get together and he's another proof of it."

"Jackie must be furious that Leo turned to you."

"She doesn't know about this offer."

"How do you know that?"

"He said so. They argued about something in their villa she didn't like. Anyway, her taste is no better than his."

"You're actually thinking about working with him."

"Why not? You're going to shoot nude photos of April, but I trust you."

"You trust me because Roper's going to be there. You actually don't care. You're indifferent and you're disappointed in me and don't give a damn."

"Don't feel so sorry for yourself."

They delivered all this without raising their voices, but his feelings were terribly hurt. He spread some of the blankets over the big armchair and ottoman facing the lake.

"You're sleeping in that chair tonight?"

"What do you care?"

"Suit yourself," she said, and spread the coverlet over their bed.

Harry went to elaborate pains to arrange a sheet and blanket, then fluffed up his two pillows and placed them just so. He brushed his teeth in the bathroom and put on the striped pajamas he often packed but never wore. As he settled himself across the chair and ottoman Zeta dressed herself in slacks and a sweater.

"You're not hungry?" she asked.

"I'm too fat to eat," he told her.

"Some of the gang's eating up at Stephano's. You know, just across from the church."

He sulked, not answering.

"You're turning in at half past eight?" she asked.

"I wish we'd never met fucking Leo Jones," he said to the night beyond the balcony.

"Then you'd never have sold your photographs to him or his friends," she said evenly. "That means we probably wouldn't own the camera shop. Our house wouldn't be paid for. We'd never have gone on those cruises or had that month in London or seen Lake Como."

He gazed out into the cold darkness of the evening.

"If I work for him it'll be a temporary thing. Like a consultant. And I'll make more money than we've ever made in any three years of our marriage. I'll be here at the lake at his villa and I'd like you to be with me until everything's finished. Not that I've actually decided to say yes. I worried how you might react and that's why I confided in Kelton. I know working with Leo will be awkward. Maybe he'll try to compromise me. I wouldn't put it past him, but I don't think he'll try anything. My car's seven years old. I'm tired of Austin. From time to time when the villa's finished you and I might stay there ourselves—without Leo or anyone else. But right now I'm walking up to Stephano's. I'm going to smile and sit down to eat. It's probably just Leo, Roper, and April, and you can come along too. I wish you would, okay?"

When he didn't respond she went out the door.

After an hour or so Harry removed the bedclothes from the chair and ottoman, spread everything back on the bed, then climbed in. Zeta returned late—slightly tipsy from the sound of her movements—and when she got in beside him she reached over and touched him lightly to make sure he was there.

TWO

The world consists only of the vulgar.
—Machiavelli, *The Prince*

The Hokey Pokey had become such a successful ice cream parlor and bar in Menaggio that its owner, Carmine Rufo, opened another in Como and had hopes for franchises that might reach all the way back to London and cross the Atlantic to the riches of America. Both establishments were fitted out like Victorian music halls with velvet drapes, slow ceiling fans, shiny tile floors, and assorted electronic machines. Both had regular bars at one end—for mum and dad—and ice cream counters with soda fountains at the other. Built for the town's British clientele who with its children filled the cheap hotels along the quay, the business offered something for everyone—pints of ale or the local wines for the parents and cones or sundaes for the kids. Rufo himself served as bartender while he wife, Lucia, worked backstage at the puppet theater to direct her daughters in their presentations. The girls and their mother dramatized popular American movies, often clever parodies, of everything from *Frankenstein* to *The Wizard of Oz*. Lucia and her oldest daughter, Monica, created and sewed the puppets and all the girls—down to the youngest, Cinda—had become skilled with the puppets' voices and movements.

The crowds came and money flowed.

Parents often stayed around for two or more puppet shows, sipping wine and watching their children. Two large video screens also featured cartoons, the Three Stooges and animal shows. Kids were often there without their parents, too, even the children of the locals. This was because two policemen, one in uniform and one in plain clothes, kept long hours at the Hokey Pokey and every resident of the town knew it. Cameras were in use, too, and could be played back as a recording of every customer's visit. The Menaggio establishment had become a regular stake-out since one of the missing girls had been known to go there.

At the new ice cream business in Como security was being planned and developed. Cameras would soon be installed. The *polizia* kept a man on the premises as much as possible, but as the crowds grew and the hours lengthened problems arose. The *comandante* of the detective squad, the big man named Benzetti, urged Carmine Rufo to hire his own guards, but this suggestion was hotly argued. Not my problem, Carmine made clear. I am the businessman. You catch thieves and killers. It is much too expensive to pay guards. In turn Benzetti pointed out that his squad was stretched to the limit—especially in the month of August—and the business could possibly be closed down.

In the weeks after their business opened in Como the wife, Lucia, and Carmine drove back and forth between the two towns on that curving and dangerous roadway tending to their businesses. They finally bought a used van, though, and dispatched Monica, age twenty, to manage the new place. Two other sisters went along during the summer months to help with the puppet shows: Danielle, age sixteen, and Cinda, age ten.

In the middle of August little Cinda disappeared. After two hours Monica phoned her parents who immediately drove down from Menaggio. By the time they arrived in Como the *investigatore,* Terminella, was on the scene with members of the Como and Milan squads. Roadblocks went up and the ferries were watched.

But she was gone. And the cameras, waiting in crates ready to be mounted, recorded nothing.

That afternoon as everyone fretted inside the

new Hokey Pokey in Como little Cinda stood beside a stranger near the old ruins at Lago de Annone. She was in the last minutes of her life and they would never find her body.

Terminella learned that he would be pulled off the Rufo investigation and sent over to Bellagio to ask questions about a wife beating. He told Benzetti about the Americans staying in Lenno at the Villa Cappeletti.
"I wanted to hear the men's alibis," the detective explained.
But Benzetti was in no mood for hunches, intuitions, or whatever Terminella wanted next. "Your ideas are wrong," he argued. "Wrong. I've listened for years while you've dreamed up this kind of scenario."
"Boss, no, listen to me."
"Groundless," Benzetti said firmly. "Wild. *Idiota.*"
The *Comandante* was the largest of all the Como officers. He had started in the tough western sections of Milan working as a motorcycle cop and eventually passed his exams and became a detective. In the army he won a boxing championship -- although sharply criticized for hitting below the belt in the title fight. Although he shaved twice a day and once in the evening before slipping into bed with his wife, the shadow on his face remained black.
"I'm telling you: go up to Bellagio," he said, restraining himself. "The woman is related to the mayor."
"So is everyone else," Terminella complained. "Let Mario do it."
"Mario is at the ice cream parlor dealing with Rufo, the hysterical wife, and the screaming daughters. Enjoy a peaceful ride on the ferry. Do this, please, without giving me more shit."
"I guess I could come back through Lenno," Terminella suggested.
"No, you won't do that either."
"Why not?"
"I heard all about your meeting with Madame

Cappeletti and her guests. When you mentioned DNA testing she went crazy. One drop of blood extracted from her guests and she says she'll never see them again. She also said you dropped ashes on some lady, then insulted and threatened everybody in the room."

"I didn't threaten anybody."

"There's more. The doll found by your photographer? The parents now tell us it isn't the same doll."

"When did they decide this?"

"Yesterday. The one that belonged to their daughter had a wine stain."

"And they just remembered it?"

"They once tried to wash out the wine stain, but couldn't. So this doll found near Madame Cappeletti's villa looks the same, but isn't. They gave the doll back to us. So your photographer just found a similar doll. There must be hundreds of them. And there's no link between this case and your Americans who come visiting in August."

Terminella gazed out the window toward the Piazza del Duomo. Bicycle riders in bright spandex sat in an open café among the pigeons and gulls in the street below. A cobalt blue sky. He thought how he spent far too much for an elaborate burglar alarm system in the modest apartment where he lived with his wife and daughters, an expenditure that came out of his own fear for his family.

"Can you look at me when we're talking?" Benzetti asked.

"Sorry," Terminella replied, then he started again. "Did you see the report on the Rufo girl? What she was wearing when she disappeared?"

"Yes, I read it. So?"

"She was wearing a cowboy baseball cap. Did you notice that?"

"What's the connection?"

"A cap from a Texas football team. The Dallas Cowboys. Sometimes they're on television. Big blue stars on their helmets. The connection is Texas."

Benzetti let the silence gather, then he sighed heavily.

"Terminella, please, get your mind off Texas. We don't even know precisely about the murder weapon. We've never had a single suspect. We haven't found half the girls. Probably because they're at the bottom of the lake. We have a limited budget and the Milan squad wants to embarrass us. DNA testing is out of the question. You told me about that book. How they tested everybody in some English village, but how even then the killer avoided giving his blood. We need evidence or a real break. Some mistake on the part of the killer. Not a detective with hunches—no matter how experienced he is or how hard he has worked. Now, please, go to Bellagio. A woman took a terrible beating and deserves to hear from us right away, understand?"

Terminella held the *comandante*'s gaze and nodded.

"Remember, also, do not go back to the Americans in that villa. I will give you three good reasons. Madame Cappelletti doesn't want you. The doll doesn't fit. And this is my direct order. Never go back there. Not even for tea or a glass of wine. Not ever."

Roper had spent two hours on top of a step ladder and wanted no more of it. While Harry worked with April and the camera and while their little host fussed with the lighting, made tea, and kept up the chatter, Roper, as instructed, had sprinkled a few grains of talcum powder—just a bit, please, there, between thumb and forefinger –so that it floated into the shot below. Meanwhile, art for art's sake: the dark velvet backdrop, April lying there quiet as a zombie, the reflectors just so, umbrellas here and there to filter the light, and both Harry and Bernard running around the tripod and peering into the viewfinder.

"How much longer we gonna do this?" Roper wanted to know.

"It's a series of shots," Harry explained again. "First a few grains of talcum. Dozens of exposures doing that. Then I'll develop the prints to see if we have it. If we're getting the effect I'm after, we'll drop larger amounts of talcum. Later, even more. So much talcum we'll have to clean up between takes."

"So we're talkin' about a guy up the ladder for days?"

"Yeah, maybe days," Harry confessed.

"Then, buddy, it can't be me."

"I can do it," Bernard volunteered. "Or you can do it, Harry, while I open the lens if that won't violate something for you."

"Either way suits me," Harry said. "You awake, April?"

"In my zone," she replied, not moving.

She lay with her arms stretched above her pillowed head, a breast exposed, her hip jutting up, her flat stomach sloping into the pubis. Harry wanted at most just the lower part of her face: lips and chin. He'd maybe later crop those out, too. So her body was a landscape, impersonal, and he meant to capture the tiny flakes of talcum as they descended white through the darkness. As the series progressed he wanted a blizzard of talcum until her curves were covered with it: black, stark white flakes, and the nude grey presence.

Harry checked the exposure meter again and Roper came down the ladder.

"More mulberry brandy?" Bernard offered.

"No, that's terrible shit. Got any coffee?"

"It does have a bit of aftertaste," Bernard agreed. "How about a nice cup of tea?"

"You got coffee or not?" Roper asked.

"Sorry, no."

Harry wanted to take a break on the terrace. April slipped on a robe and reached for Roper's hand, but he was out of sorts and made his excuses. He said he might go jogging and needed to make some phone calls to Texas. As Harry arranged chairs on the terrace Bernard went down the path to his rural mailbox.

"Honey, I think a jog would do you good," April told Roper. "Poor guy. You've been up a hot ladder working. Knock off."

"I'll go back to the villa, make my calls, and pick up my jogging shoes," he said, relieved to be free.

"See you in the lounge before dinner," said Harry, and Roper allowed April to kiss his cheek.

As Roper went down the path he passed Bernard trudging back and acknowledged him by slightly raising his chin.

Harry and April talked about composition and Bernard joined in when he returned. "Photography is about light," Harry was saying. "For instance, there's your face in the sunlight. There's a side of your face turned toward the sun and a darker side. Your eyes are in shadow. Your hair is shiny. You're April, yes, and I see you and know you as April, but you're also a composition of shadow and light—and I'm trained to see you as that."

"I'm just a composition to you?" she asked, disappointed.

"You're both April and a composition. This hillside is a composition: the trees and the shadows they make. The terraces that create perspective, all this."

"So my body is just a composition?"

"And a very lovely composition it is," Bernard said. "Harry's trying for a peculiar effect. But, dear girl, I'll climb any old ladder and sprinkle powder down on your very shapely bum with absolute pleasure and excitement."

"Thanks," April said with a smile.

"Those trees," Harry asked. "What are they?"

"Mulberry. For the silkworm trade. The ones with the white berries feed the silkworms and the ones with the purple berries—and there's not so many of them—make the sweet brandy Roper didn't much like."

April folded herself inside her robe, leaned back, and studied the terraced trees. Meanwhile Bernard talked on about mulberries, the silk trade around the lake, and how the region served in ancient times much the same as the famous marble quarries had served the Italian sculptors.

"I could stay here forever and listen to you two," said April with a contented sigh.

They were all smiling as Harry picked out the newspaper from Bernard's mail delivery.

"Does this say what I think it does?" Harry asked, pointing to the banner headline.

"My god, another little girl!" said Bernard, taking the newspaper. "And Carmine Rufo's daughter!"

"When did it happen?"

"Yesterday down in Como. I know this family and go to their bar in Menaggio from time to time. Horrible."

Harry asked Bernard to read the details and translate, but not much was known. April watched their faces and brought a hand to her throat. As he listened to the translation of the news Harry began wondering about everybody's whereabouts yesterday. They hadn't played golf. Everyone had gone his own way, but he couldn't remember anyone's particular plans. Were the wives with any of them? What was said at dinner last night? Who had gone where?

He also thought about the *investigatore*.

Terminella would be frantic.

Again, Harry knew, the detective would take this personally.

While Harry, Roper and April visited Bernard's studio at the old factory the remaining women of the group enjoyed a long lunch and covered several topics. They speculated over Jackie's departure, the detective's curious visit to the villa, April's posing nude, their husbands—all of whom were off in different directions again today—and they even came to a literary consensus, rare, because both Zeta and Val had read and liked a novel entitled *The Poisonwood Bible*.

"It's about this religious fanatic," Val explained to Robin. "He takes his wife and daughters off to Africa. He's a missionary who blunders around doing evil."

Robin had grown away from her hardshell Baptist roots in Texas and disliked religion in general, but held to a number of traditional values. She strongly felt that Jackie—no matter what her argument with her husband—should have stayed, made up with Leo, and carried on as the good wife.

"Leo drives too hard," Val offered in rebuttal. "All his phone calls and e-mails, giving orders to people all day long. He builds himself a castle, but doesn't want Jackie's suggestions. He's a control freak and she got fed up."

"It's my fault," Zeta said. "He kept asking my opinions and I should've deferred to Jackie, but didn't."

"I hear he wants you on his payroll," said Val, pushing the pasta around on her plate.

"Something was said, but nothing specific."

"You know he's nuts about you," Val went on. "But if he puts you on his payroll he'll certainly want to get his hands on you."

"He wants his hands on anything that jiggles," Zeta said, smirking.

Robin put on an earnest expression and asked, "Do your husbands still want sex all the time?"

Their forks stopped in mid-air.

"Harry does, poor thing," Zeta finally managed.

"Wade, too, but he's getting fat and I don't have the acrobatic skills I once did."

"Olan's getting kinky," Robin revealed.

"Like what?" both Val and Zeta asked in unison.

"He needs helpful pictures. Porno. And he bought me these two boxes of lingerie to wear. From one of those stores. Crotchless and so on."

Val couldn't muster a response, but Zeta said, "Hot diggity."

"And when I wouldn't wear the stuff he got mad and cut it all up with a pair of scissors."

"He cut up the lingerie?"

"Olan loses his temper. Maybe you've never noticed."

They had noticed, but let it go. Instead, Val wanted to know what sort of porno Olan preferred.

"I'll tell," Robin answered, and a trace of a grin flitted across her thin lips. "But if we're going to gossip about our husbands you have to share something."

"Okay, Wade tried Viagra, but got dizzy," Val quickly revealed. "So he cut the pill in half. That worked pretty well. We both got off. So he decided to double his fun and went back to a whole pill, but he passed out. Sometimes nowadays I think we're pretty much through with sex, but then occasionally I think he's getting something on the side."

"Why do you think so?" Robin asked sweetly.

Zeta leaned in for the reply.

"Honey, I can tell. From time to time he shows up without his underwear."

"What?" Zeta said, laughing. Robin squealed.

"But, hey, girls, what's a few pairs of undershorts in a long marriage?"

After they laughed some more Zeta turned to Robin and said, "Go back to Olan's brand of porno."

"Well, he goes to this store out on Lamar Street. He buys videos and magazines, all kinds. Black guys with white girls. Girl on girl. Orgies. We have this special chair where we sit and watch together."

"Robin, you sly little thing," said Zeta.

"What about kiddie porn?" Val asked.

"That's illegal," said Robin.

But important to know about, said Val, adding, "In case Olan's the pervert shagging little girls around the lake."

With that they sipped their white wines.

"That detective who came to speak to us," Zeta finally said. "I thought he was yummy. A small version of the Italian stallion."

I thought Kelton acted *so* weird," Val said.

"How's that?"

"The way he told the detective he didn't feel well and wanted to leave."

"Poor Kelton never feels all that good," Robin observed with a sigh.

"Wade thought the detective was a prick," Val said.

"Olan didn't like him either," Robin added. "Olan believed he said quite a few inappropriate things."

"I suppose he had to say what he did," Zeta remarked. "Now what were you saying about Kelton?"

"He looked desperate to get out of there," Val said. "In fact, he looked guilty."

"Our Kelton? C'mon!"

"Sometimes I wonder," Robin asked, putting on her earnest stare once more. "Do you think Kelton's possibly, you know, gay?"

"Not a chance," Zeta assured them. "I knew his wife Isabella and she was a very satisfied woman in that way. I'll let you in on a little secret: Harry's actually been jealous of Kelton recently."

"On this trip? No way," Val said, and they drank some more wine. "And if anyone should worry, my dear, you should worry over Harry with April."

"Oh, Val, Roper's right there serving as chaperone."

"Roper's little girl April looks at your Harry like he's a strawberry lollipop."

"I don't see it," Zeta said.

"Remember when we all went skinny dipping?" Robin asked in her wistful and little girl voice. Her mind had achieved a new ethereal orbit. "I felt real inadequate. You were the one with the great body, Zeta. You were even in a book. And, Val, you had all that up top and I was skinny as a boy. But now I miss it. Nowadays I love everybody so much that I wouldn't mind a hot tub even if April came along!"

"April with me in the same hot tub? Forget it," said Zeta, and they began to laugh.

"Wade would need a nice big Olympic-sized tub," said Val. "And he's not all that healthy, you know. He suffers from a little enigma of the heart."

After a beat Zeta corrected her. "You mean *angina.*"

"Whatever."

"Roper and Kelton aren't fat at all," said the wistful Robin, and they began to laugh again at her earnestness. As their laughter continued they realized they had consumed three bottles of wine.

After his interview with the beaten woman Terminella walked down a narrow back street high above the port in Bellagio and found an espresso bar. He ordered a double then found that he had a light but no cigarettes. The bar had no cigarette machine and he actually surveyed its three tables to see if one of the ashtrays contained a good butt.

Disgruntled, tired, and badly in need of a smoke he thought about all these women in the hill villages: rural types, overworked, living with rough and unemployed men. Many village wives were prisoners in their own houses and neighborhoods: *confino.* In the evenings after preparing a meal and cleaning the kitchen they sat outside with their husbands, but with their chairs facing the doorway of the house so strangers passing by couldn't admire them or charm them with a glance. They did their knitting and mending and spoke in low voices with their household or neighborhood companions while their husbands smoked, drank another glass of wine, and glared at the passing world. The detective's own mother was such a village wife, and although he conceded that times were better for these women they still had a hard lot.

Perhaps unluckier were those who went off to the towns with their boyfriends or young husbands. Such a woman was Madalena who lay in her upstairs apartment not far away with her jaw shattered and her nose broken. The aunts who attended her told him the story: how she worked long hours in the bakery, how the ruffian beat her almost every payday, and how he came back over and over after he had spent her money to say how much he loved her and wanted her forgiveness.

At the far end of the room sat an old man in a beret who knocked back his espresso with a single quick movement as if shooting up caffeine. Not a smoker, Terminella decided. The espresso machine hissed, choked, and produced the double that a boy soon delivered to the bar. The detective drank it thinking about his wife and daughters. They would never be like these women of the villages. His wife was already a school teacher and his daughters would have college degrees. With luck, his daughters would avoid living in the cess pools of the cities. Maybe, later, they'd have horses—or provide ponies for their own children.

He went outside and wiped his mouth on his sleeve. Somewhere nearby he had seen a tobacco shop, but where? It was back uphill, he decided, so started the climb. What was it inside some men that made them beat, confine, bully and terrorize their women? What deep cowardly anger? And now the poor little Rufo girl. What magical beast is out there?

Benzetti was probably right, he knew: hunches and intuitions weren't particularly helpful. He had stared into the faces of a thousand men around this lake and had seen nothing. From that interview with the Americans at the villa, again nothing. Their faces were all clever *maschera:* masks.

Late afternoon arrived and the narrow back streets became shadowed. He found the tobacco shop, but it had closed.

"*Merda,*" he said, and he turned back downhill on a street that led to the ferry.

These upper streets were now deserted, so when he saw a cigarette in the gutter—a whole, virtually unsmoked butt—he considered picking it up. His habit disgusted him, yet he stopped, thinking, no, don't touch it, you'll be down at the quayside bars soon enough and you can buy a fresh pack.

Then in spite of himself he reached down and took it.

He dusted it off and fumbled in his jacket for a light when a figure drew close.

He glanced up, recognized the face as one of those at Madame Cappeletti's villa, and opened his mouth to speak.

Then he saw the spike.

That recognition was instantaneous, too, because a half dozen autopsies had provided the detectives on the murder squad with a clear image of such a spike—a murder weapon somewhat like an elongated corkscrew—and it had even been sketched by the police artist from Milan.

Now it flashed before him, piercing through his summer weight jacket just beside the lapel, through his damp and wrinkled white shirt, and into his heart.

He fell against the wall of the building behind him, slumping into a daze of helpless pain.

Consciousness came and went. He was alone in the street, propped against the wall with the gutter beneath him, his legs spread out stiffly like a child's as he wheezed and gasped for breath. His urine flowed and he couldn't stop it. His hands, quivering, tugged lightly at his jacket as he endured the pain, trying to see the blood pumping out of his chest. But his strength gave way and he realized dumbly, ever so slowly, that he was incapable of calling out for help and that his time on earth had ended. The killer he sought had found him instead. With his last thoughts, then, he fumbled toward prayer as before his eyes he saw the sweet faces of his wife and daughters.

THREE

A man's true delight is to do the things he was made for. He was made to show goodwill to his kind, to rise above the promptings of his senses, and to distinguish appearances from realities.
—Marcus Aurelius, *The Meditations*

    Above Como the old Lario Cemetery looked out across terraces planted with vines and the greenish domes of the city. Mourners were strewn around among the faded wildflowers this morning and Harry could look beyond a series of elegant villas to the shimmering grey waters of the lake. Zeta stood at his side, her shoulder touching his, but none of the others in their group had made it to the funeral and thought it odd that Harry spoke of it as an obligation.
    The priest spoke on and on as Harry studied those in attendance: policemen in both uniforms and dark suits, a cluster of family, an officious looking elder, and a number of grieving couples—young couples, holding hands—who were perhaps the parents of girls who had gone missing and to whom Terminella had once devoted his energies.
    Among the stern policeman the big man stood out. He was an oak among lesser trees: broad shoulders, the dark shadow of facial hair, hands so large that it seemed he made attempts to hide them from sight. He had the chiseled face of a tired warrior. Others came to him, whispering and moving on, and by the way he acknowledged them and nodded in response his authority became

apparent. As the graveside service drew to a close the big *Comandante* turned and went directly to the widow. Flanked by the two daughters, she wore a dark straw hat fastened with a scarf. She held the scarf tightly as the big man closed his arms around her and she wept. The uniformed cops moved around this tableau like uncertain birds, watching yet trying not to. Harry knew this was Benzetti and he was determined to speak with him even in such awkward circumstances.

The crowd slowly filed downhill toward the parked cars.

"Yes, see you there," Zeta said, giving Harry's hand a squeeze, then she strolled away with the other mourners while he stationed himself on the path and waited. To the north dark clouds promised mist and cooler weather.

The *Comandante* soon left the widow and came toward Harry. Other officers surrounded him, but Harry managed to get close enough to speak.

"Pardon me!" he called out. "I'm the American who found the doll at Lenno!"

Benzetti stopped and gave him a blank stare.

Harry drew closer and repeated, "The doll? The doll at Madame Cappeletti's villa!"

Benzetti seemed to understand little and his eyes darted around until he spotted someone who could act as interpreter. "*Scusi,*" he told Harry, and he gave him a tight smile as one of his large hands came up to signal a timeout.

They waited for a big blond cop with bad acne or pox scars to make his way through the convoy of policemen. When he arrived at their side Harry repeated the business about finding the doll. Benzetti, in turn, addressed the blond cop at length.

"This is not the proper doll," said the blond cop in relay. "The *Comandante* thanks you for your help and for your presence today, but this doll the parents say is not proper."

Harry didn't understand. Proper? It was all said again slowly and this time the interpreter tried to make it clear about the wine stain. Benzetti smiled patiently and had the blond cop ask how long Harry would remain on holiday at the lake.

"Three weeks or less," said Harry and this drew solicitous smiles from all the cops. Benzetti told Harry to enjoy his holiday and to leave matters in police hands.

"But Terminella believed that someone at our villa might be involved in the murders," Harry insisted. "With your permission I'd like to meet with you in your office to discuss it."

Benzetti had turned to walk away, but as this was passed along he stopped again to give the interpreter a long and thoughtful reply. Terminella, he said, was a man of many intuitions, some of them brilliant. But further meetings were unnecessary. This was a very emotional case, the *Comandante* pointed out, and many people imagine they can help. But they should place their trust with experts. By the time all this was related in somewhat broken English, Benzetti was walking off and Harry was left to wonder about several details—the murder weapon, anything known about the killer—and he especially wanted more information about the doll.

"We are explaining to you," said the interpreter, making an effort to stay courteous, then finally raising his voice in exasperation. "The parents give back to us that doll! It is not belonging to the *bambina*. Not belonging! Understand?"

He also walked away, leaving Harry alone on the path.

Minutes later he drove back along the lake road with Zeta. When she wanted to know about his conversation with Benzetti he said only that he had expressed his condolences.

"We spend half a day driving back and forth so you can express your condolences? That's it?"

Perhaps because he and Zeta were out of synch he didn't want to share his suspicions with her. Also, she was considering this offer from Leo—and what did that mean? The two of them hardly touched. When she leaned against his shoulder during the graveside services he felt grateful, yet remembered that she turned cool toward him in the privacy of their room at the villa. Also he was unsure of his suspicions.

"I thought you might have something to contribute to the case of the little girls," she went on. "I thought you had information for the police. An idea."

He told her what Benzetti had said about the doll.

"Well, there you are," she replied. "This whole matter has nothing to do with any of us."

"I didn't know that until Benzetti told me," he pointed out.

They kept silence for a while. A lorry swerved close and honked, but Harry drove doggedly on.

"Terminella was stabbed to death," he mused. "I'll bet the little girls were stabbed, too."

"Oh, Harry, you don't know that."

"You're right, I don't."

"The detective was killed over in Bellagio after some domestic squabble. According to Madame Cappeletti that much was in the Italian newspapers."

If the police know that both Terminella and the little girls were killed with the same sort of weapon, Harry asked himself, won't that make them pay greater attention to all of Terminella's theories and suspicions?

"I do have a bit of news," Zeta said after a time. "Leo's new plans. He intends to charter a plane and fly over some of his business pals for a party. A weekend party at his new villa—unfinished or not. In the gardens, down by the lake, that sort of thing. He wants Jackie to fly over with them, of course, so we're wondering if it's a gesture to get her back."

"Big gesture."

"He tries to be thoughtful. He asked me if I thought a long weekend party would inconvenience any of us."

"He tries to be thoughtful and control us," said Harry.

"Harry, don't be petulant just because your part in Detective Terminella's case didn't work out."

It was worse than petulance. He was in the midst of insight. The murders, Terminella's observations, and a number of minor irritations contributed to it. All of us are fat nomads, he wanted to tell her. We fly around everywhere borrowing culture and in return we give back arrogance and a pop impertinence. We see the foreigners around us—just as Terminella said—as waiters, drivers, and servants getting our tourist dollars. Their lives, all their problems and all their tragedies are viewed with indifference—or worse, as inconveniences. And now at Lake Como, he wanted to tell her, perhaps we've brought them a horrible psychopathic sport.

Zeta stared at the lake, clammed up.

They couldn't even communicate. She occupied her own little zone of silliness now—thinking this about Leo or that about Kelton—so that he couldn't tell her how deeply he felt or how his suspicions moved toward wild certainties.

The men played golf, but shot poorly, became cranky, and decided to stop for a few days. Everyone wanted to do something else and seemed relieved.

Kelton asked Harry's permission to take Zeta across the lake on a Vespa ride.

"Sure, why not?" Harry agreed.

"We thought we might putter up to Bellano and watch you at work with April."

"No, Kelton, I'd rather you wouldn't."

"Oh, why?"

"We're really working," Harry assured him.

"I'm sure you are. Is Roper still helping out?"

"No, he's already bored with it."

"So it's just you and April?"

"And the Brit, Bernard. It's his studio and he's a great help."

"Oh, right, I forgot the Brit."

Later that afternoon the rain showers came again. Harry put on a light wool sweater and accompanied Wade to a little bar beyond the ferry station. While having their drinks a downpour started and they saw Roper jogging by with backpack and umbrella.

"Where does he get the energy?" Wade asked with a sigh. "I'm still bushed from golf this morning."

"I wonder what he carries in that backpack?" Harry wondered aloud.

"Maybe drinking water. Who cares?"

Maybe a dagger, Harry thought.

They stood in Bernard's darkroom looking at drying prints: angles on April's torso in near darkness with bits of talcum floating into the shots.

"Marvelous," Bernard said. "You've got it. So what do we do now?"

"Fix her in the same pose and drop a blizzard of talcum on her. You really like these?"

"Great lighting. Super."

They found April on the terrace and told her the photos were all they'd hoped for. Wrapped in two robes on another chilly day, she beamed at the news.

"Am I beautiful?" she asked.

"You certainly are," said Bernard. He went to her and cupped her face in his hands. "In fact, Harry can photograph your twat, but I want to do your face. Will you let me do that?"

"My face, really?"

"These are great cheekbones. And such sad eyes."

"Sad eyes? Me?"

"When you're not hiding the fact, yes, very sad and moving."

For a moment Harry thought April might cry.

"He wants to shoot my face, Harry. When can we do it?"

"Do it now. You've probably got too many goose bumps, so I can't shoot the rest of you."

Pleased with the prospect, April took Bernard's arm and led him inside for the session. As Bernard began the set-up Harry made tea and also began to talk about the murders again. "The killer of the little girls also got Terminella," he said to the vast space of the room. "The Como police won't talk to me, but I'll bet the little girls were stabbed just like our detective and with the same instrument. There are probably lots of clues published in the Italian newspapers over the years—clues I've never heard about. For that matter I'll bet a file of newspapers back in Austin could be revealing. I'd like to know how many little girls have gone missing around Austin in the last few years. I don't know enough. And the police aren't going to help me find out things."

"Harry, you should quit worrying over these crimes," Bernard advised him as he arranged the backdrop for April and moved lights around.

"I just can't," Harry admitted.

April suggested an off-the-shoulder pose, but Bernard said, "No, just the face in close-up, dearie," and his insistence pleased her. It also started a new line of thought for Harry.

"Terminella said he could read faces," Harry mused. "A face is a lie detector and he claimed to have a talent for reading the truth and lies in people's expressions. He was a modest guy, Terminella. I don't think he would've made that claim unless he knew he was gifted."

"Each subject has its integrity," said Bernard, coming over for his cup of tea. "Its own true presence. But the human subject strikes poses. Puts on masks. Also, the feelings of the artist get in the way. At times the artist only wants to see the mask—and is perhaps incapable of seeing more. Take the apple. An apple might be flawed with obvious bruises on it, but the artist might only want to see a perfect apple. That was the genius of a painter like Caravaggio: he saw all the flaws and blemishes and captured them on canvas. In his paintings the peasants who come to visit the holy child have dirty feet. His saints had poor teeth. It's often impossible for me to get presuppositions out of my head when I take my photographs. Maybe the objective eye was Terminella's talent."

"I'm ready," said April, waiting.

"I watched Terminella question Olan at the villa," Harry said. "Olan's one of our group, the psychologist. Terminella studied his face, really looked at him. And, oh, he said something I'll never forget. If he looked into the face of this killer he said he'd know him, but also said that the killer might see his recognition."

"Get your mind off this, Harry. Come help us."

"Nah, I'm going out on the terrace."

"I'd like you to come help, too," April called.

"It's chilly outdoors. Come help with the lighting," Bernard persisted.

But Harry took his cup of tea and went out. The trees on the hillside were dark with moisture, their trunks black, and a heavy mist weighed down the tall grass. Overhead the sky darkened, but the zephyrs moved quickly across the Alpine slopes promising a late afternoon sunlight.

Harry decided to do portraits.

Wade always wanted one more impressive than Leo's: suit and tie, distinguished, something large and important in a gilt frame to be hung at his clinic. Even Roper had mentioned a portrait for his law office. Kelton, ever frugal, would love a free portrait. Olan's ego would go for the idea and Leo would agree to another sitting. I'll use the studio here at the old factory, Harry decided, and I'll entice them over to Bellano by promising they can see my nude shots of April.

Such a strange business, the portrait.

The subject always strikes a pose—just as Bernard pointed out—yet never manages to hold it for long. If the photographer is alert the subject's face invariably shows the strain of trying to hold the pose and eventually loses it. Maybe as the mask falls away little revelations might take place.

It might not happen, Harry realized. Or maybe it won't be seen in the sessions themselves, but later in the photographs—which often give up their secrets.

Madame Cappeletti's son, Marco, worked alone in the office when Harry arrived to use the telephone.

"*Si*, please, I am dialing for you," Marco said, and as Harry gave him the numbers he obliged.

The son's bushy eyebrows gave him the look of a pleasant ape. His powerful shoulders stretched the fabric of his jacket.

"My business back home," Harry explained about the phone call. "I have a young woman running my shop for me."

At this point Madame Cappeletti swept into the room to call her son to a crisis in the kitchen. Marco handed Harry the phone and hurried out with his mother. As he listened to the phone ringing in Austin, Harry studied the room keys on their tiny hooks above the mailboxes. Having been a guest for years Harry also knew the hook where the master keys hung. Two master keys occupied the hook now, so his thoughts tripped along to possibilities.

He hung up the phone and moved to the keys.

If the portrait sessions—so far unannounced—worked, then so might a few clandestine visits to various bedrooms. He quickly plucked off one of the master keys.

Before Leo arrived Harry was back on the office phone.

"What's up?"

"Phoning the business," Harry said, and he invented a nervous grin.

"I told you, hey, use my system! Don't stand around in the office!" Leo produced a new cell phone—blazing red with chrome and lots of features—and pushed it into Harry's hands. "This ain't the one that screwed up on safari," Leo assured him. "Try it!"

As Harry punched in the Austin numbers Madame Cappeletti returned and circled the desk—chin high, haughty—to take her accustomed position. From the corridor came the sound of distressed voices from the kitchen: Marco and the cooks.

Leo told Madame Cappeletti safari stories while Harry listened to the distant ringing of the phone in Texas. No answer. He calculated the hours, thinking, damn, nobody's minding the shop. Then Wade arrived wanting the phone after Harry, so Harry quickly handed it over and edged toward the door.

"Drinks tonight, then Bruno's again, okay?" Leo commanded.

Not answering, Harry bounded upstairs, the master key glowing hot in his pocket.

Zeta had just finished her bath.

He uncorked a bottle of Tuscan red, pouring out two glasses as she emerged. He wanted to show her the key and talk about his suspicions, but she entered with some gossip on Olan.

"This was a few days ago," she said. "I was at lunch with Val and Robin and Robin was in one of her talkative moods. She told us that Olan buys a lot of porn. Then she told us how he bought her all this kinky lingerie—including crotchless panties—and when she wouldn't wear it how he lost his temper and cut everything up with scissors."

He also wanted to tell her about his decision to do the men's portraits, but she started talking about Wade losing his underwear.

"What?"

"According to Val he sometimes comes home without his underwear," said Zeta, laughing as she sipped her wine. Her robe lay open and Harry thought she looked slutty and very desirable.

"You had a weird lunch," he managed.

"We did. So tell me about your sessions with April," she urged him, and her smile altered into a soft smirk.

"Everything's going well. I want you to see the proofs."

"Ah, so you're actually using film?"

"Smart ass. Yeah, both film and talcum powder."

"And next you're going to hang little flashlights on her?"

"I have an idea or two."

"I'll bet you do. And Roper's not around anymore, right?"

"No, it's just April the sexy stripper, Bernard the fag, and me. I believe they're both slightly in love with me."

"You could possibly have a threesome."

He wanted a twosome with Zeta. Here and now. He wanted to discuss his suspicions, the master key, the crude plot in his head to do portraits and maybe confirm his worst fears. He also wanted to ask if she had given more thought to working for Leo or tomorrow's Vespa ride with Kelton.

As if sensing all this, though, Zeta moved away from him. Across the room with her back turned toward him, shielded by her robe in a little display of modesty, she slipped into her panties.

"I'm not really jealous of April," she announced to the far wall of their bedroom.

"Good. There's nothing going on. Just the sequence of shots that I really want you to see and comment on."

"But you don't want Kelton and me stopping by."

"The sequence isn't complete. I'll probably work on it for the next two days."

"Fine," she said, but of course it wasn't at all fine.

"We're going to Bruno's again," he said in defeat.

At the restaurant that evening everybody was on: good jokes, witty asides, Val's clunkers, and everyone in the attack mode.

Kelton, who often spoke with his hand over his mouth, was reprimanded for mumbling by Roper, but replied with a straight face, "A man's best friend is his mutter."

Olan and Robin kept sparring after which he managed to say, "Robin, my dear, in spite of all my explanations you're still more interested in yourself than you are in me!"

Zeta howled with laughter, others joined in, and the line was repeated so often that finally Olan had to laugh, too.

Leo ate off Robin's plate and announced his new diet plan: eat as much as you want, but just don't swallow. Everyone considered the source of this minor witticism, then gave it an undue amount of laughter. The levity then encouraged Leo to admit a defeat: Jackie wouldn't agree to come back to the lake this season, so there wouldn't be a party at Villa Franscesca after all.

"Too bad," Wade put in. "We need to punctuate our goddamned constant fun with an occasional party!"

"Instead, I'm takin' us all to dinner at Villa d'Este," Leo announced. "Saturday night. Best clothes. Limos to pick us up."

"Oh god, I need more black shoes," Val wailed.

"I've got a small announcement of my own," Harry said, standing.

"You're running away with your current model," Olan speculated.

"I wish," April quickly added.

"I've decided to do portraits of all my pals," Harry went on. "As you know, I have a borrowed studio over in Bellano. So give me one sitting, guys, and I'll make you immortal."

"Super idea," said Leo, lifting a glass. "I'll pay."

"No, this one's on me," Harry said. "It's my thing and my small contribution to a bunch of guys—each one of whom deeply believes that he's superior to all the others."

They all drank to that.

Additional bottles of wine appeared, but Bruno came to the table to announce that, sorry, there was no more prosciutto. To that Roper remarked, "If we had any bread we could make ham sandwiches if we had any ham!"

Val pulled Kelton over and gave him a big wet kiss. When Zeta raised her eyebrows at this Kelton shrugged and explained: "Val's just fond of me. She once told me I was as smart as Alfred Einstein."

One of their favorite toasts soon went up, Italian in origin: "Old age is always ten years away."

Both Wade and Olan put in loud bids for formal portraits to be hung in their offices back home. "A big framed job like Leo's," Olan boomed out.

Leo made a pun on the phrase *stunt coordinator* that Roper considered hilariously funny.

"Every time I go out drinking with this crowd I find I'm surrounded by drunks," Zeta noted.

They staggered into the night very pleased with themselves, Harry felt.

Moonlight inebriants.

Late the next day after the talcum sequences were completed Zeta and Kelton, disobeying orders, found the old silk factory and intruded on the model and photographers.

"We're bored," Zeta said casually. "Unbore us."

"Hey, glad you're here!" Harry greeted them. "You can help us clean up the mess!"

They swept and shoveled talcum while April—not bothering to place the screen around the tub and leaving her backside toward everybody—showered off. Kelton became so preoccupied with her bath that he swept up a great cloud of talcum that choked him. He claimed an asthma attack and sat down while Bernard poured him a glass of Evian over ice.

"I was already wheezing a little," he explained. "We had to push the Vespa up the steepest part of the path below."

April wrapped herself in a robe and sat beside him. "My little boy has asthma," she said with sympathy. "He's allergic to everything. We can't have pets."

"So where have you two been sightseeing?" Harry asked Zeta.

"We stopped at a roadside memorial where some cyclists got smushed by a lorry. And saw some very nice views of the Alps."

"Smushed?" said Harry. "Is that Italian?"

"From the Latin root. Where are these famous proofs of your model?"

"C'mon, I'll show you."

As Zeta and Harry moved towarthe darkroom April took the opportunity to lean against Kelton and their voices fell into the intimate range. Bernard made tea and spread cream cheese on wafers.

Inside the darkroom, crowded close so that he could smell the faint mixture of Zeta's perfume and sweat, Harry hung up the series of shots: April's body as a grey presence, the first stark white flakes of talcum, then more, then the snowdrift of white that changed the darkness. Zeta studied them carefully.

"It's not all that original," he whispered. "But Bernard and I played with the lighting. These here were particularly long exposures. What I want to do next might be more original, but difficult. I want to do a body with little points of light streaming out of the folds and crevices."

"The pencil flashlights?"

"That's right."

They were both whispering although it wasn't necessary.

"Then you've been thinking about all this for a long time?"

"Yeah, I guess so. I bought the little flashlights at a hardware store in, um, January."

"Harry, these are extraordinary."

"You think so?"

"They have the same power as our old shots in the dunes."

"Well, they're not all that original."

"Don't say that. It's like, hm, I don't know. Like darkness is the real presence. Like we're so happy to see these first little flakes of white."

He wanted to put his arm around her, but he was so grateful for her praise that he didn't want to jeopardize it.

"Harry, do the flashlight shots right now," she urged him. "Don't let a bunch of stupid portraits for your buddies divert you, okay?"

"It means everything that you like these."

"But listen to me. You don't have to flatter anybody or give perks to anybody just now. Keep doing your own thing."

He wanted to confess that the portraits were part of a greater strategy. The photos of April were merely arty, he wanted to say, but the proposed portraits were maybe life or death.

When they came out of the darkroom April was discussing her children. Kelton gave her his full attention while Bernard munched on wafers and sipped wine. A summer night descended on the terraces like soft ink.

April's son was fourteen and her daughter was eleven. The boy was her scholar, she said, and the girl was a jock. She spoke about them with such warmth that Zeta sat nearby, accepted a glass of wine from Bernard, and gave her a wide smile.

"So how'd you fall in with us?" Kelton asked, flirting.

"Oh, easy. Roper promised me Europe. Italy with you guys, then a stop in London before we head home. When could I ever afford a trip like this? Or folks in your –" She paused, took a breath, and glanced at Zeta. "Folks in your class. I've never met nicer folks, really, and the only guy who asked me to take my clothes off thinks of me as a landscape."

They all smiled. She had a Texas twang, though gentle, and could probably sing, Harry decided, like Dolly Parton. "I think of you as April *and* as a landscape," he reminded her.

"Well, I'm gettin' fat on all the good food and I'm learnin' lots about photography and if I can stay with good ole Roper's appetites I've got myself a great trip."

Bernard let out a small nervous whoop.

"On that subject I know some good gossip when you have something to trade," Zeta told her.

"Roper's an addict. That's all I'm gonna say."

"More than once a day?"

"Oh, honey, please. Good morning, good nooner, good night. The boy's in shape and I'll tell you true: back in Austin I wouldn't leave him alone with my daughter for a second."

Harry rose quickly to that. "You're not serious?"

"Aw sure, I won't even let 'em go jogging together. Once or twice, see, I've intercepted one of the boy's passes. Does he think I can't recognize that shit? I mean, he's a sweetheart to me, but at my house we're not servin' no buffet."

Zeta laughed and looked at Harry who wasn't.

"Listen ya'll," April continued. "London is gonna be a blast, but if any of you are goin' to Paris or someplace and wanta talk Roper into another side trip, I'm free. I mean, I can call my club and cancel appointments and won't lose my job or anything."

Zeta promised to think about something fun.

Harry announced that he might stay longer at the lake this year.

"When did you decide this?" Zeta asked.

"I want to finish up here with Bernard. And we're always the first to leave, so this year I want to be the last."

"Keep me up on the news," Zeta said with a whiff of sarcasm.

"You may stay on with Leo, working for him."

"I haven't said I'm doing that."

"You haven't told him no, either."

"When are you going to do my portrait?" Kelton interrupted.

"You can be first. What about tomorrow?" Harry replied.

"Great. Will you be here, too, April?"

"Will I?" she asked Harry.

"Sure. You're my lure. If I tell the guys they have to climb this mountain I'd never get 'em here. So I'm going to tell them—with your permission—that you'll be running around buck naked during their sessions."

"Harry, I want you to shoot that next sequence," said Zeta. "I mean it. Your pals don't need your help to feel important. Do your own thing."

"I want to see those talcum shots myself," Kelton added.

"Tomorrow," Harry said. "Right now I want to eat pizza down at the port. C'mon, Bernard, my treat. We don't want to eat another big meal with the gang tonight, do we?"

Zeta, Kelton and April quickly agreed.

Going down the path toward town April fell in with Kelton and took his arm while Zeta did the same with Harry. In a short time Bernard drove by in his old Fiat, honked, waved, and bumped out of sight. After the meal he would drive back uphill while they took the ferry.

"I want to help you with the flashlight studies," Zeta said, holding Harry's arm.

"Oh? Why's that?"

"Because I want to make sure you actually do them. And not just a series of stupid portraits. And because the talcum effect is—well, sensational. And because I'm the best assistant you've ever had, never mind Bernard."

"You've always been my best assistant."

They walked on, then she said, "I like April. A lot. And she's a wonderful model, isn't she?"

"She is," he agreed.

"And real. Both touching and real."

"Glad you noticed," he said, and they both took deep breaths of the evening air as they went down.

"Tell me the real story about you and that young girl in Africa," said Harry as he moved behind the camera.

Kelton wore a silk turtleneck for the session and suggested a pose looking back over his shoulder, but Harry made him sit up straight and face the lens.

"How much did I tell you about that?" Kelton said, oddly confused as Harry made the first of several exposures. "Hey, wait, did you snap a picture?"

"Relax. And tell me the truth about that girl."

"You think I lied about it?"

"You said she ran out of the hotel and got hit by a car. That sounds odd."

"Odd? What do you mean?"

"I've known you a long time, Kelton, and I don't think you ever lied to me except that time. There was just something wrong in your voice."

The look on Kelton's face was so astonishing that Harry clicked off another shot. Recovering, Kelton arranged himself on the stool, posing, but Harry waited behind the camera, arms folded. April, Bernard and Zeta had gone to the market in Bellano, so the only other sounds were those of the birds singing in the trees outside.

"It's very embarrassing, the whole thing," Kelton finally said. "That was just a story about a car hitting her."

"This happened in the Sudan?"

"You have a good memory. But are you going to take some more shots or not?"

"In a minute. Tell me what happened."

"It was the booze. I used to drink a hell of a lot, you know that. When she drank with me it got her crazy and wild."

Harry waited, feeling in control. The camera worked a curious magic. As Kelton began again a light film of perspiration formed on his brow.

"I always felt guilty as hell. This was actually after I married Isabella and every assignment was the same: I took up with someone as soon as I left home. I was always afraid that I'd give Isabella some African germ, but the irony there was that I gave her a dose only once—after some stewardess for Caledonia Airlines. Anyway, this Kenyan girl: she was the daughter of my housekeeper, did I tell you that? When she drank she got crazy in bed, so I encouraged it. I was guilty about that, too, but Isabella was never really wild. Maybe this girl was eighteen years old, but, hell, she could've been a lot younger. I took her up to Juba on assignment and we stayed drunk for days, banging away. Then she died. Probably alcohol poisoning. She was a small thing, so I figured that's what did it. Died in my bed, Harry. And the Sudan: well, what's one more life? A little money thrown at the problem and it goes away."

Harry clicked off two more exposures unnoticed.

"You said you had to leave Kenya," Harry reminded him.

"The mother made inquiries, but I denied that I took her daughter up to Juba. My editor asked me about it and I told him there was nothing to the story, but suggested he should find me another beat because of all the gossip. I left Nairobi soon after that."

"Is there anything else you're not telling me?"

"Like what?"

"I don't know. Did you get some sort of buzz out of it?"

"What the hell's that supposed to mean?"

"The drama of it. Were you actually with that young girl when she died?"

"Harry, damn, I could hardly live with the fucking guilt. After all these years I can't forgive myself. I'm like the penitent Catholic: always sinning, always guilty, then back to sinning again. It's a vicious circle. I even feel like I killed Isabella. That's right. I sat by her bed in her last days pushing that little button that raises and lowers the bed, moving her into a sitting position then back down again—just to do *anything*, Harry, because she was unconscious and slipping away from us and I had to do *something*."

Harry made two more quick exposures. The room seemed to tilt, but he continued.

"I was just wondering if you maybe got into killing little girls."

"What?"

"Little girls."

"Christ, Harry, are you thinking I've killed the little children around the lake all these years? Is that what's in your head?"

Kelton was off the stool now and away from the camera.

"Detective Terminella believed that someone in our group might be doing the killings," Harry said evenly.

"He told you that?"

"Implied it. And I know he believed it."

"He just *implied it*? Goddamn, Harry, you've just accused me of being a murderer because some Italian implied something?"

"He maybe paid with his life for suspecting us. I believe that's possible. And I saw your face, Kelton, when he questioned us at the villa. You wanted out of there."

"I got sick. He was like the fucking Grand Inquisitor."

Harry let the silence between them grow. He strolled over to the kitchen and poured out two glasses of wine.

"If you're accusing me like this," Kelton said in a single burst of breath, "then you don't know me at all and I don't know you!"

"I don't think you're the one at all," Harry admitted.

"Well, Christ, that's a relief. You know, Harry, since you found that doll on the path you might've gone off the deep end."

They sat down together on kitchen stools and Harry told him that the doll was now considered the wrong one and that Benzetti and the Como police had asked him to stay out of their business. He also told him that the portrait sessions were a concoction, an effort to get at the truth.

"Then you're going to get all the guys here and accuse us?"

"I didn't know exactly how to go about it, but I got a hell of a strong reaction from you, didn't I?"

"Damn, Harry, you're going to lose all your friends. And does Zeta know about this plan of yours?"

"The two of us are out of sorts. Maybe because of Leo's offer. Anyway, no, Zeta doesn't know I have my suspicions."

"When she hears she'll go ballistic."

They sat drinking the wine.

"Christ, you had me going," Kelton said with a heavy sigh. "I always feel people know things about me. I used to worry Isabella knew things. Or some editor. I almost went crazy when I heard Terminella wanted to talk to us. Guilt is the goddamned fuel that runs my life and I hate it."

"You're my dearest and best, Kelton, always," Harry told him. "And I wanted to do your portrait first so I could figure out how to go about this—what to say and how to do things."

"Then allow me to say, asshole, that you're a clumsy amateur and, besides, you're completely wrong about our group."

"Maybe I'm not wrong," Harry said, and his conviction caused Kelton to give him a long, thoughtful stare. "Anyway, do me a favor. I'll do Olan's portrait next and if he asks about your session with me just tell him things went smoothly, okay? Don't say much more, deal?"

"Okay, pal, but tell Zeta what you're up to. She's a rational lady, so listen to her. This is going to cut it with Leo and everybody else and if you keep on I don't think we'll be coming back to Lake Como next year."

"Right," Harry agreed. "We won't be coming back."

Kelton breathed a long sigh, perhaps a goodbye to all of Leo's perks. "This portrait," he finally said. "It's free of charge, correct?"

"Without cost," Harry assured him.

"Then let's do it. Vanity, taken in moderation, can't hurt anybody."

Olan's rooms were less of a harem than Harry imagined, but in plain sight there was a stack of porno magazines with a demure copy of *Newsweek* on top.

On the closet shelves Robin's lingerie spilled over in a cascade of silk and lace. Olan's wardrobe dominated the hangers: suits, jackets, an old tux, golf shirts, and four bathrobes.

Harry worked hurriedly.

Downstairs in the lounge Zeta, Kelton, and Bernard waited. The others had hired a launch for the evening and had gone over to Isola Camacina for dinner. Harry took Robin's little diary, then went back to the pornography, thumbing through it until he found a magazine filled with children: hairless boys and girls in woodland poses. It was an old magazine, French, with a cover as worn as chamois, and the only one of its kind among the others. Poor Robin, he kept thinking.

Before leaving he pressed his ear to the door, listening for anyone in the corridor. The whole strategy disgusted him and he felt sleazy looking through Olan's sleaze. He went downstairs, slipping the master key back into his pocket.

In the lounge Bernard was tipsy and holding forth, telling a story about Quasimodo wanting to go on holiday. He hunched his shoulder and bounced around, acting out the joke as Kelton and Zeta leaned into one another laughing.

"Where on earth have you been?" asked Zeta.

"Prowling around," he admitted.

Bernard went on with his joke and as Zeta and Kelton obliged with laughter Harry kept thinking of the frayed magazine of children's porno, serial killers, and how such killings were always sexual in nature, how sickness bubbled up from hidden depths, how like a virus it was.

Early in the morning they went over to Bellano again.

Both on the ferry and hiking up to the old factory Zeta and April talked about children, the working mother, men, money, and others in the group. Sometimes their whispers broke out in bawdy laughter.

Harry set up the flashlight sequence and prepared for Olan's portrait session. Before lunch he took the first exposures of April in the draped and darkened tent where he had shot the talcum sequence, using her hands, armpits, and legs and breasts to conceal the flashlights, trying to catch pinpoints of light. He conferred with both Bernard and Zeta between shots, played with apertures, experimented, and finally knew he hadn't found the desired effect.

The day turned hot.

After the session April stretched out in a hammock for a nap while Bernard prepared salads. When Bernard went into the darkroom to develop the first efforts Harry and Zeta found two wide-brimmed straw hats and took a walk among the circle of stones in the field. Harry still hadn't decided to speak about his suspicions, but she asked him if he felt disappointed that the doll found on the path wasn't the right one.

"Terminella," he replied, speaking slowly, "believed that someone staying at our villa might be involved in the murders of the little girls." He waited for her reaction, then continued. "Even when the doll turned out to be the wrong doll I think he kept his suspicions. He never said it exactly, but implied it. When he met us that evening at the villa he wanted to read our faces. He said he'd know the killer. And if you want to know, that's why I'm doing the portraits of the guys. I want to read their faces, too."

"Harry, let me get this straight. You think it's one of them, too?"

He took a deep breath and paused, then said, "Yes."

"Oh, Harry, for Christ's sake!"

"Benzetti, Terminella's boss, told him to forget it. The meeting at the villa got complaints, I think, and Terminella admitted that others on the case didn't agree with his methods. At the cemetery Benzetti dismissed me as well. He shouldn't have, but he did."

Zeta turned to him. Beneath the brim of her straw hat her face divided into little sunlit squares as she struggled to stay calm.

"Harry, your new work is wonderful. Your best in years. I hope you pay attention to it and forget all this nastiness around the lake. The murders have upset you, I know, but don't neglect your gift. You're a fine photographer, my wonderful photographer, but you have to keep your emotions in check, right?"

"Zeta, I know I'm right about this."

"But you aren't," she said sharply. "And if you let others know what you're thinking you'll make them furious."

"Terminella said he'd know the killer, but that the killer might know he'd been recognized. I think that happened. I don't know how, but I believe it happened and that's who actually killed the detective."

"You don't have a single shred of hard evidence and neither did your detective," she said, her voice breaking. "Admit it."

Zeta leaned against one of the stones, shook her head, waited, then finally said, "Go over that part about the portraits. You intend to do what?"

"Talk to them while I do their portraits. Study their reactions."

"What are you going to do, accuse them?"

He didn't divulge what had happened with Kelton or what he planned, but couldn't respond. She moved away, pacing off some distance between them.

"Leo will never want anything to do with you again," she said.

"Is that all you can think about? Leo's response?"

She took off her sunglasses and gave him a hard look. "It's really about Leo, isn't it? It's because he asked me to go to work for him."

"Zeta, dear love," he said, calming himself. "When you looked at my work—April and the talcum—and complimented me, god, I loved you for it. I loved us together. You're the only one whose judgment I've always trusted. And maybe you've given up on my talent, but –"

"I want to believe in you," she interrupted. "But, Harry, you're so wrong in this."

"No, I'm not wrong," he insisted, and his own voice turned hard. "Because intuition isn't just some wild fancy. It's knowing what you can't know logically or with solid evidence. It comes from the same place as that talcum—a powder that becomes light itself as I photographed April's body. It's imagination seeing something yet unseen. Listen to me. I can't get the flashlight effect, but I will—because it's a vision I've already seen in my imagination. Nobody else can see it except me, but I'm going to catch it in the lens because it exists. In my imagination and actually already in existence."

"Oh, god, Harry, I just don't know. I think you're so wrong," she managed, and he could only hope that something inside her might once again give way to him.

Harry's impatience gnawed at him. Time, he knew, was an essential element in photography: the pose, the amount of time the lens is open, the slow and careful development of the darkroom image, the emergence of the picture, and then at last the time as a viewer gradually comprehends the object and its meanings. The passage of time as one reads a book is an aesthetic dimension in narrative. One listens to music in time as the composition rises, falls, swells once more, finds its motifs, creates emotion and becomes a total experience. One views all painting in the dimension of time: no one quickly sees a landscape or a still life or Picasso's *Guernica* as a whole, but rather the eye moves over it part by part, small images making up the larger vision until one sees and understands. All artists feel time in their craft, he understood, then cleverly give it back to their audience.

The photograph stops time so it can be examined. Its occupants will never be that age again; that instant, that hour, that day, that year turn into memory, and other memories, unphotographed, grow vague and disappear into the mists of inaccuracy.

The photograph asks patience of us. We look at that person from the past, the expression in the eyes at that moment, the tilt of the head, the object in the background, so that we can come to what?

To detection.

To the rapture of knowledge.

It was agony to want to know.

But Harry waited.

He sat in the creaky wicker chair and pulled on his black socks. Before him on the coffee table Kelton's proofs were spread out for his perusal while Zeta, legs crossed at the dressing table, fussed over her hair and went through the complaints about his dark suit.

"You'll be the only man in the group without evening wear," she told him. "Again."

"The suit's a Givenchy," he reminded her.

"Givenchy schmenchy," she answered.

Harry studied Kelton's face in the proofs. If Kelton were a movie actor he'd be Gary Cooper or Harrison Ford, a trusted American type: honest, open, without irony, the sympathetic listener. Olan on the other hand would be the sly, sardonic fat man: Sidney Greenstreet from the old Bogie movies or a wicked Peter Ustinov with a touch of Anthony Hopkins.

Zeta answered the knock at the door. Val had arrived to hurry them along. The limos were downstairs.

Harry delayed until Zeta gathered her little black beaded purse and stood at the door with Val, then announced that his socks didn't match. Zeta cursed, sighed, and told him to hurry.

When they were gone he quickly took Robin's diary out of its hiding place. Making sure he had his master key he locked up and hurried down the hallway to return the little book to Olan's room.

Nothing remarkable had turned up in Robin's day-to-day except for a few scratchy marks, perhaps code. The rest was wistful drivel. From time to time she had crushes on Roper and Kelton. She listed her minor weight changes and took a couple of shots at Zeta although the recent entries seemed friendly. But those scratches: one of them aligned itself with the date of Terminella's death. Was she possibly keeping a chronicle of Olan's wanderings around the countryside?

Inside their room Harry casually dropped the diary behind a desk and it fell perfectly, wedging itself between the baseboard the leg of the desk. Olan's silver case was there: his breath mints. Harry had the urge to take one, but didn't.

Everybody fluttered around the waiting limos, Leo ordering who should sit with whom. Harry slid in beside Val who wanted to know how she looked, patting her ample bosom. "Can't see you all that well, but you smell delicious," Harry responded, and Leo snapped at the driver to get moving.

They drank heavily all the way down to Cernobbio and the men did most of the talking: golf on the hotel course, the dinner Leo had arranged, the women's cleavage, and the possibility that they soon might need bodyguards.

"If I ever go back to Africa I might actually need one," Kelton admitted. "Old colonial Nairobi isn't the same. We used to stroll uptown from the Norfolk Hotel, a quarter of a mile through streets lined by trees around the university. No more. Muggers everywhere. It's getting to be a bandit economy."

"Get too far off the beaten path in Austin and you might need a goddamned bodyguard," Leo added.

They talked about living in gated communities and the benefits of private security, then Kelton told about his reporter buddy who took a taxi in Mexico City and was delivered into the hands of bandits who shot him six times.

The two women in Leo's limo, Robin and Val, remained silent. All the women would act as mirrors tonight, Harry decided, reflecting the egos around them. Did they suspect, he wondered, that they were laboratories where the men practiced loving themselves? Jackie had quit and flown home—maybe sent away—and April traded her favors to Roper for this cultural excursion. Val endured the dull doctor and Robin had the fat man on top of her. And what about Zeta? She was changing, sliding away from him, he feared, and what would they become? Or was it all that dire?

Curving into the driveway the limo passed floodlit gardens until Villa d'Este appeared. The statues on the grounds gave them greetings until they stopped at the waiting doormen and butlers. As everyone spilled out of the limos the women invoked the names of old celebrities—yes, Robin, the duke and Mrs Simpson—and they staggered a bit as they moved under the gothic archways, entered the great doors, and followed Leo as he headed toward the bar. April gawked at the chandeliers while Olan cursed that he had forgotten his silver case of breath mints.

Between the bar and dining room a doleful quartet played: piano, guitar, horn and bass. Leo ordered champagne, then grabbed Zeta and danced her onto the floor. As she was whisked away she tried a laugh that failed. Robin made overtures to Kelton, wanting some return on her investment, but he avoided dancing by pretending a strong interest in Wade's monologue.

Val moved beside Harry.

"Hey, wanta give me a try?" she said in a slutty Mae West voice.

"Why not?" he answered in his W.C. Fields best.

At the bar Roper's hand crept inside April's gown, his fingers somewhere in the vicinity of her nipples.

As Harry and Val danced by Kelton they exchanged glances and acknowledged Roper's crudity.

On the dance floor Val began her own beat and Harry tried to follow.

"I'm more of an armful than your little wife," she boasted.

"You're in my weight class and you're winning," he said, smiling as if he didn't mean it.

"Oh god, you and Zeta are so unlovable."

"Really? You've noticed?"

"You're both so critical. But all of us enjoy watching you try to love one another. Love's difficult, isn't it?"

"Careful, don't try to be profound."

"That's what I want in my books. Things that are truly profound."

"I suppose one has to choose between wit and profundity."

"Well, wit just isn't funny anymore," she replied, pulling him along, and he thought, for Val, that was rather profound in itself.

At the edge of the dining room the maitre'd signaled that their table was ready, but Harry ended his struggle with Val and returned to the bar for his champagne. April, having disengaged herself, lifted a glass in his direction. Olan, checking to assure himself that it was Dom Perignon, found himself joined with a happy drunk—in a tuxedo even more ancient than his own, the white jacket having turned yellow with age—who moved himself to tears saluting their group, especially April.

"*Grazi fiasco!*" he called out as they moved toward their table—which Kelton promptly translated as *thanks for your disaster!* The drunk was perhaps German and seemed truly joyous to see them.

Dinner began with citrus marinated salmon with navel oranges, Beluga caviar and pea shoots: a small portion with additional champagne. The main course consisted of game: a venison chop with braised shallots, *quaglie en tegame*, and a saddle of rabbit in applewood smoked bacon. They ate the quail with their fingers, pulling the meat off the bone, but then

Olan announced that a pricey bottle of Lombard red wine had gone bad.

"Vinegar!" he shouted as if someone might not hear.

The steward, a little ferret of a man with a pencil mustache who wore his silver tasting cup, smiled only slightly and ordered the bottle replaced. Olan, though, wouldn't sit down as the *sommelier* strolled over to stand beside him and wait. A silence befell the table and Harry, fearing the worst, polished off his venison. In time the second bottle arrived and was uncorked.

Olan quickly pronounced it bad as well

The steward without expression drew his silver cup to his lips, took a sip, then said, "Please?" It didn't come out with any arrogance.

Leo leapt to his feet and joined Olan.

"Take that bottle and drop it on the floor," said Leo.

The drunken German, suspecting confrontation, ambled over from the bar for close observation.

"You try the wine," said Olan to Leo.

"Your word's good enough," said Leo, and he jerked the bottle from the steward's hands and gave it to Olan. The *sommelier* started to speak and the maitre'd arrived just in time to see Olan follow orders. He dropped the bottle to the dining room's marble floor where it exploded like a rifle shot. The incident now had the attention of the entire dining room.

A spray of wine and glass caught everyone nearby in the little tableau.

Harry found himself standing.

"Goddammit, guys," he said, and he was blind with anger.

Leo began to count out a fistful of American dollars. Both the maitre'd and the *sommelier* accepted their portions although their faces had turned crimson.

"Sit down, Harry," said Wade. "You're not paying."

The maitre'd spoke sharply in Italian and the dumbfounded server ran off for mops and towels.

"I have in mind a nice burgundy," said Leo

calmly. "Something aged that would go well with our game course. You choose."

The *sommelier* nodded and hurried off and the maitre'd uttered something that might have been an apology.

Harry, hating the whole display, left the table and crossed the dance floor to find the men's room beside the bar.

True, he reminded himself, he wasn't paying. Nor would he pay for the limousines, the champagne or food. He was behind paying for green fees with no real worry that he should ever catch up. Before they departed for home Leo would undoubtedly buy them more gifts and Harry knew he'd accept what was offered. Yet now his hands trembled as he washed his face in the basin.

Roper and Kelton appeared as he toweled off.

"The steward kept his hand out," Roper opened. "So for a little embarrassment he got a hell of a nice tip, hey buddy?"

Before Harry could answer the drunken stranger entered, standing with his legs wide apart and waiting to see if further drama might unfold.

"It doesn't matter that the steward kept his hand out," Harry argued.

"Sure it does," said Kelton.

Roper stood at a urinal and addressed the wall. "You've gotta admit it was sorta entertaining."

"Olan was born stupid, then had a relapse," said Harry.

"Zeta's worried about you," Kelton noted.

"Oh, is she?"

"Okay, she's probably just pretending."

Harry wanted to smile, but had trouble with it.

Roper approached, zipping up. "I hear there's gonna be a hell of a dessert," he said, grinning at Harry's discomfort.

At the bar Zeta placed her arm through Harry's and without saying a word accompanied him back to the dining room. Harry nodded at everyone without smiling on his return, but badly wanted to leave. Wade was in the midst of a long, dull story.

The dessert arrived: a brulee made of chocolate and blackberries and set in a tart of delicate pastry. After that they drank two nice bottles of a Lombard wine.

They rode home inebriated, filling the limo with silence. A fatigue beyond drunkenness weighed on Harry, a deep weariness with these people, and the drizzle from a dark gunmetal sky confirmed his mood. Droplets of rain wept down the window beside his face as the dark lake passed by. Everyone slept.

A slow rain lasted through the night until finally he heard Zeta in the bathroom running water from the tap. He drifted back to sleep, then Zeta was on him, naked, stroking his hair, and he turned to her with a grateful kiss and they joined in their familiar routine. It became sex without a word, but with promise: even if they weren't yet patched back together the old physical need overtook them. As always, sex ebbed then surged up again, reminding them who they were together.

They slept late until April knocked on their door asking if they were going back to Bellano.

"Yeah, but today's Olan's portrait," Harry called through the door, and he heard her disappointment as she said goodbye and left. When he came back Zeta sat on her knees in the middle of the bed, her hair wild, looking well fucked and pleased.

"I'm not going to work for Leo," she said. "You must know that."

He walked across the bed on his knees and kissed her. She had bad wine breath, but he didn't care.

"Don't say no to him just yet," he suggested.
"What's that mean?"
"I'd like you to do me a favor instead."
"What?"
"God, I love you naked."
"Never mind that. What favor?"
"See if you can get the key to his new villa. Tell him you want to look around."

"He'll want to be with me. I'll never be able to inspect it by myself. And what? You suspect Leo, too?"

"I want to think about everybody. Besides, I've got a master key to everyone's room here at the villa."

"How'd you get a master key?"

"Swiped it. I've already used it. But, really, put the charm on Leo for this."

"He doesn't require much, but I won't get his key. Your breath's terrible."

"So's yours."

"Anyway, here's my theory," she said. "If anybody in our group is killing little girls around here –and I don't believe it for a minute—then it's probably Roper."

"How'd you get this special insight?"

"What April said. He's a sex maniac and she won't let him get her young daughter alone."

"She said that?"

"She meant it too. Oh, do that some more."

"For right now don't have any theories, okay?" he asked, stroking her backside. She moved her fingers through the hair on his chest and for a moment they kept silence.

"Except for Kelton," he said quietly, "these aren't our friends."

"It was a bad scene at Villa d'Este," she admitted. "But we've known them all for years, haven't we?"

"In Austin we don't see any of them except Kelton. Years ago I did Leo's portrait, then he bought some of the dune studies and helped me sell a few of my other works to a couple of his friends. We made a lot of money that first year, remember? We flew down to Mexico on his plane and met the others. I started playing golf with the men, then we all started coming to Lake Como—and we had some fun. But we don't go to their homes in Austin and they don't come to ours. We've never met any of their family members and we don't know anything about Leo's money except for what we read in the business pages."

"All that's true."

"Remember how Kelton got into the circle?" he went on. "He wrote that magazine piece—which wasn't altogether unflattering. Olan, Wade and Roper work for Leo. We really don't know much about any of them. Leo's loaned Wade a lot of money, did you know that?"

"How'd you find out?"

"Roper told me. Leo's money brought us together and holds us together, and we haven't asked many questions. We see the others at Leo's parties—again, except for Kelton. And through Isabella's sickness and death we grew closer to Kelton, but as for the others I've said to myself, okay, Zeta likes them well enough. She likes going to Europe with them and drinking the expensive wines we can't afford. I've blamed it on you, but I'm just as bad. And these people are strangers."

"I plead guilty. And listen, sweet: Leo's offering is flattering. He said he'd make me a millionaire and I've had all sorts of fantasies about the money, but I can't manage Leo. We both know that."

"He wants to pry us apart. That money's meant for you alone."

"That was part of the attraction. Kiss me."

They kissed until they agreed to go brush their teeth.

In the bathroom Harry lathered his face while she drew water for a bath.

"Harry, if we never see any of this group again—except for Kelton, of course –I'm okay with it. But nobody here's a killer. I just don't believe that."

Harry shaved under his chin, not answering.

"I trust your work and I love you," she said quietly, sitting on the side of the tub with her fingers in the bath water. "But I'm skeptical. I feel as though that beautiful Italian detective got you excited."

"We'll be back in Austin before long," he said, talking out of the side of his mouth as he shaved. "There will be little girls who've gone missing in Austin, too. And one of our guys will have been cited somewhere in his past for child molesting or worse."

"Then wait, sweet, and don't do anything now. You're not a detective. You're an amateur."

"Maybe nothing will come of it, but I'm doing the portraits. In the meantime keep your mind open, okay? Even about Kelton. And don't have any theories yet."

"You believe you're right in this, don't you?"

"Don't have any theories and also come to Bellano and work as my assistant. Starting today with Olan."

"You want me to listen in?"

"I want you to pretend you're not listening. But I want you with me."

Zeta strung drying wire across Bernard's kitchen, across the width of the factory, and around the backdrop and camera so that Olan could enjoy a selection of April while Harry worked. These included her torso adorned with talcum, her body illumined by little flashes—early efforts, yet interesting—and a few candid shots on the terrace, asleep, at meals, and strolling about. In each shot, carefully selected and hung by Zeta, April revealed more than she cared to hide, and in a couple of photos she gave the camera a direct and provocative gaze from her old days as a stripper. One of them prompted Zeta to raise an eyebrow at Harry.

"Sometimes my technique turns her on," he explained.

Bellano's only taxi delivered Olan at noon.

He emerged in his silk business suit, the Gucci tie perfectly knotted, and gazed up at Bernard's ramshackle factory with the disdain of a Mafia lord. Indoors, though, he warmed to Zeta's kiss of greeting, Harry's solicitations and a cup of Bernard's tea.

"The portrait," he said archly, "should be, you know, distinguished. I know I may not be the distinguished sort, but –"

"You're absolutely that sort," Zeta assured him, avoiding sarcasm.

"Good tea! And, ah, look at this one!" He loved the candid poses in which April gave the viewer her seductive best. "What a girl, my, my, what a girl!"

Without mention of the ugly incident at Villa d'Este they made smalltalk while Harry set up the chair and camera. The topics were orchestrated by Harry: golf, Leo's new villa, and finally the detective's death. During this time Bernard and Zeta disappeared to distant chores.

"Fascinating man, that detective," Olan allowed.

"When you told him that evil exists I thought the two of you might give us a philosophical discussion."

"Did I say that?"

"Hold that expression." Harry clicked off the first exposure.

"I wasn't ready," Olan complained.

"We're after a number of different poses and expressions. Just make yourself comfortable."

"I'll have to decide where to hang a fine portrait. In my office or home, what do you think?"

"You know my theory of the detective's death? I think the one who has been killing the little girls also killed him."

"Possibly. Want me to turn slightly?"

"Sure, go ahead. Tell me about going to medical school. You attended a medical school and flunked out, didn't you?"

"Who told you that?"

Harry made a quick exposure.

"Can't remember. Somebody recently."

"I withdrew from medical school. I was going to become a psychiatrist. This was years ago. I wanted to get into practice and became a psychologist instead. The course of study was just as rigorous. Who told you I flunked out?"

"You and I really haven't ever talked about our careers. You met Leo when he became your client, is that right?"

"I don't suppose that's a secret. Yes, it was after his big deal with that computer company. He cleared millions and needed to clear his head. Harry, let me ask you something, too. Do you like Leo Jones?"

"Well enough. And I figure he likes Zeta so much that he invites me places, too."

"I sense you don't approve of him."

"Oh? Why's that?"

"You were very angry when he paid off that wine steward."

"I was angry with you, too. You guys were assholes."

Olan slapped his knee and laughed, taking it as a joke and an impertinence.

"Tell me about your practice," Harry went on.

"That steward was arrogant," said Olan, puffing up. "And he kept his hand out, didn't he?"

"Hold that," said Harry, making another exposure.

"I really can't discuss my practice or clients, but allow me to say, Harry, that there's a lot about Leo you don't know or understand."

Harry adjusted the lens. "Does Leo like little girls as much as you do, Olan? I would like to know that."

"What the hell's that supposed to mean?"

Harry moved a light fixture. "Child porno. You're into that, aren't you Olan?"

"Did someone say that about me?"

"I saw you coming out of that big porno shop on Lamar Street in Austin," Harry lied. "But, yeah, I've also heard some stuff."

"Goddammit, has Robin talked about me?"

"Not at all, She wouldn't."

"Then who? This is absurd!"

"You have porno in your room. I hear it includes a bit of child pornography."

Harry made another exposure before Olan left the chair in anger, pacing the room, puffing up as he did. He then stopped at another photograph of April before he caught himself and turned away.

"If you're trying to disturb me, you've succeeded."

"I don't care one way or another," Harry replied.

"You should. Our friendship is at stake."

"No it isn't. We're not good friends, Olan. We just tag along after Leo. I've been to your house once and you've turned down a couple of Zeta's invitations. We play golf in Austin—what?—once a year at most. Usually just in August here in Italy. We never really talk. But something else I've wanted to ask. On the days here when you don't play golf exactly what do you do?"

Olan attempted to compose himself. He returned to the chair, smoothed out his trousers, and sat down. "Now look here, Harry, I want this portrait. It's very generous of you, but I want it. Leo regards you as a top photographer and, well, Robin would undoubtedly give a good picture great value."

Harry moved behind the camera and clicked off a shot. He marveled at his own control, but also how the session was like a vise that held Olan. The last exposure caught an expression like that of an angry toad, yet Olan seemed determined to sit there in spite of insults and provocations.

"Where do you go when you aren't playing golf with us?" Harry repeated.

"You know very well that I go hiking."

"Let me tell you about Terminella. He was a very intuitive detective and he suspected you."

"Impossible."

"Let me finish. He thought his killer might be someone with a medical background. Someone with odd sexual habits. Someone who knew the paths around the lake. I watched him observing you. And I can't help wondering, Olan, if you search out little victims on your days off and if you've followed this god awful hobby all the years we've been coming here."

Another quick exposure as Olan left the chair again. Harry thought for a second that he might charge.

"I can't overlook what you've just said, Harry, and I'll never forgive you for it!"

"I'll try to live with that," Harry said with indifference.

"Let me tell you a thing or two!" said Olan, his voice rising. "You're right about Leo's interest in you! He just interested in Zeta, always has been, and you're excess baggage! His tiny little villa won't have room for you, count on that! And what's more, you're a damn bad golfer! I'd like to punch you out, you bastard!"

Olan's fists were balled and his face had turned an odd shade of lavender. His brow beaded with perspiration.

"You're a violent man," Harry said calmly. "Not at all the steady professional.

The only thing you care about is your authority and when it's threatened you want to hit somebody. I'll bet you cuff little Robin now and then. Is that what goes on in your marriage?"

"I am not violent!" Olan said loudly, trying for control and failing.

"You wanted to hit me, but knew I'd probably knock out half your teeth. You wanted to hit that little wine steward who served you a perfectly good bottle."

"Nothing of the sort!"

"He questioned your judgment and you almost decked him."

"I'd have been entirely justified!"

"There, see. And Leo egged you on. And, by the way, Olan, that's cruel about my golf. I know I don't have much of a backswing, but that was unkind."

At this point Zeta and Bernard bounced in, smiling, rattling bags of groceries, as if they hadn't heard all the shouting.

"How about some wonderful tea biscuits?" Bernard called out.

"My, it's warm in here!" Zeta added. "You should wipe Olan's brow, dear, can't you see he's perspiring?"

The two of them became instantly busy in the kitchen, clinking dishes together. While Olan took out his handkerchief and mopped his face Harry once more tinkered with the lens and lighting. Amazingly, then, Olan regained his control and returned to the chair.

"Here, let me straighten your jacket," Harry offered, and went over to pull down Olan's lapels.

"Perhaps I was off base at Villa d'Este," Olan conceded. "You were visibly upset and so were the ladies."

Harry also smoothed Olan's silk tie.

"And you don't seriously believe I could do such a thing as you suggest, do you? The crimes. Here at the lake."

As Olan continued to allow Harry's attentions Bernard called from the kitchen.

"Let's see, you both take milk, correct?"

"I can't think who might've noticed my magazines and videos," Olan went on in a half whisper. "You have me very upset, Harry, if you want to know, and I can't think straight. I do have one old magazine with photos of children in it. Should've tossed it out a year ago. It could be very offensive to some people. But, Harry, I could nothing of the sort you imagine!"

Zeta arrived with a tin of biscuits. Harry moved behind the camera and made another quick exposure so that Olan protested that he wasn't properly posed.

"I apologize for that scene with the steward and the *sommelier* at dinner," Olan told Zeta.

"Think nothing of it. Why don't you remove your jacket while we have tea?"

"No, please, no hot tea right now. I'd like to finish the sitting, Harry, if that's all right with you."

"Sure," said Harry, biting into a tea biscuit.

Zeta and Bernard soon withdrew again.

"You haven't yet answered my question," said Olan as Harry clicked off another shot. "You don't really think I could harm little children, do you?"

"Just don't know," said Harry calmly. "You're a violent guy, Olan, and a real pig. Maybe little girls have the nerve to resist you, so you kill them. Then what? Fuck their little dead bodies? You tell me, Olan, 'cause I can only guess."

As Olan leapt out of the chair for the last time Harry clicked off a final shot.

"You and I are not friends anymore!" shouted Olan, enunciating each word in his peculiar stuffy accent.

"Never were, as I told you, so who gives a shit?"

"Don't speak to me again! I'm leaving!"

Olan went striding out, probably surprised as he passed through the front door that his taxi had gone and left him on top of a mountain. Harry looked out a window to see him trudging down the path. Zeta arrived at his side with Bernard.

"Loved the part where you accused him of hitting Robin," she said.

"You heard all that?"

"I've always thought he cuffs her around a bit."

"Really? You never mentioned that to me."

"I suppose I could fire up the old Fiat and give him a lift," Bernard said with a sigh.

"He's a hiker," said Harry. "Let him walk."

Olan obviously went directly to Leo with his complaints about Harry's insults, but Leo laughed at him and hurried to hear Harry's side of it. Plans were quickly made to split the group for the evening with Robin, Olan, Wade and Val going back to Bruno's. Val told Kelton she hoped Bruno had more of that Gestapo soup, her favorite. "You know," she explained. "With chilled tomatoes."

The others went back to La Fugaride, Leo having forgiven them for catching fire during their last visit. On the way to the restaurant Leo stayed in a high mood, laughing and saying to Harry, "Olan says you went crazy and accused him of being a serial killer."

"The only reason anyone ever talks to Olan is to annoy him," Harry replied.

That night April and Roper announced their plans to dance the night away in Mennagio, so Harry decided to snoop in their rooms. Leo phoned Jackie in Austin to tell her about the Olan portrait session, but she wasn't at home. Zeta kept laughing about Gestapo soup. When Kelton sneezed he announced that he was allergic to the chickens wandering in from the backyard.

"I may have the pip," he said. "Do human beings get the pip?"

"In your case, very likely," Zeta told him.

"What exactly would that be?" April asked.

"The spots on dice are called pips," Roper informed them.

"It's also an unspecified minor disease," added Zeta.

"Which?" April wanted to know.

As Leo paid the bill Harry drew Zeta aside and persuaded her to linger with Leo in the lounge of the villa while he snooped upstairs. On their arrival back at the Cappelettis, then, Leo found himself lucky to get Zeta for himself. As Harry went off to the elevator Zeta mouthed a single word: "Hurry."

He tried to. First he found the sexual miasma of April's and Roper's large room: rolled panties everywhere—pencil thin, removed in haste, tossed aside—along with chewing gum wrappers, piles of sweat clothes, empty water bottles, loose coins, unread books, unused condoms, a phone system like Leo's, adult videos—perhaps borrowed from Olan's collection—and a lot of clothing that appeared to have been stripped from the body, wadded up, and fired at the walls like missiles.

April's children occupied a large framed photograph: a girl of perhaps ten with her arms around her older brother, both of them with curly mops of hair and resembling their mother.

In a bureau drawer: April's knee socks and a neatly folded nurse's uniform. In Roper's backpack: a single dirty sock, a half-eaten health bar and no daggers.

Roper's memo book contained dozens of numbers and addresses for Leo's business contacts. The last page bore a single reminder: Call Jackie Again. Was Roper arranging a settlement, separation or divorce?

A simple room, all in all: two sexual athletes in an explosion of apparel.

With Olan, Wade, and their women still out dining and the corridor empty Harry hurried along to Leo's room. Inside the suite—why didn't I stop here first?—he found two unlike rooms: Jackie's orderly closets, made bed, everything neatly in place, and Leo's crowded workroom with phones, computers, headsets, wires and gadgets.

Leo had more than Harry could quickly study: a new palm computer, cameras, a scanner/fax, e-books, pocket PCs, a super laptop, even electronic games. Missile Command and Super Poker. More electronic surprises: two US Army monitors, one portable. Harry had never seen Leo with a camera in his hands, but everything seemed cutting edge. He recognized all the software including some web cams. Leo, clearly, could talk across the world, actually viewing the faces of his business pals, and it gave rise to a single thought: Leo touched many more people than those who hung out with him on this annual trip, moved through several markets, bought and sold, lived at another dimension, and had access to power. His collection of magazines caught him with congressmen, a governor, the golfer, the Dell people, the Beaumont oil man, and a number of ranch owners. Leo's ego was in his stack of magazines and why, Harry wondered, has he bothered with our modest group for these seven years? Don't the rich naturally fall in with other rich people? Olan, Wade and Roper had decent yearly grosses—although Wade was rumored to be in heavy debt—but Kelton lived on a couple of pensions and Harry himself just got by.

From the corridor he heard heavy keys turning in nearby locks: the others back from dinner. Time to get downstairs.

A last few items caught his eye: a roll of architectural drawings, undoubtedly Villa Franscesca, then, more curiously, a cluster of Rolex watches beside one of those monitors. Unboxed wrist watches, shiny, five of them. These will be our gifts at the end of the holiday this year, one for each of the guys, Harry knew, wristbands coiled together. And he knew more: they were fakes, probably purchased from that guy in the turban on the street in Tremezzo, that odd guy selling Chinese knock-offs of Rolexes outside the trattoria that day he and Kelton had lunch together.

Olan's voice drifted down the corridor, no laughter in it, as Harry waited for the night's last goodbyes and silence. Finally he hurried downstairs to find Zeta and Leo at a table in the lounge.

"Couldn't sleep," he announced, breezing in. "So I decided to join you two for a nightcap."

Leo covered his disappointment and Zeta said brightly, "He's telling me about all his collectibles. He has a whole storage unit filled with Limoges."

Harry managed, "Hey, great."

"Waterford and Westwood, too, but maybe I'm sellin' everything," Leo added, and he pushed a bottle of wine, a glass, and a quart of Bushmill's toward Harry as he sat down. "Zeta's got me convinced I gotta go for different stuff."

Zeta crossed her eyes with boredom.

"What stuff?"

"The serious collector goes for the old masters. That's what I'm thinkin'."

"Leo was asking how one goes about finding and buying, say, a Monet," Zeta informed Harry.

"I got too many toys. Electronics, cars, a goddamned jet, collectibles. But now I wanta go, you know, European."

Harry nodded gravely and sipped his wine.

"Let's face it, I'm acquisitive. I gotta believe in upward mobility in art collections. Think there's any chance at all, Zeta, I could buy the David?"

A moment of silence.

"The David in Florence. Maybe I could put it, you know, someplace like the rotunda of the state capitol in Austin."

They stared at him until he finally grinned, letting them know he was kidding, then the three of them laughed.

Before noon the next day Harry and Zeta took the ferry with Leo. In Bellano they rode up to Bernard's studio in the town's rickety taxi. The sky was silver with bright sun and the day had turned hot, so they cooled off at Bernard's with gin and tonics as Harry went through the setup.

Leo wanted his wavy hair set aglow with backlighting. "My brother Cooter has this big mane that grows down to his goddamn shoulders and I wanta make him jealous. You know how to get something backlit, doncha?"

"Like a shampoo advertisement," Harry replied.

"Exactly. This sweater okay?"

"Perfect," Harry told him again. Leo's dark silk sweater had been thoroughly discussed at the villa, on the ferry, in the taxi, and on arrival.

Leo liked the old factory had told Bernard with

all sincerity that something could be made of it. He also studied the photos of April strung everywhere and took notice of the unsheltered bathtub. When told that April had washed off the talcum in plain sight of everyone including Kelton, Leo responded with a single appreciative, "Damn!" When he knocked back his G&T and asked for another Bernard supplied it.

Again Zeta and Bernard drifted away to the terrace and darkroom, out of sight yet not quite out of earshot as Harry set up the camera and chair. Tactics, Harry knew, would be awkward and he fretted on how to begin, but Leo relieved him of an opening gambit by quickly bringing up Olan's experience and by leaping forward to add, "So you think somebody at the villa—maybe in our bunch—is knockin' off the little girls, do you?"

"Terminella, the Italian detective, thought it was possible."

"How do you want me? Have we started?"

Harry had already made an exposure and said, "Yeah, we're up and going. That light falls on your hair just right."

"That night the detective stopped by the villa?" Leo said. "I knew he was suspicious, but he was smooth, don't you think? And I'll tell you a weird creep: Madame Cappeletti's son. Big guy. Them damned eyebrows of his."

"I've been thinking about you," Harry replied, getting right to it. "And I've been thinking about why. But of course there isn't any why if you're a genuine pervert."

"Well, I never had enough pussy, Harry, and I never will. If that makes me a pervert, then I'll put Roper and maybe another two hundred guys I know in that same category."

"Okay, stop talking for a second. Hold it."

Harry photographed Leo's lustrous hair.

"What I'm going to do," Harry said, then stopped. "Hold it. That's good. What I'm thinking about doing back in Austin is a little detective work on my own. Maybe somebody in our group has some prior violations with little girls. I mean, hell, there are probably hundreds of children who go missing in central Texas."

"Don't get tangled up with some incompetent private eye," Leo advised. "Nine outta ten don't do anything. Lemme fix you up with this cop I know. State police. He'll get you what you need."

Leo paused and struck a pose. Harry took another exposure with the thought: hey, he's good, he's all mask, and I can't upset him in the least.

"Sure, I could use help and I'll be glad to meet with your guy, but I have a couple of ideas on my own."

"Now, Harry, I wouldn't want my financial dealings given a hard look. I mean, shit, check up on me and pussy all you want to. But all business is in the shade, you know, buddy, if not way over on the dark side."

"I'm only interested in your perversions."

"Same as Jackie. She don't care how I make the money, but she worries about women. Since she's been gone I've been goin' over to Lugano. Betcha didn't know that, did ya?"

"Got a lady friend over there?"

"For six years, Harry. Widow lady in her forties. Horny as a hot stove. I don't ever do without."

"I wouldn't think so. Hold that."

Leo smiled for the camera.

"But, look, humor me," Harry began again. "If you like little girls, admit it and tell me about it."

"Okay, to a certain age, sure, I like little girls and it's all mixed up with hormones in our food nowadays."

"Oh? How's that?"

"See, the little darlin's used to stay younger much longer. Thin little arms and legs, no titties, no downy hair on their little crotches. That's when I liked 'em, Harry, if you want to know. Now our food is so damned full of hormones so the kids mature more quickly. Little tykes getting' their periods at eleven years of age. You can't hardly find children anymore. Except overseas. Here it Italy they eat outta the gardens and don't use hormones. Natural meat and vegetables over here. So the little ones stay little, hairless and such."

Harry might have looked appalled until Leo broke out in loud laughter. He was kidding again—or was he?

"Dammit, take my picture," Leo commanded him, laughing. "Or are we gonna sit around all day talkin' kiddie pussy?"

"You had me going," Harry admitted.

"I bet ole Olan puffed up like an adder. And what about Kelton? I reckon you accused him, too."

"Yeah, and he gave me a long story about a young girlfriend in Africa. I think he wanted to confess."

"Damn, Harry, you're a case."

"Turn sideways a bit. There, hold that."

Leo sighed and asked, "Harry, how long've we known each other?"

"More'n seven years."

"And you've never asked me for special favors, Harry, and that's why I made a generous offer to Zeta. I think I can make a little money for you two. I hope you see it that way. In fact, I told Zeta I'd make her one million dollars if she'd agree to help me out for awhile."

"That much?"

"I know you two've talked about it and I realize what you might be thinkin'. But I'm not hittin' on Zeta, honest, and if I can speak candid, Harry, Jackie paints only fair and don't always have the best taste. I'm thinkin' of buyin' some real good art, though, and Zeta, well, she's classy and you know it."

Now Harry didn't know—in spite of what Zeta had told him—if she had refused Leo's offer or not. It sounded as though it was still on the table. He said only, "Zeta has to make up her own mind, Leo, on whatever you've been talking about."

Soon after this exchange they finished up. Zeta and Bernard appeared on cue, fixed lunch, and Leo told stories about his safari, his brothers and their ugly wives. As lunch finished Zeta risked a question about Jackie and Leo's face wrinkled with concern as he shook his head sadly.

"Not a good situation," he admitted, lowering his tone into an intimate range. "Not good. I irritate Jackie. Maybe folks just shouldn't stay married for all that long."

"I was wondering if I should phone her," Zeta offered.

"Oh sure, call if you want to. But she won't say much. You know how she is. And I may be givin' her a settlement that gets to be all the consolation she needs."

That evening before dinner Kelton and April paid a visit to Harry's and Zeta's room.

After asking Roper's permission Kelton had taken April for a day's outing on the back of his Vespa. With her arms tight around his waist he had covered some of his favorite trails on both sides of the lake. They had stopped for a fancy lunch in Bellagio, then everything altered. Over a glass of wine, listening to a mandolin, and gazing at the lake they had kissed. It was a gentleman's kiss, April said, with no tongue, but somehow they knew. They checked into the hotel above the restaurant. After a few hours in the hotel he asked her to marry him—in the vague but not too distant future—and she accepted. They planned to leave immediately for Florence, Venice, Rome and Capri.

"What?" Zeta asked, her mouth open.

"That's about it," Kelton said. "I'm not getting any younger and, well, you know, time's winged chariot and all that."

"Does Roper know yet?" Harry inquired.

"That's where we were hoping you and Zeta might help us out," April put in, grinning.

"Oh no," Zeta answered. "Do your own dirty work."

Kelton went into his Gary Cooper imitation, stammering, pausing, and finally saying, "The thing is, uh, until we get organized, well, see, I want her to move into my room."

"You had a hell of a Vespa ride," Harry commented.

"Uh, tell you what," Kelton went on. "If you come with me, Harry, maybe I'll go and speak with Roper now. You don't have to say anything. Just come as a witness. Or a referee—however it plays out."

Meanwhile, April and Zeta strolled out to the balcony and could still be overheard. "My children will meet us in Rome," April confided. "And he wants me to quit work. He's retired, see, so his checks get banked in Austin no matter where he goes or what he does. So we can travel. And, god, Zeta, he's a gentleman, I just love him. He says he knows a private school where we'll put the kids."

"Sounds all planned," Zeta replied, and by this time the men were at the door, leaving.

"Such a gentleman. Well, not exactly in bed."

"Don't tell me," Zeta quickly put in.

This was the last Harry heard before he and Kelton started toward Roper's room. As they went along Harry knew that his friend wasn't in a mood for much levity, yet said, "You realize, buddy, that this still leaves us one woman short?"

"What about dinner tonight?" Kelton asked, thinking ahead.

That evening they all occupied the large round candlelit table beneath the eaves at La Valuu: Roper, alone, with amazing insouciance down beside Leo, Kelton and April at the other end of the table, Wade with Val, and Olan, cool toward Harry yet telling stories, nudging Robin, laughing and slapping the table.

"Don't you think the lovers could've waited until we all went back to Austin?" Robin asked Val, nodding toward April and Kelton who boldly held hands between courses. Roper overheard the question and answered it.

"It's a clear alienation of affection suit if ever I saw one," he called across the dishes. Everyone laughed nervously and Harry's guess was that Roper's temper was just barely held in check in spite of the light-hearted remark.

Kelton replied but with his hand over his mouth so that no one quite heard his response.

Olan once more began talking about a client so he could talk about how he solved a problem with superior analysis. A woman claimed to have red streaks coming up her body, but he reasoned with her and convinced her that a childhood memory was the source of the obsession.

"Did she really have red streaks?" Val asked.

"Of course not," Olan told her. "She was bloody neurotic. I fill up my appointment book with idiotic obsessions. Sometimes we never find the root of a client's distress. If a man tells me monkeys climb into bed with him at night I might finally suggest putting bananas out on the windowsills, lots of bananas to keep the little bastards outside eating all night."

"But what about truly disturbed people?" Val persisted.

"Like our serial killer at Lake Como? Or to put it right, Harry's killer of children and detectives? My guess is such a monster could never properly be analyzed or cured. Best thing in that case is shoot the fucker and stop his mischief."

Olan laughed at his own broad advice, thumped the table and gave Harry a glance as if to say, there, I'm not the beast, I even brought up the subject, screw you.

They discussed, in order, cigar smoking, Tolstoy, diets, and action movies before Val launched into her newest spiritual plans. She wanted to go on the Hajj to Mecca, then visit India. She went on about metempsychosis, the transmigration of souls—using the word *metempsychosis* often and enunciating well—then concluded her nightly essay by remarking that her favorite Indian god was Sheena.

During coffee Leo handed out his gifts: thin diamond bracelets for the women and those Rolex watches for the men.

"Real diamonds!" April exclaimed, holding her bracelet up. "Can you *believe* this?" Harry felt tempted to lift up his new watch and say, hey, maybe those diamonds are real, but not this baby.

Wade stood to make his earnest annual toast to Leo. "Thank you again, dear heart," he began. He cleared his throat for an attempt at ironic wit. "Leo's great ambition is to become a greater and greater snob with a villa far from the lowlife of Austin. At the present he's stuck with us and we have the taste and sensitivity of mongrels."

Mild laughter and response.

"We do, however, love all flamboyance, gross sums of money, vulgar gifts, and expensive baubles," he continued. "So if Leo is the duke of Como, we are his court. And if you refine yourself so that you never show off again, we still love you!"

It was far too much and wrong, yet everyone tapped on his plate with his silverware.

Soon they made their way back down the stone stairway toward the car park. Zeta clung to Harry's arm.

"I called Jackie, but couldn't reach her. Left a message on her machine," Zeta told him.

"She might be happy to be out of this. I don't expect to hear from her."

"You think she had a part in anything?"

"Yeah, but I can't say exactly what."

"Harry, everybody's laughing about your obsession. Even Olan scored on you tonight."

"Something's here," he insisted, and she left that unanswered.

Kelton and April quickly took a taxi to the Milan airport and were gone. Leo announced he was driving over to Lugano to see a friend. Roper went jogging while Olan and Wade prepared for separate hiking excursions. Zeta and the women went shopping in Varenna.

After a suitable lapse of time at the villa Harry looked into Wade's and Val's rooms after the maids finished cleaning.

The rooms belonged entirely to Val. Wade was possibly allowed to sleep on his side of the big bed, but the closet held only her clothes and the drawers of the chest and dressing table contained only her things.

Wade appeared to live out of two pieces of luggage

shoved underneath the single bed in the smaller second room and his toiletries occupied a forlorn dop kit on the floor beneath the lavatory in the bathroom.

The desk was strewn with her notes and pages, and Harry stopped to read a passage, a florid description of the sex act between the fictional heroine and her lover that read:

> *She settled herself luxuriously*
> *on the feeling of his impalement.*

Harry decided it was possibly the most inadvertently funny and most awkward euphemism he had ever read and he tried to memorize it so he could share it with Zeta. But he moved on, wanting to see if the room answered any of his questions. The books and magazines were froth, nothing Wade might read. Val's cigarillos. The case of wine everybody collected and usually donated to the Cappelettis.

Poor Wade. He had receded into his practice: the futzy, dullish doctor. He took care of old people, of Val, of dull speeches in noisy restaurants. Did he resent it? Was there some deep anger no one saw? Probably not. Did that malpractice suit years ago signal an interest in young girls? No. Like Harry himself Wade had lingered in Leo's group for a long time because of Val—who, like Zeta, had a gift for life, although Val's talent had long ago lost its luster. Poor Wade. If his wife spoke in malapropisms, he wandered in the dull pastures of cliché. A teddy bear. Not a killer.

Harry stepped out on the balcony getting a slightly different angle of vision on the lake and when he turned Wade stood beside him.

"Wade," he said stupidly, his mind tripping along.

"What're you doing in here?" Wade asked casually.

"The maids left the door open," he lied. "So I called and came in. I thought you might be here on the balcony."

"The *loggia*," Wade corrected him

"Yeah, right, I thought I might catch you for lunch."

"I'm off on a hike. Thought I told you that."

"Maybe you did."

"Maybe we can grab a bite later on the piazza."

"Sounds fine," Harry agreed, relaxing.

"Anything special you want to discuss or shall I bring Olan? He mentioned lunch, too."

"Nothing important. The portrait session. You have a dark suit, don't you?"

"I'll have to get it pressed," Wade allowed.

Of course you will, Harry wanted to say. It's a wrinkled mess. It's wadded up in your luggage under the damned bed.

Roper traded portrait sessions with Wade, though, because he wanted an opportunity to scold and threaten Harry.

"When we get back to Austin, you're not going to investigate any of us or I'll personally sue the hell outta you," Roper snapped at him.

"Oh? On what grounds?"

"Invasion of privacy. Malicious mischief. You name it."

"Hold that pose," Harry said gently. "You look exactly like a lawyer."

"And if Leo gets on your case you've really got a shitload of trouble and I'll help him see to it."

"Is it Leo who's so upset with me?"

"So am I and so is everyone!"

"Maybe you're upset because April ran off with Kelton and he's my friend and you want to blame me for it."

"Not fucking true."

"He's gone and you can't threaten him, so you decide to threaten me?"

"I repeat, you will not investigate anybody."

"Hell, Roper, you're one of my prime suspects and raising all this hell just confirms it."

"You cheap little picture maker."

"Here's my hunch: you're an oversexed guy and you've been punching April day and night and also chasing these little girls around the lake—same as you've done for years."

"That's goddamned slander!" Roper yelled, leaving the chair. For a moment Harry thought they might throw a few punches, but instead Roper walked to the kitchen and stood by the open bathtub. Bernard, hearing the ruckus, stayed in the darkroom and Zeta hadn't arrived.

"There's other evidence you could be my killer," Harry pressed on. "April told us she won't let you near her little daughter."

"She said that?"

"She wasn't kidding and I believed her."

"There's a photo of April's kids, Harry, framed, we've kept in our room at the villa. She carries other pictures in her wallet. Those photos are two years old, maybe more, and her daughter, for your information, is a terrible goddamned little flirt, believe me, buddy, and she throws her little twat up against me if I even get close to her! She knows damn well what she's doing, too!"

"And she's how old? Twelve? Thirteen?"

"Hotter'n her mama! I can't keep her off me!"

"You should hear yourself. That testimony would sure as hell play in a court of law, wouldn't it?" Harry checked the chair and area with his light meter. At last Roper pulled up Harry's stool, sat down, and tried to calm himself.

"Listen to me, Harry, you don't have children and you probably don't know the little teenagers nowadays. The belly buttons. Makeup and breasts. Hand jobs. The sport fuck. You don't have a clue, and April's daughter is what we used to call pure jailbait. So I never once touched her. Which brings up this craziness of yours here at the lake—your Texas killer theory—which is an altogether different matter, Harry, separate and unconnected to the little devil at April's house!"

"So you say," Harry replied evenly.

Roper took a deep breath—his courtroom pause—and began again. "Harry, pal, you're accusing your friends. Olan's furious. Leo's upset, but laughs about you. If you accuse poor Wade, he'll have a fit. And here outta the blue you suggest I'm a fucking killer because something cockeyed April said—which probably got misconstrued. Anymore of this shit, Harry, and believe me, you're out."

"Out of what exactly?"

"The group. The new villa. Leo's thing."

"Is this Leo talking or you?"

"Harry, we're all talkin'. You've gone weird on us."

Zeta came in breathlessly and smiling from her uphill climb, tossing her hair back, greeting them, waving hello with a bottle of wine. Bernard, on cue, emerged from the darkroom.

"Want to finish this?" Harry asked, moving beside the camera again. "We've only got a couple of exposures so far."

"Nah," Roper said. He gathered up his backpack and manufactured a smile. "I'm really not into the portrait game. I just thought we should talk."

"Hey, I just got here!" Zeta complained with a grin, and she was so charming that Roper, uncharacteristically, moved over to her and kissed her hand.

"Leo wants us all back at that island restaurant tonight," Roper said, and he turned to Bernard and added, "You, too, chum. Join us."

"Can't make it," replied Bernard with a brittle smile.

"Well, then, I'm off. Remember what I said, Harry."

"And what's that?"

"You know. Curiosity killed the cat."

When he was gone Zeta, Bernard and Harry stood looking at one another and Zeta said, "What? Did I miss something?"

"We had a couple of rough spots," Harry admitted. "And I think I was just threatened. Maybe he was speaking for himself or maybe he spoke for his boss, but I think it was definitely a threat."

"Definitely," Bernard agreed.

Zeta finally reached Jackie by phone in Austin and told Harry about their conversation.

"She said they were arguing about the villa and so I naturally apologized for invading her space. But she insisted it wasn't just the villa. And she said things won't ever be patched up and that she thinks Roper has already started divorce proceedings on Leo's behalf."

"Roper said as much to me," said Harry.

"The other news I got from her is that she's going to Mexico, an art class in San Miguel. She specifically asked us to keep the information from Leo."

"Why do you think?"

"She just said it wasn't any of his business. Or whom she went with. She did add that—now that I think of it. Think she might've already met somebody else?"

"Very likely a woman friend. Who the hell knows?"

They sat together on their balcony, their legs covered with blankets as they watched the last rays of the sun and the blue shadows across the lake. In such moments Harry felt himself sliding into old age, but without regret. These should be the years beyond career or mischief or the annoying competitions. Sex should be less of a frenzy and taken with ease. He looked at Zeta. Her wrinkles would deepen and expand, the web of time in her face, yet she should become more mysteriously beautiful than ever.

In his reverie he thought of all the Romans before him who sat by the shores of this lake with these same senior contemplations. They wanted serenity here, as if nature could give it to them: the old generals of the legions and the merchants of the Appian Way. Did it ever come to them, serenity? Probably not. The generals had enemies, old scores to settle, worrisome children, political regrets, and the continuing moil. The same with the merchants whether successful or not. Did some senator or poet or retired warrior sit here in search of the last pleasures, yet fret over justice undone, over murders unpunished, and feel incomplete?

Zeta interrupted his meditation, saying, "Jackie told me about a gallery for sale and thinks I should go into business."

"Does she want to be your investor?"
"She was very sweet and encouraging."
They sat for awhile without saying more, then she started again.
"This hunch of yours that you'll find something revealing in the portraits, Harry, it's wrong."
He didn't reply.
"You'll lose friendships," she went on.
"Hmm," he managed.
As they dressed for the cocktail hour Harry fastened Zeta's new diamond bracelet for her. Sadly, it was her best piece of jewelry. She didn't wear rings because of her arthritic fingers, had never owned diamonds before this inexpensive gift from Leo, and wore only cheap wristwatches that she usually misplaced. As he fastened the bracelet he kissed her bare shoulder and said, "So. A gallery?"
"In Dallas. Actually, that appeals to me most."
"With or without me?"
"Oh, it's all fancy right now. I doubt anything comes of it. Maybe I'll talk with Jackie again when everyone's back home." She began on the night's dining: Leo had reserved the entire restaurant on the island and a special chef had been hired for the evening, Bruno's cousin, Enzo, who was probably auditioning for a permanent job next year at the new villa. Enzo had come up from Milan to work for Bruno as a pastry chef, but the kitchen, Zeta said, wasn't yet big enough for both of them.
"We're getting some sort of Wellington," she said with a sigh, and as they left the room she borrowed Harry's new Rolex, scooping it off his bedside table and dropping in her beaded purse. He told her it was a fake and probably wouldn't keep time, but as usual she couldn't find her little decorative timepiece.
They took the elevator down to the lounge, then Harry took her hand and led her outside onto the terrace so they could admire the lake again in the gathering twilight. Near the door, alone, smoking a cigarette, was the big blond cop Harry remembered.
"Good evening," Harry said, and the policeman replied in a stiff Italian.

"Come on, you remember me," Harry persisted.

"*Como sta?*"

"We met at Terminella's funeral. At the grave. You served as my interpreter, so I know you speak English."

"Yes, I remember," the policeman admitted, unhappy about it.

"This is my wife Zeta."

Zeta smiled and spoke, but the awkwardness increased. The big policeman had placed himself against a pillar so that he couldn't escape.

"What are you doing here?" Harry went on, smiling.

"Seeing a friend," came the reply. Harry decided that was a fabrication. It also became apparent to him that he had to set the cop free.

"Good seeing you again, but we're meeting our friends," Harry managed, and he took Zeta's arm and steered her away.

In the lounge the others were drifting toward the car park as Harry and Zeta arrived.

"That was odd," she remarked.

"Don't you see what it means?"

"What?"

"They're watching the villa."

"But why?"

"Because they probably now believe what Terminella insisted on telling them."

Leo called everyone to the vans.

"Go over this again," Zeta urged Harry.

"Don't you see? Terminella was killed because he suspected one of us or somebody here at the villa. Now the cops are here. This isn't a public hotel, so what's he doing? He's watching everybody. Maybe it took a while with forensics. Maybe the killer used a weapon—a knife, say—that was also used to kill some of the little girls. The cops had to be familiar with the killer's weapon and maybe forensics finally proved –"

"I don't follow," Zeta objected.

Leo called again, impatient. Robin had the hiccups.

"Why would a policeman be here at the villa?" Harry repeated.

"Maybe he's dating one of the servants."

"Let's go have dinner. Think about it. We'll talk later."

With that, they put on their smiles, arrived at the vans, and went toward the evening's entertainments.

Enzo the cook turned out heavy sauces, overcooked pasta, a thin soup, and a pastry that contained an inedible meat, yet Leo poured lots of wine and stayed in a high good humor. From a nearby alcove a string quartet—also provided by Leo—attempted to play easy listening favorites while out at the island harbor a water taxi waited.

Architecture became the subject, everyone agreeing to go visit Gehry's new masterpiece in Spain, then Olan cleared his throat to predict that all new architecture would be free form, no timbers, no squared corners, just curves and vaulted arches. Roper, ever sensitive to Leo's feelings, quickly predicted that renovations of beautiful old structures—such as Leo's Villa Franscesca—would never go out of style. Wade caught on immediately and voiced his agreement.

Val launched into her usual mystical ideas on creativity and originality. "Genius is a wild spirit and a great heart!" she proclaimed, waving her rings. "First comes Byron the genius, then comes his poetry!"

Zeta drank off her wine and looked at the ceiling.

Great mounds of spaghetti arrived.

"Oh boy," said Olan in despair. "Chef Boy-r-Dee."

Harry and Wade gave up on the food so drank wine and chatted.

"Got my suit ready for tomorrow," Wade told him, anticipating the portrait session.

"We'll take an early ferry and catch the morning light," Harry suggested.

"You won't take me over to Bellano and try to upset me, will you?"

"In what way?"

"By accusing me and calling me a killer. Word gets around."

"Don't anticipate my methods of interrogation," Harry answered, grinning.

"I know you've been trying to get everyone animated, Harry, but, really, you've ruffled a few feathers."

Roper picked up on their conversation and began a story that won everybody's attention. "I was out jogging," he said, "when I saw Wade crashing through the woods. Coming down off a hillside up near the old Roman bridge. He stumbled and fell halfway down!"

"You must've seen somebody else," Wade called down the table.

"Hell, Wade, you were unmistakable! You wore your standard green outfit! And you rolled downhill until you caught yourself on a bush! My first thought was, hey, Wade's the killer Harry's worried about! Didja leave a little body up there in the woods above the bridge?"

"I didn't actually stumble or roll," said Wade, surrendering.

"You were headed downhill, buddy, a hell of a lot faster than you meant to be going!"

Leo laughed and Olan guffawed and slapped the table.

"If you must know, I was being followed," Wade announced. "A big guy in a dark suit. I thought he was probably a mugger because he wasn't properly dressed for the hiking trail. So I went around a corner, left the upper path, and scrambled down to the lower path. No stumbling. And I resent like hell, Roper, what you just said about a little body left in the woods."

"Yes, shame on you," said Val to Roper.

"Right you are," Leo added. "That's Harry's thing, calling us killers, and you shouldn't make accusations, Roper. But wait, Wade: you're runnin' off from a mugger in a business suit?"

"He was a big rough looking guy!"

Harry gave Zeta a look, but she failed to read it.

The remaining courses were disasters and the coffee was one of those flavored blends everybody hated. By the time the poor cook appeared, expecting compliments, Harry knew what was coming and excused himself. As he headed for the door Leo began his attack.

"Tonight's dinner, pal, hey, it was indescribable. Make that unspeakable," Leo said, and the cook, who understood little English, beamed with pride as the insults flew.

The night was chilly. Out on the dock the captain of the water taxi, a cavalier type with a pencil mustache, held his cigarette between his thumb and forefinger and blew smoke at the moon. Voices drifted across the lake: indistinct syllables from a far shore or a distant boat.

Zeta came outside and leaned against Harry for warmth, so he placed an arm around her and drew her close.

"What was that funny look you gave me during dinner?" she asked.

"Don't you see? Wade was followed by a big guy in a business suit. Very likely another cop."

"So Terminella thought the killer was one of us and now all the other cops agree with him?"

"Yeah, something like that."

"Harry, that's pure speculation. But suppose it's true. Just suppose. You'd be in danger, wouldn't you? Especially since you announced that you might go back to Austin and comb through a few police records."

"I've thought about it. The danger. But the killer wouldn't murder one of his own because that'd certainly get him caught, wouldn't it?"

"You'd be right, but you'd be dead."

"You're shivering," he said, and he took off his windbreaker and wrapped her in it.

"Feels good," she told him. "I'll wear this tomorrow while you do Wade's portrait. I'm going to Bellano's big attraction. Something called the waterworks. It's a cave or something with a waterspout. Bernard says I should see it. Do you mind?"

"This windbreaker goes well with all cultural attractions," he said. "And, listen, I'll finish up by noon, so let's meet at that same little trattoria in the port, okay?"

"Noon at the port," she agreed, and they huddled

together as the others emerged from the restaurant and as the captain fired up the engine of the water taxi.

Harry and Wade took the early ferry and arrived at the studio to find Bernard coming out of the darkroom. The factory wore its morning chill, but hot chocolate simmered in the kitchen and they poured themselves steaming cups.

Bernard had finished running proofs and they were mounted in the darkroom for Harry to inspect: Kelton, Olan, Leo, and just a couple of Roper. While Harry went to view them Wade strolled around the studio sipping his chocolate and gawking at April's photos, moving slowly from picture to picture, curiously formal in his dark suit.

Bernard joined Harry as he studied the proofs.

"See your killer in those faces?" Bernard prompted him.

"You're skeptical," Harry answered, smiling.

"It would be a very long shot, don't you agree?"

"They're just masks, aren't they?"

"Seems so to me. I'm not sure your acquaintances have all that much life underneath their eyes. If you don't mind my saying so. Oh, maybe this one." He tapped Kelton's photo.

Kelton's intelligent eyes, Harry thought. Were there some deep demonic urges back in there? No way. He was probably lying in bed with April at this hour, a goofy smile fixed on his mouth, addled and exhausted with her, while the Italian sunlight spread lazily over their bodies.

Wade called from the studio.

"Coming," Harry answered back.

"I'll turn out the proofs on this morning's chap when you've finished today," Bernard told him.

"You've been a great help," Harry said. "And you've indulged me in all my wild ideas."

"Anything to catch a psychopath," said Bernard with a smile, revealing his skepticism, and Harry decided against telling him that the police were probably watching them all at the villa. Instead he went out to Wade and began the rituals with the lights and camera gear.

Wade launched into the subject himself. "I understand that you went to that detective's funeral," he said.

"That's right," Harry replied.

"I felt insulted by what he said to us. We're aristocrats on holiday, he told us, and regard all Italians as waiters or servants. He didn't have to put it that way. And it occurs to me, Harry, that you agree with him."

"What makes you think so?"

"Your attitude toward the rest of us. Clearly, it's changed. I can't say exactly how, but I know it. You somehow disapprove—and not in the way Zeta disapproves of Jackie's painting or Val's writing, not just as a matter of taste. I feel you've withdrawn. That you deeply dislike us. You'll not be coming back to Lake Como with us next year, will you?"

"Wade, I don't think any of us will come back here. At least not as a group."

"I'm not surprised to hear you say that. Do I sit here in this chair?"

"Please. I'll be ready in a minute or two."

"How do I look?"

"You could run a comb through the hair over your temples."

Wade pulled out a pocket comb and obeyed.

"What's happened to you, Harry? Have you gone radical on us?"

"I don't know, Wade. Sit down. Shift a little to your left and let's do this."

"Do you agree with that detective that we're all superficial? Look, Harry, take Kelton: he's seen the dirt of the world, but he still likes good wine, sunny days, and a pretty woman—as he just proved by trotting off with April. What's different with you? Lighten up. These local murders—they've got into your head."

"Hold that," Harry said, and he made two quick exposures. Wade remained stiff, his chin up, posing, but Harry really didn't care.

"Talk to me," Wade insisted.

"Look at yourself, Wade. You're asking what's wrong with me? You don't enjoy yourself at the lake, not anymore. You're under a ton of stress. Everybody sees it. You push yourself on hikes. You drink too much, eat too much, and kiss Leo's ass. I'll bet you joined right in with that cook last night, didn't you?"

"Well, it was some awful spaghetti."

"You're unhappy here and I know you've got money problems back home."

"Sure, I lost that goddamned malpractice suit and, yes, I'm stressed out and short. But I enjoy this month at the lake every year, I really do."

"I don't believe that."

"I leave my practice every year and come here!"

"Because of Val. You get off on your own and try to make the best of it, but I think you're lonely here. You get drunk as quick as possible every evening. You're not Leo's doctor anymore. He quit you and he's probably leaving you out of the new villa—at least Roper thinks so and he should know."

Wade rested his head in his hands.

"I know we're out of Leo's villa," he managed. "It'll break Val's heart. She has this status thing in her head. It'll kill her and she'll blame me. And about my money problems, you don't know the half of it." He rubbed his hands nervously while Harry resisted more exposures. "Even so, don't suggest that I'm involved in any of this shit around the lake. On that you'd be dead wrong."

"Tell me about the little girl and the malpractice suit," Harry said, pressing.

"My insurance company settled. Naturally I should've appeared before the jury, but it looked like a lock. But we settled, then I couldn't get insurance right away. The premiums went sky high. I made some bad investments trying to cover myself. But I had to touch the little girl, Harry. Her mother was sitting right there watching us when my nurse was called away, then it happened. Just suddenly happened. Christ, Harry, I thought the little girl had tuberculosis, so I had to examine her. Then it became a goddamned game: how to get money out of the rich American doctor."

"I believe you, Wade, but I hear some strange shit about you—things I wish I hadn't."

"C'mon, Harry, don't give me that."

"Val told Zeta you sometimes come home without your underwear."

"Goddamn, she said that?"

"Maybe there's something your wife doesn't understand."

"Goddammit. I go to that X Store out on Lamar Street. Hell, I've seen Olan there too. They have booths where a guy can watch porno. Goddammit, Harry, a man should be left alone with his habits. But you think that makes me a psychosexual killer?"

"Nothing of the sort. Look, go wash your face. Bernard will get you a glass of seltzer water."

"Right, I'll take a break. I want this portrait."

Wade visited the toilet, then stood around in the kitchen with Bernard and Harry gulping down a glass of water and taking deep breaths.

"We've known each other for years," Wade finally said evenly. "Not all that well, true, Harry, but we can be friends. I know you and Kelton play golf together in Austin, then go to that old pub over by the university. Maybe I could have a drink with you guys occasionally."

"Sounds good," Harry said. "And I really don't mean to upset you, Wade, I don't, but I've got this fixation."

"That's right, Harry, it's your problem, not mine, I know that."

Harry guided Wade back to the chair and smoothed his suit. It still had the musty odor of Wade's luggage.

When they resumed the session Wade struck a number of poses as Harry clicked off exposures. Poor Wade. As he worked Harry remembered something Wade had mentioned over drinks more than a year ago: methods for committing suicide. Harry didn't invite the memory, but it bubbled to the surface of his awareness as he worked, and he saw the man before him plainly, getting older, overweight and overwrought, a doctor about to lose his clinic, married to a woman about to lose status with her friends and who would undoubtedly blame him for it. The memory came back clearly: they were sitting in a booth drinking Shiner beer. You can take an empty syringe, Wade said, and you can inject a vein with air, just air. If you pick a prominent vein on the underside of the arm—a nice, blue, fat vein—you can watch the air drive out the blood and snake its way up the arm. Put in several good inches of air, he told them. Then wait as the air moves toward the heart. It usually stops the pump, said the doctor, laughing. Just a short jolt and you're gone. Harry recalled the exact words: snake its way up the arm, a short jolt. And he remembered how Wade's hollow laughter had created a moment of premonition, and a feeling, now, that led Harry to believe for a moment that this would be the last photograph ever made of the doctor.

 Struck with poor Wade's state of mind Harry invited him to lunch down at the port, but the doctor refused and thanked him.

 An hour later Bernard drove them down to the quayside in his old Fiat and Wade took the ferry back toward Lenno. Bernard and Harry had a bottle of wine and some pizza at the trattoria, but Zeta didn't show up.

"How long does it take to see this waterworks?" Harry asked.

"Not all that long," said Bernard. "But it's pleasantly weird. She probably sat down on one of the benches to watch the waterspout."

 They finished the wine and she still didn't arrive. Finally, Bernard made his excuses. "It's the bloody wine," he said. "I've got to have my nap."

 When he was alone Harry began to feel uneasy.

FOUR

Men in the same quarters who had eaten together by day and rested together by night took sides and fought each other. The shrieks, the wounds, the blood were unmistakable, but motives were mysterious, the fates unpredictable.
 —Tacitus, *The Annals of Imperial Rome*

The crevasse above Bellano, a deep stone fissure in the side of the mountain, contained a roaring waterspout—it boomed sideways out of the rock face—and the thundering torrent eventually hurled itself into the lake. In prehistoric times the fissure perhaps served a primitive people as a cave-like spiritual center, and it still had the dank and mysterious feel of a greystone cathedral, a fierce place where the noise, movement, and rushing water echoed off the walls and seemed to place the visitor in the belly of a beast. Above the fissure in the high meadows at the top of the mountain stood those monoliths beside the ramshackle old silk factory and one could imagine cavemen or Druid-like priests moving in ritual column from their sacred stones in the fields to the dark interiors of the crevasse, back and forth, light to darkness, sunlight and vegetation to the loud netherworld of shadows and dread.

Years ago the hydraulics of the crevasse had been harnessed to supply power to the silk industry on the heights and water to the town below. A century ago a series of metal catwalks had been constructed along one side of the fissure. These led to shelves of rock that became precarious footpaths and crude stone stairways made safe by guard rails, everything climbing higher and higher until visitors had views of the cascading waters more than ninety feet below. Halfway along the climb was a platform of rock so visitors could view the waterspout and further on where the fissure opened onto the sky stood a cluster of benches where visitors could sit, warmed by a slant of sunlight, and contemplate the gorge.

Zeta rummaged around in her shoulder bag until she found the wallet containing her money. The woman at the ticket kiosk—it cost only a euro to see the wonders of the crevasse—smiled and responded with a friendly greeting in Italian, using the word *nessuno* which Zeta understood to mean that nobody else was touring this morning.

The crevasse was a noisy cave, windy, with a cold mist and Harry's windbreaker felt warm and comforting. She found a plastic bank card in one of its pockets before getting caught up in the monstrosity surrounding her. As she moved on the roar became deafening although she couldn't yet see the waterspout.

An eerie advance: she felt like a dragon awaited her.

Mounting a stairway carved out of stone she finally saw it: tons of water booming from a cleft in the stone, hurling itself at the opposite wall of the fissure. She gripped a hand rail and moved across a shelf of rock, climbing higher. When she finally climbed more than fifty feet above the spout she could look straight up and see a patch of sky and the morning sunlight through a narrow crack at the top of the walls.

Looking back down, then, a movement caught her eye.

Someone was on the catwalk below, yet hidden.

A strange feeling came over her: fright. Above it all the waterspout roared away, creating confusion.

She waited. Whoever it was remained out of sight, hugging the wall away from the guard rail. Someone was there, definitely, and she wondered if one of the policemen might be following her, but that couldn't be, no, wait, Harry said they were only following the men, not the women.

She climbed higher, feeling the cold chill of the mist. She went up a series of clanking metal steps, shifting her shoulder bag, and found another spot where she could view the catwalk below, a vantage point halfway hidden behind a jut of rock.

Minutes passed while she watched.

She began wondering if she had been mistaken, yet she concentrated on that turn in the catwalk below, thinking, okay, he'll come into view, just wait, calm yourself.

Another minute. A weird, noisy, shadowy place. All right, there's nobody here, *nessuno*. She began to convince herself.

Then she saw him as he turned away.

He had moved much closer—far beyond that turn in the catwalk she'd been watching—and as she pressed against that wedge of rock he had spied on her, seeing her plainly. Now, curiously, he turned away.

Trembling, she kept her position and watched. It was far too noisy to hear his footfall on the metal catwalk, but once again he'd have to pass that turn so she could see him in retreat. Waiting, she held her breath and brought her fists to her mouth.

Then she saw him.

An altogether familiar figure.

She had a sudden impulse to call after him and her lips opened to form his name.

But she didn't. Instead, the cold paralysis from her hands seemed to move into her mouth as she burrowed into this wedge of rock. She shivered. Fumbling in her shoulder bag she found the Rolex, deciding to wait another ten or fifteen minutes. I won't move, she told herself. I won't move. Yet before ten minutes had passed a woman arrived with her little boy, making that turn on the catwalk below, warning her son who hurried along unafraid. At the sight of them Zeta started back, relieved.

Even so, she couldn't account for how frightened she had been.

* * *

Outside the trattoria Harry paced the cobblestones. Those still at the outdoor tables seemed oblivious, laughing and chatting, and the tethered boats bobbing at the quay lent the afternoon a peculiar nervousness. Although unsure where the waterworks were located he almost started out when he saw Zeta hurrying toward him.

She grabbed his arm, spun him around, and said breathlessly in his ear, "Leo! I saw Leo hiding from me! It was so weird and, god, to tell the truth it scared me!"

"What? Slow down."

He steered her back toward the trattoria, her urgency confusing him.

"Up at the waterworks! When he saw me he ran off!"

"Leo at a tourist spot? Doing what?"

"Hiding in the rocks! It's this sorta cave with a big noisy waterspout! He followed me, but then ran off!"

"Let's get a drink," he said, guiding her back toward the outside tables. "Aren't you hungry? Go over all this from the beginning. By the way, have you got some euros?"

She rummaged in her shoulder bag as they claimed a table, telling him about the catwalks, the creepy mist and the general claustrophobia. "I thought, hey, what's he doing? Maybe he wants to get me alone. Maybe to pitch his offer again. Or to wrestle a kiss out of me. But then he scurried away!"

She found a wad of euros and tried to summon a waiter and in all this she produced the Rolex and pushed it toward Harry.

When he saw the fake Rolex he made a connection.

"Leo's the one getting the little girls," he said.

"What are you talking about?"

"I'm calling the detectives in Como," he said, rising and looking toward the rear of the bar. "There's a phone back there. You want a drink?"

"Double Scotch. You better have one, too."

"I'm fine, honey, and I'm dead right about this."

Harry ordered a drink for Zeta then went through a pantomime with the bartender in order to use the house phone and put a call through. A female on the other end, seemingly offended that he asked if English were spoken, proceeded to stall matters. Harry wanted Commandante Benzetti while the woman insisted that she would pass along any message. Besides, she finally revealed, the Commandante was in Bellagio.

"Can he be reached?"

"And what," she wanted to know, "is your business?"

"The murders," he told her. "The murders of the little girls."

Having heard dozens of such urgent messages, she stalled again, finally asking, "Yes, and you have a tip for the police?"

"I'm the one at the Villa Cappeletti who found the doll."

A long silence. She knew nothing about a doll.

"I know the identity of the murderer," he said in exasperation.

Name please? She meant Harry's name and seemed to be taking longhand notes.

He made the mistake of explaining further about the doll, saying that the one he gave to the detectives might be important after all and that it might need to be retrieved.

"I am not knowing," she explained with strained patience, "about any doll."

He suggested that she phone Benzetti, then gave her the number on the bar telephone where she could call him back.

"I will try to say all this to the Bellagio police," she agreed. "But is better if you say to me what you know."

With that he decided to ferry over to Bellagio and find Benzetti himself.

When he returned to Zeta she had finished her drink and ordered a pizza, but he rushed her away. They hurried to the dockside station to find they had just missed the Bellagio ferry.

"What do you know that I don't?" she asked breathlessly.

He said that the Rolex was very important.

"How? In what way?"

"Let's hire a water taxi," he told her, pulling her along. "There's really no time to waste."

The Bellagio police headquarters occupied a battered building near the quay, an old ruin held up by jacaranda and draped with flags. In the center of its foyer—a space half the size of a basketball court—a young cop with broad shoulders and a quick smile stood behind a rickety card table bearing a single black telephone whose wires went off fifty feet across the floor to disappear beneath a door. The cop had the smile and healthy good looks assigned to make an impression on visitors.

"Tell me, please, your business, then I am deciding what to do with the information," he kept repeating in careful English.

Harry wanted nothing less than Benzetti and it took ten minutes to determine that the Commandante and two *poliziotto* had just left by boat for the journey back to Como.

"Can he be reached by phone or radio?" Harry wanted to know. "This is an emergency. *Emergenza, si?*"

This made little impression. Zeta tried to explain that their business had to do with the killer of all the children around the lake. The young cop warmed to Zeta, but he had obviously heard many such claims. Harry went on to say that Benzetti's men were currently watching the villa in Lenno. He dropped Terminella's name. He asserted that he had positive identification on the killer, wondering for only a moment if this were as true as it seemed. At last the young cop sighed, nodded, and went off to find his immediate superior.

"So tell me about the Rolex," Zeta insisted as they waited.

"Don't you see? It gave off a signal. He wasn't following you to the waterworks. He thought he was following me. When he saw his mistake he turned around and left."

"Why'd he follow you?"

"He probably wanted to kill me. What else?"

"Oh, Harry," she said, and the skepticism returned to her voice in spite of herself.

"Zeta, we don't know him. We don't know any of them."

The young cop returned with an older man, grey haired, who introduced himself as the *investigatore* on duty.

As Harry once more went through the lengthy explanation the man's smile became a disbelieving smirk.

"Look, you knew Terminella, right?" Harry persisted.

"*Si,* yes, of course," the man answered, working a finger beneath his collar and scratching.

"I'll bet Terminella was killed by the same weapon that killed the little girls," Harry argued. "And this information hasn't been in any newspaper, so how would I know this? Benzetti's officers are at the villa where we're staying, you see, because Terminella strongly believed that somebody there was the killer. And his hunch was right! So now Benzetti believes this, too, because he knows Terminella paid with his life for this theory! So take me to Benzetti or call him back, so I can tell him who the murderer is!"

During all this the detective studied Harry's face, glancing once or twice at Zeta. "Perhaps you are correct," he finally said. "*Forse.* Perhaps."

"If I'm right and you don't believe me, think how foolish you'll look," Harry went on. This proved to be a winning argument.

"Very well, the Commandante will decide," the man said, and he raised a hand to calm Harry.

Weary of the caution of the police and their constant deference to superiors, Harry walked across the room and looked out a window onto the street. A vendor sold roses wrapped in bright tissue beside the curb.

"Madame, would you like coffee?" the young cop asked Zeta.

"Yes, please," she replied, then went over and stood beside Harry.

"Do you think Jackie knew about Leo and that's possibly why she left?" Zeta asked.

"I've thought about it. How could she not know? She'd never leave Italy if they were just arguing about the décor at his Villa Franscesca, would she?"

"I don't know," Zeta said, and she still seemed far less convinced than Harry wanted her to be.

The detective came back with two espressos in double paper cups. Benzetti had turned the police boat around, he informed them, and was headed back. For a few minutes they sipped the coffee and made smalltalk. Zeta asked the detective about some scratches on his neck.

"My two sons," he said with pride. "Eleven and twelve years old and—how do you say?—*echimese,* very strong. We wrestle and I always hold back, never wanting to hurt them, but they never hold back because they don't understand. So they are always injuring me."

Zeta remarked that she always wanted a daughter.

"Yes," said the detective. "A woman needs daughters."

Later when Harry stood apart with Zeta again he spoke about Leo's villa once more. "There's something important there," he said, convinced.

"Tell the police."

"Yeah, I will," he agreed. "They need to search it."

They sat at a chipped oval table in a conference room that also contained an elaborate coffee and espresso machine for the entire force, so officers constantly entered, made coffee, heated milk, and disrupted privacy while Harry spoke with Benzetti, the unnamed detective with the neck injury, and a uniformed cop who took notes at Benzetti's side. The room had high windows so that if one stood up and paced, as Benzetti liked to do, the lake and mountains could be seen, but Harry, seated, only had a view of the sky as the Commandante's thick body moved around.

Benzetti, as it turned out, spoke a crude English, also adding an occasional nod or grunt while Harry related how his suspicions led him to take the villa's master key and to visit the rooms of his friends. He spent a length of time telling Benzetti about the monitoring equipment in Leo's room and car.

"It finally occurred to me that he could follow anyone with a microchip receiver," Harry went on. "He has the usual stuff—a GPS directional system, for example—but also some military equipment in the same category."

"He is a military man?" Benzetti inquired.

"No, but he's a wealthy man with powerful friends including a congressman back in Texas. He could acquire what he wanted."

They went back over the matter of the Rolex watches. Zeta had borrowed Harry's gift from Leo, she explained, then discovered Leo following her.

"I think he gave out presents—dolls, caps—to many children around the lake," Harry said. "Items bugged with microchips. Then he followed them electronically."

"Ah, so why does he follow you?" Benzetti asked.

"Possibly to kill me," Harry quickly replied. "Because I'd announced that I intended to look into everybody's possible criminal records when we went back to Texas."

The police officers went over all this to one another in Italian.

"Let me ask you," Harry interrupted. "Wasn't Terminella killed with the same weapon that killed all—or many—of the little girls around the lake?"

"You are clever to imagine this, yes," Benzetti replied. "A curious weapon. But also I am asking you this: did your Leo give something to Terminella? When my detective comes to the Cappeletti villa to speak with the guests?"

Harry paused, thinking.

Then Zeta replied, "Yes, a cigarette lighter. Leo handed him a cheap plastic cigarette lighter that Terminella kept."

"Very probably with a microchip inside it," Harry added. "And I believe the doll found on the path—and all other dolls assuming there're others—contain microchips, too. I don't know how or why the doll was thrown down beside the path—Terminella could never figure that out, either—but if you still have the doll I believe you'll find a directional chip inside it."

The officers again conferred while the aide took notes. They also waited for two young policemen to enter the far end of the room, to make coffee, and to depart.

Benzetti began to pace again.

"You are saying to me that your friend Leo is repairing an old villa?" the Commandante asked.

"And I think you should look at it," Harry suggested. "Maybe you'll find dolls or toys there. Children's clothing, that sort of thing."

"Yes, we will look," Benzetti agreed.

"But since your men are already watching us at the villa, maybe you're already ahead of me in much of this," said Harry.

"But we are not watching the Cappeletti villa."

"You're not? We saw one of your men there. Lucchio. I recognized him because he was my interpreter at Terminella's graveside."

"Perhaps he visits someone there," Benzetti offered. "But he has no such instruction from me."

Harry felt confused, but Benzetti smiled and consoled him.

The detective with the neck injury spoke up. "At this hour," he asked, "where do you think we will find your friend Leo?"

"I thought he was going to Lugano, but then Zeta saw him at the waterworks."

"And he goes to Lugano for what reason?"

"He told me he visits a lady friend there."

"At this hour," said Zeta, answering the detective's question, "we usually gather for drinks at the villa, then eventually go to one restaurant or another."

"You don't eat at Madame Cappeletti's table?" asked Benzetti, smiling.

"The restaurants are very good," said Zeta tactfully.

"The lady friend in Lugano," said the aide with the notepad. "Does she have a name?"

"I don't believe there's a woman in Lugano," Harry answered. "Not anymore. I think he probably goes hunting instead."

"Very *interessante,* all this," said Benzetti, pacing. "Because we live in new times. Many scientific advances. It makes sense, the microchips that show the killer his directions. And it hurts to think that such a man as this could be, hm, *superiore,* more advanced, you see, than we could imagine. But we have already think of this. Electronics. Finding directions in such a way, this we have thought about. We are being clever because the *maligno,* the evil man, is often clever, and if he is the hunter, so are we. And better hunters, I believe, than he will understand. You are thinking on all this, Harry, because you care and I am giving you our thanks. We will inspect the doll and look at your Rolex watch. Also the villa that your friend makes new. We will do all this. But for now, please, I think you should join your friends for the evening."

Benzetti then spoke to the local detective and the aide, giving them their orders and watching them hurry away.

"I can offer you a ride across the lake to Madame Cappeletti's villa," he concluded.

"A directional system," Harry asked, making sure. "You've thought of this possibility before?"

"Ah, yes. We have the expert from Milan. Come, please, our boat is ready."

They motored across the water in a darkening twilight, the sky overhead filled with interstellar currents, a pale beauty, and on the deck of the police boat with its glowing red and green running lights Harry watched Benzetti and Zeta speaking to one another, their words drowned out by the booming engine. Benzetti was a large man with an angry mouth that somehow struggled to smile as he listened to her. Harry saw the distress in her face. In this new turn of events, Harry surmised, something deep inside both of them had ruptured, and if they didn't know Leo Jones then somehow they didn't know themselves. A tinge of paranoia also arrived as he watched them together: did she still doubt his theory and was she admitting this to the Commandante? Could I possibly be wrong? he asked himself. A hundred scraps of circumstantial evidence, bits of chance, he follows her and frightens her, yet could I be wrong? Doubts arrived then he waved them aside.

A dozen officers gathered at the ferry dock, moving around Benzetti for a discussion. Harry and Zeta waited, his arm draped around her, then everyone walked up the path to the villa.

"Please, be with your friends," Benzetti urged them. "Behave normally if possible, please, while we question your friend Leo."

As they approached the verandah they could hear Olan's laughter and the slap of his palm on a tabletop. Then Leo's voice. It surprised Harry that Leo was present and he realized that he had somehow expected Leo to be in flight.

"Ah, yes, your friends, I believe, are waiting for you," Benzetti said as they mounted the steps to the verandah, and Harry suddenly knew that the police were skeptical and that his story was itself under suspicion. They would question Leo, yet they hadn't inspected the doll or the Rolex, so they couldn't possibly believe anything they had been told.

In the lounge everyone turned and gaped as Harry arrived with his squad of policemen.

"Harry, this does it!" Roper shouted. "Leo's some mad fucking child killer? Up yours!"

"I don't believe it for a minute," said Val.

"Total nonsense!" Olan said to the ceiling.

Benzetti had invited Leo into the library, so with everyone in the lounge Harry encountered a furious disbelief. Roper had his fists balled as if he might attack. Only Robin stayed calm, sipping her white wine, but her eyes went wide when Val started shrieking at Zeta.

"You're the reason Jackie left us!" Val accused her.

"Not true. I just talked to her on the phone and everything's fine between us. If you don't believe me, phone her yourself."

"She's too much of a lady to tell you what she really thinks of you! You've always been a snobby bitch, Zeta, and I don't know why we've put up with you as long as we have!"

"Girls, girls," Wade interrupted, but then turned to Harry. "You have no proof in any of this, Harry. Nothing substantial."

"Proof will come," Harry promised.

"No, goddammit, it won't!" Roper said. "You and that little chain-smoking detective just stirred up a little drama, that's all."

"Detective Terminella was murdered with the same weapon that killed the little children!" Harry shot back in his loudest voice.

"What weapon is that?" Olan demanded.

"I don't know. The same weapon."

"See, you don't know fuck all," Roper told him.

"Harry, what in hell did you tell these cops?" Wade asked.

"What he told them they believed," said Zeta, coming to his defense.

"Because they'll believe anything!" Roper shouted. "Face it, they're desperate fucking amateurs! They've had all these murders in their backyard for years and nothing to show for it! So now they're with Leo running down a false lead!"

"After all Leo's done for you two!" said Val. "He bought Harry's out-of-focus pictures! He's given you both dozens of gifts! And all those upgrades on the airlines!"

"Don't forget the wine," Zeta prompted her.

"Exactly, the wine! You're both so ungrateful!"

"Don't forget the fake Rolex watches," Harry put in.

"Those were fakes?" asked Wade, somewhat more suspicious.

"I love Leo like a big brother," Val continued, starting one of her speeches. "A perfectly wonderful big brother. You've never seen me flirting with him, not once, because he respects me as an author and I respect him as the genius businessman he is. And he helped Wade. Helped him financially and without hesitation, didn't he darling?"

Wade gave that a mild shrug.

Olan cleared his throat and began a speech of his own in his most authoritative bass voice. "I can say with confidence, Harry, that you're way off base. I've attended Leo and I know he's a ruthless man in business, crude at times—we all know that—but a killer, no, impossible. He hasn't the psychological profile. I mean, he plays golf, doesn't he?"

"Oh, please, Olan, you don't know shit," Zeta said with a sigh.

This started the shouting match once more. Harry enjoyed being somewhat defended by Zeta while Olan, Roper and Wade sent up a chorus of protests.

Robin in her quiet little voice said, "I suppose supper is out of the question tonight?"

"Not at all," Zeta answered. "Let's go into the dining room, Harry, and see what Madame Cappeletti's serving."

"I'll need a drink first," Harry said.

"Why not? Everybody else is tanked."

"Don't think I won't tell Leo exactly what you've said about him," Val called after them as they departed.

"Go somewhere and compose a bad sentence," Zeta responded over her shoulder.

A short time later the detectives, officers and Leo filed out of the library. From their table in the dining room Harry could see Benzetti and Leo pausing to speak in the corridor. A uniformed policeman stood guard while the waitresses, already wide-eyed because of all the shouting in the lounge, gawked from the entrance to the kitchen. Leo glanced into the dining room, saw Harry and Zeta at their table, then averted his eyes.

When Benzetti finally came toward Harry and Zeta he was intercepted by a drunken and loud Roper.

"I should've been allowed in the library!"

"Ah, and you are?"

"If you want to know I'm Leo Jones' personal attorney!"

"Very good. He is soon perhaps needing legal counsel."

Their voices carried clearly over the dining room. Both Madame Cappeletti and her son peeked out with the waitresses at the kitchen door.

"Leo Jones will soon be flying back to the States and getting away from this whole damn farce!" Roper went on.

"Advise him, please, not to leave the country. Also, he is invited to see us in Como tomorrow, so please to join him if you prefer."

"You haven't got a damn thing on him! All you've got is the crazy conjecture of that guy sitting over there—who used to be Leo's friend!"

"Please," said Benzetti. "And your name is --?"

"Up yours," Roper replied, and went back to the lounge.

Benzetti sighed, attempted a smile that failed, and strolled over to Zeta and Harry. He sat down, but declined a glass of wine.

"Your friend," he began, "says he is all day in Lugano."

"Not all day because I saw him," Zeta interrupted.

"He says no. And he is giving us the name of his lady friend, so we are calling her. So far, no answer. But he is very embarrassed and prefers his wife is not knowing."

"Maybe he has someone to provide an alibi, but my wife saw him," Harry asserted, and with this Benzetti tried another smile, one of profound and weary patience.

"My men, they are searching the villa of Mr Jones," Benzetti went on. "They are saying they find only the tools of many workmen, but I am having them search again. Sometimes in old villas are hidden places, even whole rooms. So we are very careful. Also, I am not forgetting the doll—which is temporarily misplaced—or the Rolex watch. It will be returned to you, of course, if it gives us nothing."

"You'll find something," Harry assured him, yet some of his certainty ebbed away.

"Tomorrow we are speaking with Mr Jones again. With his attorney, I am thinking. Here is my card. Call me if you think of anything else."

"Can't someone look at the Rolex tonight?"

"Ah, no, we have in the morning our expert."

Benzetti stood up slowly, a tired man.

Harry felt foolish holding the business card.

"I did see him," Zeta insisted once more.

"Yes, perhaps," Benzetti replied. "But the waterworks, it is a place of many shadows and much noise and—how do you say?—distractions. You know this is true, do you not?"

Lying in bed beside Zeta that night Harry kept thinking about Leo's villa, wondering if it had a secret entrance or dungeon, a room filled with shackles and torture equipment where Leo could butcher his little victims, letting their blood and entrails drain down a stone outlet into the lake. Maybe Jackie discovered the room and that's why she flew back to Texas, he speculated, or maybe she found his hidden stash of toys, tee shirts, caps, fountain pens, and all the items to be handed out to children as their deadly gifts. From all this conjecture he also began wondering about himself and the recent flood of intuitions. The talcum and tiny flashlights on the female torso: he had seen those images in his mind's eye before leaving Austin, the precise effect he hoped to recreate in the lens. Inspiration and insight: the picture that once seen can never be unseen or dismissed.

After seeing all the electronic equipment in Leo's room a bit of time passed, then certainty arrived. It came replete with imagery: the poor children giving out signals, the omniscient predator.

Before Zeta went to sleep—half drunk on almost a full bottle of red wine—she said that when Leo turned away at the waterworks she saw this strange posture, the posture of guilt. Normally he would've called out to her, come to her, kissed her cheek, and certainly would have remarked on the coincidence of their meeting in such a place, but instead he tried to make himself small and inconspicuous, trying to steal away, and she knew something was terribly wrong, something she couldn't assess at the time.

The luminous clock beside them showed half past two.

Am I still certain? he asked himself. Yes.

He wondered if Jackie had placed the doll near the path. But why? To stop the monster and his hunting trips? Did she possibly do it, then flee to Texas, then hurry off to Mexico? Did she fear for her life? Did she go to San Miguel as she announced or was that a fabrication?

He watched Zeta sleeping. Did she actually tell him that he was superficial? If so, maybe he was. Kelton, after all, had spent his life in the middle of important political events as a seasoned reporter. Even Olan and Wade knew the dirt of the world, helping their clients. And Roper had followed the law—or near enough. But I've dawdled around with baby photos and family groups that any local guy could do, he told himself, and I run a storefront photo shop. But now: this thing with Leo. Maybe I've lived all my life for this—to find him out and stop him.

With this last thought Harry fell into a dreamless sleep.

The next morning—never mind Benzetti's request for a meeting in Como—Leo and Roper were gone. Madame Cappeletti's son had driven them down to the Milan airport in exchange for Leo's big new sports vehicle, the promised gift to the villa, and Leo had placed notes of farewell in the mail slots. In Harry's mailbox the note was addressed to Zeta alone. Waking late and coming downstairs Harry ran into Wade who informed him that everybody else was packing. Wade's own sad pieces of luggage waited at the door to the car park.

"By the way, thanks for what you did to Leo," Wade said. "By my reckoning your fuck up puts me and Val back into Leo's good graces and assures us a room in the new villa when we come back next year."

"There won't be a next year," Harry answered.

"Oh, you're sure of that, too, are you?"

"Certain enough."

"Listen, one more thing. I do want the portrait if all works out. I'll pay for it."

"I'll think about it," said Harry, not giving him any satisfaction.

By the time Zeta arrived Wade had departed and breakfast was no longer served, but Gladyce and the other kitchen help concocted a brunch of pastries, omelettes, curls of prosciutto, tea and coffee. Harry delivered Leo's note and watched Zeta open it with a butter knife. She read it and folded it back into the envelope.

"Private business?" he asked, wishing he hadn't.

She shrugged and studied the lake. It glinted with sunlight, making them squint as they waited for the food, and without his morning's *Herald Tribune* he was forced to pay attention to the far shore. At last, though, Zeta told him the contents of the note although she didn't let him see it.

"Leo still wants me to work for him. He says the offer stands."

Harry attempted a noncommittal wave of his hand.

Instead of talking over the important events of the previous day they fell into a conversation about Kelton and April, speculating if they'd see them as a couple when everybody returned to Austin. After that they figured the tips for the maids and servers and when they finished eating Zeta announced that she meant to start packing.

"I want to visit Bernard again before we go," said Harry.

"How long will that take?"

"A day over on the ferry and back."

"A whole day?"

"All the prints and negatives have to be sorted out."

"Your pals aren't going to want the portraits now."

"Wade wants his. But I'm talking about the shots of April. The ones you liked, remember?"

"Oh, right," she said absently, and it seemed curious that she had so quickly forgotten.

"Anyway, are we in a hurry?" he asked.

"Not really. We have open tickets. But I do think I'll go upstairs and decide what to leave and what to take with us."

"I'll leave the tips in the office," he said, and she went off.

Soon afterward the big blond detective, Lucchio, came to the verandah, spotted Harry, and came forward. Harry rose and they shook hands in the glaring sunlight.

"I thought Benzetti might come," said Harry.

"He sends a message. No microchips anywhere and we found nothing after two searches at your friend's villa."

Harry tried to take this in.

"There wasn't some sort of sensor in the Rolex?"

The detective smiled. "This Rolex, I think you know, was a fake."

"That's not the point. It wasn't bugged?"

"Our expert found nothing."

"What about the doll?"

"With the doll there is a slight problem. The secretary in our headquarters in Como takes it home to her daughter. We will get it again later today, but the Commandante expects nothing."

"But the Commandante knows nothing for sure, does he?"

"He said you would be upset by this," said Lucchio, catching the sarcasm.

"And I am. You need to look at the goddamned doll."

"The wristwatch is more important. Both you and your wife say that Mr Jones followed her because it gives out a signal, yes? But it does not. It cannot. It is just a cheap watch."

"Does Benzetti know that Mr Jones has gone to Milan to catch a plane back to the States?"

"Yes, this he knows. Mr Jones, he telephones. Also, we have no evidence to detain him."

"There's a tremendous amount of circumstantial evidence," Harry argued.

"The Commandante thanks you. He knows you care. We all appreciate this. Not so many visitors care."

Harry felt too overwhelmed to speak again.

FIVE

*The years as they pass plunder us
Of one thing after another.*
—Horace, *The Epistles*

When Harry went back upstairs Zeta and Robin were speaking together in low voices—about him, obviously, and the mess he had caused—and abruptly ended their conversation when he entered.

"Robin and Olan are leaving," Zeta said, making an effort to smile, and Robin stepped forward to give Harry a dry kiss on the cheek, a definite goodbye kiss.

"See you in Austin," Robin told him, not meaning it, then she turned back to Zeta to give her a fierce hug, and Harry heard the words whispered in Zeta's ear: "So sorry."

"Have a safe trip," he managed, and Robin tugged at her lace collar, nodded, and got out of the room without anything more to say.

The untidy room held their silence for a moment, then Harry began telling Zeta about the decision of the police to follow none of his information. She listened as if she already knew.

"Well, I definitely saw Leo and he acted weird," she said with a sigh of resignation. "Maybe he drove over to Lugano and his lady friend afterward." It was her weakened defense of Harry's elaborate theories.

"So before going off for a little sex on the side Leo ferries over to Bellano to visit the fucking waterworks?" Harry snapped back. With that he began going over the particulars again, feeling alone and stupid doing it. Zeta listened without meeting his gaze, giving her attention to her clothing and an open piece of luggage.

At last he stopped and said, "I guess you want to leave right away?"

"I'm dying to," she admitted. "Maybe you could ferry over to visit Bernard and to pick up your photos and gear, then be back here at dinnertime. I'll look into flight arrangements while you're gone, okay?"

A reasonable request, so Harry agreed. At least Zeta's tone was helpful, though clearly she didn't want to talk about the affair with Leo anymore.

He took the ferry, then, and a taxi uphill to the old factory where he and Bernard had a final drink together. He also went through the whole story for the little photographer: Leo's gifts, his theories about directional microchips, Benzetti's conclusions, and his own subsequent embarrassments. Bernard listened with empathy, then asked the important question.

"Do you believe you were possibly wrong?"

"I believe I was right. I believe so now. But nobody else believes me."

"What about your wife?"

"Maybe she never believed me, but I know she doesn't now."

"Then how can she account for seeing Leo?"

"I don't know the answer. Events have confused her, maybe, and the police and pressure from our friends have had an effect on her. It's possible she doubts what she saw with her own eyes. But that's unlike her. Zeta's convictions are usually unblinking. And, Bernard, I believe Leo was looking for me, honestly, and I'll always believe that. Never mind the wristwatch and the opinions of the police."

They drank mulberry wine diluted with seltzer water and ate cashews. As they gathered up Harry's cameras and gear, then the negatives and prints of April as well as the proofs of the portrait sessions a cool north breeze arrived, rattling the leaves outside the windows, and a hint of late autumn weather came with it. April sprinkled with talcum and the first crude experiments with the tiny flashlights still looked convincing.

"These shots promise everything you want," Bernard assured him. "You should always trust yourself, Harry."

"Thanks, my friend."

"About photography and about Leo Jones," Bernard made clear.

Harry's mouth tightened and he managed another grateful nod.

After that Bernard donated an old duffel bag and insisted on driving Harry down to the port. As they piled everything into the battered Fiat truck Harry looked back with an admiring sigh at the circle of stones in the overgrown field.

At the ferry Bernard grabbed him in an embrace. "May we meet again," he said, his voice cracking. "And give my best to Zeta and to April when you see her." With that, overcome, he turned away and didn't look back.

On the ferry over to Lenno, Harry felt something in his pocket: the master key to the villa's rooms. He decided to tell the Cappelettis that he found it in a corridor.

Back at Lenno he struggled up the path with his gear, barely managed to stuff everything in the tiny elevator at the villa, and went up to the room. Except for his clothes the closet was stripped. Zeta had gone. In a wave of panic he sat down heavily on the bed and looked at his forlorn camera, the crate of leftover wine in the corner, and at last spotted the folded note wedged into a corner of the mirror at the dressing table. As if his body were weighted down with iron he finally went across the room to get it.

> Harry dear: I've decided we
> should fly back separately.
> Your ticket is with your passport,
> but remember to make specific reservations.
> I've decided to work for Leo. If this greatly
> disappoints you let me say that it's strictly
> temporary and for financial considerations.
> I need to buy some time and space of my own.
> Also, Leo promises that we won't come back here
> to work on the villa unless Jackie is with us—

and he promises she will be. I'll phone as soon as I know you're keeping hours at the shop.
      Deepest love, Z

He hurried to pack, thinking he might get to Milan before Zeta's flight left so they could possibly fly back together. His photographic gear, golf clubs, luggage and liquor supply dismayed him, though, and at the height of his confusion he went downstairs to ask Madame Cappeletti if she could confer with the airline and get him the next available reservation.

In the office he encountered her son and an argument started that he didn't understand. *Punto,* the son kept repeating, and eventually Harry decided that he was getting scolded for leaving small tips for the maids and waitresses.

"No," he countered, holding up fingers and entering into a pantomime. "Thirty percent! *Trenta!*" but the son was adamant and wouldn't be calmed until his mother arrived to shoo him away.

After that Harry explained the favor he needed and Madame Cappeletti said curtly, "Yes, yes, I will do it, but we are very busy! Other guests are arriving! You are not the only guests we have here!" She accepted his plane ticket and dialed a number, then added that her son wouldn't be available to drive him to the airport.

"But I'm leaving the villa more than a case of excellent wine," he told her, and his argument, he knew, sounded pathetic.

"Take a taxi," she said with a brittle smile, then she turned to a courteous conversation on the phone with an Italian airline clerk.

When Harry entered his house in Texas he saw immediately that Zeta had never arrived and wondered if she had ever left Italy. His disappointment turned into anger that she might be with Leo. Later he reached Kelton by phone and asked him to find out where she was and with whom.

"Zeta's left you?"

"It appears so. Definitely."

"So what're you going to do about it?"

"Get drunk."

"Then hold on. I'm coming over to get drunk with you."

They slumped down in the deck chairs that evening, drinking to the limestone cliffs around them, to the fixed stars, and to buddies who would never change. Their grief seemed absolute: Harry had somehow blundered and lost Zeta and although April was now in their lives they would never be a foursome.

Harry kept going over the scattered pieces and Kelton indulged him: Leo's electronic equipment, a mysterious woman in Lugano, the neglected doll, the waterworks, and the seemingly inept attitudes of the Italian police. He hated Zeta's failure to credit his theories and her capitulation to Leo.

"Now I'll spend the rest of my life getting her back and trying to prove what I think I know about that little sonavabitch."

"Chase Zeta and forget Leo," Kelton advised, slurring his words.

A rational suggestion. Even in his growing stupor, Harry decided, Kelton was a pal capable of clarity.

They drank until their drawls and slurring observations rendered them unintelligible. After midnight Harry went into the kitchen for another bottle, but forgot why he stood before the pantry door. Kelton came to find him.

"We need ourselves a Texas ranger," said Kelton, pronouncing it as *rang-cher*.

"I need help remembering what I'm looking for," Harry agreed.

"We need a cop who doesn't like rish guys like Leo. Rich guys. A cop with computer skills. Who can hold his liquor. What was that pun somebody made in Italy?"

"If it happened at Lake Como, I don't want to know about it," said Harry, his voice trailing off.

"I love Zeta like a sister," Kelton sobbed at the kitchen.

"Yes, and where is she?" Harry asked, and from this plaintive question they both had to recover themselves.

A week passed before Zeta phoned from Dallas where she was investigating a gallery for sale, an opportunity Jackie had urged on her.

"I thought you might still be in Italy with Leo," Harry said.

"That didn't work out. Jackie wouldn't come back from Mexico and I wouldn't go back to Lake Como without her."

"That's a relief. When're you coming back to Austin?"

"Not soon. Jackie arrives today to look at the gallery situation with me. The building housed a boutique, then a martini bar. But it may be perfect. By the way, I'm staying with my cousin Julia in Kessler Park. You have her numbers in the Rolodex. Remember Julia?"

"Okay, so when are you getting back here?"

"Not anytime soon."

"I'll drive up, then, so we can check out this gallery together."

"No, don't, you have a business to run."

"Not much of one. And not this weekend. We need to talk."

"Harry, no, I want to do this my way."

"But how? What'll you use for money?"

"Jackie's helping. Remember, she has money of her own. Leo's not in this at all. And I'll handle it."

The faint static on the telephone became interstellar: light years of distance opening up, the far galaxies colliding.

"Zeta, tell me. Are we separating?"

"Right now we're apart," she answered, remaining deliberately vague.

"True. You're in Dallas and I'm here."

"Harry, you've known for a long time that I've wanted to leave Austin. You said it yourself: our friends aren't really our friends there. It was true long before the mess with Leo."

"I'm not worried about our friends—although, by the way, Kelton has been a hell of a great pal. I'm worried about us. You and me."

"It's just for now," she said, but her tone sounded permanent.

The conversation then deteriorated into pieces of news. Jackie had gone to Mexico with a bodyguard—or maybe an armed man who could have been a new boyfriend. Val was writing a book about a tycoon who resembled Leo. Robin was somewhere in the mountains of Arizona and Jackie speculated that she had left Olan. Kelton and April lived with her kids in a big leased house on Lake Travis. Wade's stress test proved that his heart was okay. Roper finished third in a golf tournament.

"I want to come see this gallery," Harry finally said, returning to matters he needed to talk about.

"Later," Zeta said. "We haven't even plastered and painted yet."

But two days later he drove north to Dallas.

In the Oak Lawn section of the city he sat in his car at a fancy suburban strip mall: boutiques, patches of mown grass, sidewalks of colored tile, and vehicles far newer than his parked beneath the trees. The shops were adorned with discreet brass markers and Zeta's read, simply, AMNESIA—clearly, Harry decided, the name of the defunct martini bar, but so very appropriate.

He arrived unannounced, tried the heavy glass door, found it locked, so took a nickel out of his pocket and rapped on the window. Zeta came out of a back room wearing shorts, a sweat shirt, and a dusty apron. Her hair was the color of pewter, so that she looked older yet no less sexier. When she opened the door he wanted to kiss her, but she turned away talking fast.

"It's a mess, but come on in," she started. "See, I've been moving partitions around so the skylights are even more effective. There's super storage in back. I'm thinking of getting my license so I can authenticate art pieces for clients. Lots of people here buy and sell art and I might even want to fly to Europe occasionally to, you know, make purchases and such."

"You colored your hair," he managed.

"Like it?"

"You look different, but great. I take it the deal's done on this place."

"Roper was here and everything's signed," she informed him.

"So Roper's helping you to leave me?"

"I'm just leaving Austin. Roper's representing Jackie who's putting up the money. So Roper's not between you and me."

"What's with Jackie and Leo? You said she ran off to Mexico with some guy with a gun."

"Jackie and Leo are friends. I don't know the whole story."

She took off her apron, then put it back on. Keeping busy, she turned on a hot plate and started making coffee.

"Harry, I'm very happy you've made a new start with your work. The shots with the talcum, they're terrific, really." She seemed to be reciting a speech to the coffee pot. "Your gift, you know, it'll come around again. You still have a great eye. But I'm going ahead with this, I have to. It's just the time for it. There's a hole in my life. Are you listening to me?"

"A hole in your life," he repeated, and the words stabbed at him.

"And what's wrong may be my fault entirely, I don't know. It might belong to both of us, too, but I intend to solve it for myself if I can."

They stopped and listened to the coffee pot spewing and popping.

"Zeta, we've had a lot of years together," he began, then stopped to clear his thoughts. "I can't stop loving you, sweetheart, and I can't imagine living apart."

"Things have just gone terribly wrong for me," she said evenly, and her calm started a hemorrhage inside him. He wanted to talk about Leo and what happened in Italy, but he just stood there looking at the little coffee pot. He wanted to tell her that she was embarrassed for him, but that she was embarrassed in front of people she didn't even know or like. He wanted to remind her that it was her contribution that started it—seeing Leo as he followed her that morning.

Time seemed to leap forward and the coffee finished making. She asked if he wanted a cup and he wanted to accept, to prolong the visit, to find some alchemy that made things right, but he felt lost.

"Nah, coffee would just upset my stomach," he said, and he gave her a last look, turned, and walked out.

The lush shores of Lake Como were forever gone, the Alpine mountains melted, the pleasant shadows burned away. His serenity, like the Texas landscape itself, had been blighted and what remained was hard thorn, cactus, the dust storm, the tornado, the rattlesnake, the scorpion. Two days after seeing Zeta in Dallas his heart had become as arid as dry stone. Only Kelton and April stood by him; to everyone else he was the guy who had accused Leo Jones of murder over in Italy.

He went to dinner at their new place out on Lake Travis, a noisy contrast to the peaceful memories of August. Water-skiers, zipped around by screaming powerboats, sent up plumes of spray and yelled to one another. The restaurants on the distant shores resembled beer and food fights. Echoes of boom boxes spread across the tepid waves at twilight and the rocky beaches made Harry feel that he sat at the edge of a doomed reservoir on the outskirts of hell.

October had arrived still hot as a furnace. Around him in the shade of the deck April's children sniped at each other, complaining about the new fall term at school. While Kelton manned the barbeque grill, April listened to Harry's determination to sell his business and tried to console him.

"I'll never find a buyer," he told her, drinking whiskey over ice.

"Sure you will," she answered. "And in the meantime I've found you a nifty new model for the flashlight sequence. Her name's Darla and she also happens to be a licensed masseuse."

"Just what I need," he said with a smirk.

"She used to dance at the clubs with me, but now she's way too old for it. I think she might've hit thirty five."

"You're a devil."

"You gonna be hungry tonight?"

"Not much."

"Then don't drink too much because Kelton's got some news that'll brighten you up."

"Better news than Darla the masseuse?"

"Maybe so. Now I'm gonna bring out the potato salad."

Harry finished his drink and listened to the distant ruckus on the lake while Kelton and April set up the outdoor table. At dinner he pushed his food around on his plate and watched with satisfaction as April's children seemed to like their new father and only fussed a little when he sent them off to do their homework. As the last twilight edged into darkness April served coffee.

"I've found us this source," Kelton finally confided. "Cartwright told me about her. You know him, maybe: works at the magazines sometimes, knows all the cops, that guy. Anyway, she's kinda crazy and when you meet her don't get hung up on all her western clothes. She likes cowgirl shirts with fringe, the whole dude thing. I think she used to sing for some shitkicking band here in town."

"If she's supposed to be my new girlfriend, forget it. I'm in love with my wife and, besides, April's fixing me up with Darla."

"No, this woman works for the State Police. She's a technician and research person now because her husband got shot down while on highway duty. He was a patrolman who pulled somebody over down toward San Marcos, went up to the car window, and caught a bullet in the face. Died on the spot. So the police gave his wife a job and trained her. She hates all criminals and devotes herself to breaking the rules to get 'em. You with me?"

"You're talking about Leo."
"Why not? He's suspected of a crime."
"In a country far, far away."
"Maybe not. As you once said yourself, little girls also disappear here in Texas, don't they?"
"Kelton, old pal, you've been thinking on all this."
"Harry, either you get Leo—if what you know is true—or in his way he gets you."
"He's already cost me Zeta. Maybe that's irrational but it's how I feel."
"So I'll set it up with this cowgirl. By the way, I hear she's hefty. And I don't want to invite her to the Dog and Duck. Someplace fancy, I'm thinking, so our cause looks a bit more important."

Before that arrangement could take place Harry received a phone call from Jackie inviting him to lunch at Sullivan's.
"You look great," he told her as they unfolded their linen napkins, and she did look buoyant: a black dress and a Hermes scarf featuring burnt orange. The restaurant was somehow a comfort, a reminder of meals shared with the group.
"How're you doing?" she began.
"Not great. I think about Zeta all the time and I worry she's not okay."
"She's going to be a major success," Jackie responded, and it sounded vaguely spiteful. "She has great taste and talent and oddly enough we're now friends like never before."
A young waiter with a dark tan materialized at their table, smiling, and quickly took their orders for fancy salads. At nearby tables coveys of well-dressed women continued to wear their sunglasses indoors—it was a hot October noon—and Harry felt that he was being closely observed from behind all those dark frames.
"I'm glad I could help Zeta financially," Jackie went on when the waiter departed. "She'll pay me back. Have you seen Amnesia?"
"Yeah, last week. I have to tell you, Jackie, that

I'm a little pissed with you for financing Zeta so she could leave me. On the other hand, I love you for it."

"Of course you love me for it. Because you love her and want what she wants for herself. By the way, she asked me to invite you to this lunch."

"Oh? This is Zeta's idea?"

"Well, naturally, my pleasure. But at least ten women here today will see us together. And that matters. A few of them will probably phone me and I'll report that you've always been a dear friend—and still are, Leo's and mine—and also the most wonderful photographer in the city. You'll get the benefit of the doubt, I believe, and maybe even some new commissions."

"Ah ha," he replied, listening to the surrounding lunchtime chatter as it rose above the sound of plates and silverware.

"Everything is in the past, Harry, and now we're alive and well in Austin. What people think, that counts. You should have your portrait business intact—and of course your clever experimental art. Perhaps you'll meet someone new. And I can have my generosities. And, oh, look at this wonderful food around us. I'm starved, aren't you?"

"You are generous, Jackie, and thanks," he said, and he wanted to ask a dozen questions, but waited.

Without being prompted she answered one question immediately. "Leo and I aren't together. Maybe you've heard that."

"I heard, but wasn't sure. I've also heard that Robin left Olan."

"True, but she came back. You can see them yourself next weekend at my house. I'm giving a little lawn party and I hope you'll come."

"Will Zeta be down for it?" he asked hopefully.

"No, but I want to invite Kelton. Is he still with the stripper?"

"They're married and living out on the lake. And April hasn't been a stripper for years."

"I knew that, but I've really just wondered if such a marriage will—you know—hold up?"

"I saw them two nights ago. I believe they'll last a lot longer than some of the rest of us."

"Point taken. Anyway, invite them both if you see them. By the way, I'm happy enough that I won't be seeing much more of Wade and Val. He's so boring and I don't know why Leo always wanted Val in the group. The author thing, I suppose. But Zeta was always dead right about her: a terrible romance writer at best."

"I'll be there and bring Kelton and April," Harry promised. "Thanks for including me."

He still had questions to ask, but their salads arrived and they began eating. As he picked out wedges of veal he wondered if Zeta would show any of Jackie's bad paintings in the Dallas gallery.

"How was your Mexico trip?" he asked instead.

"Nice. Ever been to San Miguel?"

"Yeah, once, I heard you went with a bodyguard."

"Who told you that?"

"Can't remember. Did you?"

"Of course not. To protect me from whom?" She did a thing with her fork, a jerky little movement he had often seen that revealed her nervousness. Had he caught her in a lie?

They ate in silence for a moment until he ventured out with, "Don't you want to ask me, Jackie, what happened between Leo and me in Italy?"

"You accused him of murdering those little girls at the lake, but I assumed you were angry—that the two of you had some sort of argument—and for some reason you just blurted it out. By the way, did I tell you that Leo sold our villa?"

"Really? Did that disappoint you?"

"No, I always hated the place. And it was unfinished to the last."

"Why'd you hate it?"

"It was all pretension. As it was renovated Leo also grew more pretentious himself—or didn't you notice?"

"I know he wanted Zeta to furnish it with great art."

"Exactly. He once asked me if I knew the price of a Rembrandt."

"Can I ask something else?"

"Anything, Harry, and isn't this salad super?"

"Did Leo go back to Lake Como to sell the villa?"

"Go back personally? As a matter of fact, yes, he did. Why?"

"Oh, selling the villa—well, that's something an agent could do. But possibly there was something he wanted to retrieve. Or possibly hide."

Jackie paid close attention to her salad. Harry decided to go forward as if he actually knew a great deal.

"There's something else," he said. "I know you dropped that doll beside the path. The doll I found that morning that brought the detective to Madame Cappeletti's."

"Why would I do such a thing?" she asked, manufacturing a twitch of a smile and once again doing that thing with her fork. He knew somehow with certainty: yes, Jackie had placed that doll on the path.

"Maybe because it was one of many such dolls. Dolls that belonged to Leo."

Jackie placed her fork on the table and leaned forward, lowering her voice. "Harry, please, you must never repeat any of these things about Leo. Never again. If you do, you'll only manage to hurt yourself terribly. Word travels around the city. Please."

"Jackie, sweetheart, did we come here today so you can ask me to shut up?"

"Truly, Harry, this isn't for me. Or for Leo—who can always take care of himself, believe me. It's for you, Harry, because you need to get back to normalcy, back to your old self."

"You put the doll on the path," Harry went on gently, "because you know Leo's sick. There was something the police never found that Leo had to go back for. And you were afraid. You went to Mexico with a bodyguard and you still know too much. You're still afraid, but you're trying to smooth things over."

"You have a vivid imagination," said Jackie, recovering herself, but still twitching her fork and trying to get her smile to work. "You want to get Zeta back and you believe you can do it only if you can prove all your accusations against Leo."

"Actually, that's true," he admitted. "And you're being very brave coming here with me, Jackie, and I love you for it. You want to tell Leo that I've recanted. Because all of us who suspect too much or know too much are in danger, and –"

"Don't be silly."

"Jackie, you're afraid, don't say you aren't. But I won't put you—or myself—at risk anymore. Promise. To say these things about Leo, that's slander, I know it, and I want you as a friend. Okay? Am I still invited to the party?"

"Absolutely, dear heart."

"Leo's afraid, too. That's our advantage. He had a close call at Lake Como this year and now he doesn't know who knows or suspects what. If you want to, Jackie, tell him I know I was wrong about him. Want some dessert?"

"Dessert? Why not?" she said, recovering an airy smile and attitude. He could read the relief in her face, but she added, "And, Harry, I swear, I don't know half of what you're talking about."

She was present when they arrived, sitting in her Dale Evans outfit on a big leather couch beneath the mounted head of a Longhorn steer. Except for that mounted head the bar in the Driskell Hotel remained tasteful and traditional: big chairs, soft lamps, a grand piano, and an old fashioned pressed tin ceiling.

Tilly Britt sipped on a salty dog and had already finished a dish of mixed nuts as Harry and Kelton approached. She rose to greet them—plump and perfumed—and during introductions professed to know them both. "I've read your stuff a lot," she told Kelton, and he responded to the flattery with his familiar blush. She also claimed to know Harry's photographs, then proved it. "Girl on this sand dune," she said. "Trash all around. And somebody told me that the model became your wife."

"For lots of years," he confirmed. "Her name's Zeta."

They sat down to chat, starting with the hotel itself.

"My husband rented the Cattle Baron's Suite for our wedding night," she revealed. "Goddamn, the man loved me. I remember the big bed, the red drapes, and the fancy ceiling—which is about what I saw of the room, if you get my drift."

"I heard about your husband's death," said Harry. "Sorry."

"He woke up ev'ry mornin' mad as hell," she said with a laugh. "Hated anybody who broke the law. When he read the mornin' newspaper he got madder. When he got to work and heard what went on during the night shift he got furious. Cops, he said, held back a wall of shit so it didn't fall on the women and children."

"You believe that, too, don't you?"

"Abso-fucking-lutely," said Tilly.

By the time fresh drinks arrived Harry had indicated that their target was Leo Jones. Tilly geared up into her professional voice.

"Lemme put you straight. I'm sittin' here in my yellow boots, but I'm really a computer geek. And if you're goin' after somebody on a business deal I can't help. I just do criminal searches. So if somebody wants to tap into Leo Jones' financial profile he's gonna get a quick trace and know exactly who wants what."

"This is definitely criminal," Kelton assured her.

As they sipped their drinks they explained the murders in Italy and their suspicions.

"Boys, that's heavy," Tilly said with a sigh when they finished, and she turned to Kelton and fixed him with a crooked grin. "You go along with all this, do you?"

"I trust Harry and I do," he answered firmly.

Tilly cocked her head and considered Kelton, paying him deference, perhaps, because he was an established and reliable journalist and not just some crazy guy with a camera who took photos of naked girls out in the dunes. She also wanted to know how they started going to Lake Como and why—a place she'd never heard of—and how they came to know Leo. While they explained it she leaned back, crossed her boots, and finished off the second drink.

"Okay," she finally said. "I've sure as hell heard of Leo Jones and he's so rich he's gonna have his tracks covered. I mean, he's got lots of pals with major clout and any poking around about a criminal record he's gonna know about. If he tries to trace it back to me, I have to tell you he won't be successful because I cover my own tail pretty damn well. If you wanta know, I cheat. Any good law officer does and I do it better'n most. Anyway, it'll take a couple of days, but I damn near guarantee he's gonna show up clean."

They both said they appreciated the effort.

"Just curiosity," Harry added, "but could you also check a statistic? How many little girls under, say, twelve years of age disappear year to year in central and south Texas?"

"That'll be easy information. Sure, I'll get that too."

"We owe you," Kelton said.

"Not at all. Glad to help, but you're gonna get zero."

A day later Harry, April and Kelton went back to work on the sequence with the lights—not tiny flashlights this time, but small portable lasers. They built a space inside Harry's darkroom at home, talked about it all morning, then went for lunch at Rosa's Tex-Mex. There they speculated about Madame Cappeletti's weird son, wondering if he could possibly be the killer-in-residence at the villa. Kelton suggested that he fit the profile: a mama's boy, strong, secretive, never seen with girlfriends or boyfriends. They also wondered aloud if something besides the doll on the path might've brought Terminella to the villa, but they kept coming back to Leo, to the month of August, and Zeta's curious sighting at the waterworks. "Leo's the one," Harry said again, and he recalled Bernard's observation that darkness is a presence the same as light.

Back home alone that afternoon Harry stretched out to sleep off the Mexican beer when Zeta phoned.

He sprang to attention on the side of the couch when he heard her voice. They went through a few courtesies, then she asked him about the photos with the talcum and he told her, sure, he had them all, and that he had gone back to work that very day with Kelton and April on the new sequence.

"I'm thinking about a show with some great watercolors I've acquired and maybe some of your photos mixed in," she said.

He waited, hoping, until she went on.

"Are your talcum shots framed? And could you send them to me framed or not?"

"I'll drive to Dallas and deliver them," he volunteered.

"No, Harry, I really don't want to see you just now," she quickly answered and his hopes sank.

A brief silence.

"These watercolors I found," she said again, cheerfully. "They show the bare limbs of trees in winter with objects in the branches: bicycle wheels and things the eye has to discover. Super stuff."

Another silence as he tried to invent a pleasant response.

"Harry, do send the photos, please, they're really special and I think I can sell them. And if they aren't properly framed I'll do it for you—if you trust me to get it right."

"I've always trusted you," he said. "And, sure, I'll package them up and send them. By the way, you wouldn't consider coming down for Jackie's little lawn party, would you?"

"I just can't, darling, sorry, I'm far too busy."

Once again he recovered, telling her about his lunch with Jackie—omitting anything about Leo or Italy—and about Kelton's and April's house out on Lake Travis. They soon went into their goodbyes, sending one another love without great warmth, then afterward he added up his losses and gains.

She phoned me, he told himself, and she's thinking about me and my work. She also called me darling.

    In the dead of the Texas night you go driving and think about evil. It occurs elsewhere, you decide, and happens to strangers in distant cities and faraway countries and doesn't touch your life. Yet the dark of night is out there like a rebuttal: fields that contain the shallow graves of the missing, of all those bludgeoned and raped and stabbed and hidden in the ground. On summer nights these fields are lit by softball diamonds where the children gather for games, and the starlit sky intoxicates them and the earth calls to them although they don't yet know its true voice, and they hear only the crickets and nightbirds and the comforting sound of friendly voices. Later, much later, they recognize the deep sensual hum of their own bodies singing back to the earth, but for the very young the night dazzles their senses and they call out to their mothers, "Don't worry!" or "I'll be playing just over there!" never suspecting that the hunter draws near or that the cold earth awaits. Innocent softball nights and stops along the highway: a Dairy Queen playground illumined by a pale streetlight or an interstate rest stop where the father waits, smoking a cigarette, then finally goes timidly to the door of the women's toilet to call his daughter's name, getting no answer.
    Long after midnight, restless, you drive a stretch of dark highway listening for the voices of children no longer there. Bits of clothing cling to thorns near a fence row or in a culvert a small shoe waits for the seasons to change. These aren't my children, you say to yourself. These are the children of others, of aliens and strangers, of people far away from here.

    Tilly had a hick voice, easily recognizable: nasal with a touch of baritone, a raspy smoker's sound. She phoned to tell Harry that Leo Jones had no criminal record whatsoever, not even a speeding ticket.

"I went all the way back to juvenile court," she reported. "Maybe he later cheated on his taxes or skinned out some guy in business, but whatever he's done hasn't concerned the cops."

"He could've paid to take things off the books," Harry suggested.

"Oh sure, bribes happen. But I think you'll wanta give up the chase. And, oh yeah, that other matter. Little girls who disappear around here? We've had five in three years—which is about normal considering the population. We've also had tons of child abuse situations, but that's another category."

"Did Leo's wives ever accuse him of breaking the law? Maybe in divorce court records?"

"Another category again," said Tilly, getting bored with it.

He thanked her for her efforts.

As he dressed for Jackie's party he wondered if he might be crazy: a deep and obsessive dementia that had driven Zeta away. Then, again, he decided his intuitions were correct. There is no such thing as coincidence, he told himself. And lots of coincidence is hard evidence.

Giant live oak trees tapered down two acres of lawn toward the river and from Jackie's terrace one looked over a crowd of several hundred guests, tented bars, buffet tables, a barbeque pavilion, a western band, and roving waiters in orange jackets.

"Small, intimate gathering," Harry remarked to Kelton.

"Yep," Kelton answered, covering his mouth with his hand and doing his cowboy imitation.

"And did you see Leo over by the pool?"

"Yep," said Kelton, keeping it up.

"Does this mean Jackie and Leo are together again?"

"Nope, don't reckon so."

"I don't understand the rich," Harry confessed.

"Same kinda cattle run with each other," Kelton explained.

"Drop your drawl, okay?"

"It's the western band."

April stayed home with the kids that late afternoon so Harry and Kelton strolled around sipping beer and discussing Tilly's disappointing report. They leaned on the stone wall of the terrace noting who was present and who wasn't. No Wade or Val. No Olan or Robin. So far, one astronaut, one ex-football coach, one minor actress, and several legislators. Many middle aged women draped in too much jewelry.

"Who do you suppose they are?" Harry asked.

"Wives of legislators and art patrons," Kelton informed him. "Leo's giving a million dollars to some arts association this afternoon."

"How do you know this?"

"Gossip is history. And it grieves me there's no dirt on Leo. You figure on giving up the chase?"

"Don't want to, but I guess so. At the moment I can only think about Zeta."

"You believed that if you could nail Leo you'd win her back, right?"

"Maybe, I don't know anymore."

"You could get her back without all the trouble."

"If you say so."

"Look at that guy eating barbeque."

"Where?" Harry asked, and Kelton pointed out a squat little man with wavy hair who resembled Leo and fumbled with a plate overfilled with food.

"Gotta be one of Leo's brothers," said Kelton.

"I can't recall any of the brothers' names except Cooter."

At this moment Roper appeared, smiling and tanned. Although Kelton returned the smile, nodded, and exchanged courtesies he used the moment to withdraw. "Think I'll go find our hostess," he said, departing.

"Surprised to see you here," Roper told Harry.

"I was surprised to see Leo. You follow at his heels, don't you?"

"Fuck you, Harry."

"Fuck you, too."

That settled, Roper finished off his champagne and together they took a few deep breaths.

"You and Zeta still apart?" Roper inquired.

"Afraid so."

"I take no satisfaction in that."

"Thanks for saying it."

"And, Harry, Leo would like to see you this afternoon. He doesn't understand why you said that about him in Italy, but, hell, he likes you. He's always liked you."

"Did he tell you to come fetch me?"

"Of course. You could see him now. He's in the house talking to the arts people. In the study. He's giving them big money and they're giving him a plaque."

"So I heard." Harry thought about this overture. Keep your friends close, he decided, and your enemies closer.

"Should I go tell him you'll see him in the study?" Roper asked.

"Tell him I'll see him someday soon," Harry replied.

Harry went looking for Kelton, but found Jackie. She offered her cheek for a kiss and made a show of introducing him to a state legislator, a pudgy man with broken capillaries in his cheeks, a glowing whiskey face. Afterward Harry made his way toward the barbeque pavilion where the little man with all the hair—clearly Leo's kin—finished off a plate of tamales.

A breeze arrived, cooling and unlike the recent assault of autumn heat. The men could comfortably wear their jackets this evening and the women could wear stockings and sleeves, but, even so, the little man with the tamales stood covered with perspiration. He also had a vacant look in his eyes as if he only barely acknowledged the crowd and had appeared at the party solely to gorge.

Harry waited, uncertain of how to begin a conversation, and thoughts of Zeta leapt in, how she might enjoy this party on the river and how she might look: lips in a smirk yet smiling, eyes bright, very beautiful.

"Hey, guy, try these," said the little man, nodding at the plate he had filled again. Harry obliged.

"Big doings," Harry ventured, nodding at the crowd.

"Hell, Leo's givin' away a million bucks," said the man, and he shook his head in disbelief so that a trickle of sweat dived toward his nose.

Harry introduced himself and extended a hand.

"Nobby Weston here," came the reply, and the grip that found Harry's was hard as oak.

"Come again?" Harry asked, making sure.

The little man repeated the name then added, "You notice how all the gals here tonight are downright old? I mean, damn, I've checked out every old gal who's showed up for barbeque. That actress? I talked with her some and she's no spring chicken. Maybe art just ain't for the young. You meet that actress?"

"Didn't talk to her."

"Ever fucked an actress?"

Harry grinned, thought about that for a moment, and replied, "Yeah, I think so. I can't really remember."

This partial admission established Harry's masculine credentials and Nobby laughed, then ate another tamale. His topic became rich women: artists like Jackie, poetry lovers, and the horse set.

"You from around here?" Harry asked with a smile, exploring.

"Grew up in West Texas. Got a place now in the Davis Mountains. Ever been out there?"

"Nope, haven't," said Harry, concocting his own friendly drawl. "Always sounded like a pretty country."

" The altitude makes it a tad cooler. Lotsa trees. Most of the land is state park, but money buys you in. Or used to, anyhow. As Leo proves, money and pull always gets it done."

Harry agreed, smiling, and took the opportunity. "You come see your brother much?" he ventured.

"Not really. I reckon I'm an embarrassment. But I told Jackie I was crashin' her little hoedown and here I am."

"How could you be an embarrassment?" Harry asked, pushing on.

"Well, like this art thing. Leo now fancies he likes art. Lemme tell you. I saw this big painting out in—let's see, it was in Pecos. Know how the painter did it? This was maybe forty years ago, and this painter squeezed out tubes of paint—you know, like toothpaste—and laid on big globs of colors that intersected. Guess how much for this? I heard it got valued at millions of dollars and I'm not talkin' just thousands. I mean millions."

Harry shook his head in mock dismay. Jackson Pollock in Pecos?

He listened to Nobby's new topic: coyotes that preyed on the cattle out west. Harry nibbled at a mini-taco, but his nerve ends were singing with new information and he could scarcely pay attention. In a short time Leo's brother returned to the favorite family topic, the pursuit of women, and it occurred to Harry that Leo had perfected a predator's game and that Nobby still chased down conquests in the old fashioned way.

"It's a sad damn shame when a mature guy like me starts payin' attention to food and gives up hittin' on the gals," he said earnestly. "I mean, I've checked out the Mexican help, that ole gal that plays fiddle in the band, and I guess I'll go back to the actress. You know actresses start out in classes where they take off their clothes and do love scenes? None of 'em have inhibitions. Same as hospital nurses. Show me yours and I'll show you mine. And play acting can get personal real quick. My problem has been meetin' some actresses. So I crashed this shindig hopin' to meet this gal, but I think her best years might be way back. I bet she's had five husbands by now."

"Leo know you've crashed?"

"Hell no. That's why I'm stayin' out here by the barbeque and tamales."

Harry started moving away as if he regretted going. Nobby had a new topic—high school football and the majorettes of yesteryear—but held up a taco in farewell.

When Harry found Kelton again he pulled him aside.

"Well, that was definitely Leo's brother, Nobby, and I've got a new angle of attack. The family name isn't Jones."

"It isn't?"

"Not if brothers have the same family name. I had him give me his name twice just to make sure. I think I'll try Tilly again."

"I doubt she'll help you," Kelton said. "And Leo wants to see you. Maybe you should go say hello."

"No way," said Harry.

"Harry, be rational. And pragmatic."

"And let this thing go? Can't do it, old buddy."

Zeta phoned to say she liked the photographs and that they framed beautifully. In turn, Harry suggested that he should come to the opening and charm potential buyers. "I still have charm," he assured her.

"Oh? Says who?"

"It's well known. Talked about everywhere."

He knew she was smiling at the other end of the call, yet she didn't invite him to Dallas. Later, though, he concluded, okay, she's still thinking about me, she bothered to phone, she cares.

"You again," said Tilly, greeting him with something less than a smile.

She wore jeans, an embroidered shirt, and soft black boots. Harry ambushed her at the coffee machine on her break: uniformed cops passing by, a nearby bulletin board crowded with rules and regulations, and the distant male voices of state police headquarters.

"I've come courting," he said. "Any chance?"

"Didn't you once use me and toss me aside?"

"I can offer lunch. Chicken fried steak or such delicacies."

"C'mon back here," she said, and Harry followed her back to an alcove filled with plastic chairs and formica covered tables. She fired up a Marlboro and allowed her paper cup of coffee to sit there.

"What kinda books you read?" she began.

"You go first."

"Okay, let's see. Jim Crumley's a favorite. Also Robert B. Parker. Anyway, I read a lot of mystery and cop novels and I figure you do the same because you're a sucker for detective shit and want to practice the art yourself."

"You're a whiz," he told her.

"Harry, listen to me. So you peek into a guy's records and you get something that looks incriminating. But what you have is circumstantial bullshit at best. Nothin' definitive. Lemme tell you what I do. I'm a tracer, mainly, and I can find damn near anybody. At present I'm tailing a big black—and I mean big—who started a killin' spree as soon as he got paroled. We call him Black Rider. He went into a bar down at Loyola Beach, drank himself two beers, then broke the bottles and started in. Killed two and wounded three. He even took a coupla bullets for his trouble, but never slowed down. This case, Harry, is more or less urgent. What you want on Leo Jones is more or less private speculation without priority."

"I don't think his name's really Jones."

"How'd you come to that?"

"His brother's family name is Weston. They grew up someplace in the Fort Stockton or Davis Mountains area. Naturally, there could be different fathers involved. But somehow I don't think so."

Tilly took a long draw on her cigarette. "So you want me to start again?"

"My wife's in Dallas and won't come home," said Harry. "She thinks I'm a fool for these suspicions—and I know they're true. My best friend's beginning to give up on me. Nobody believes me except me. Can I bribe you with something?"

"Not chicken fried steak and not money," she replied. "Lemme ask you. Did you cheat on your wife?"

"Never. And at the moment my heart's broken if that matters."

"Did she run away with some other guy?"

"No, she opened an art gallery. And she thinks I've gone crazy."

"Because of Leo Jones?"

"Weston," he said, and he spelled it for her. "And the name's really vanilla, not ethnic and not some terribly embarrassing or unpronounceable name, so why would he want to change it unless he's hiding something?"

"There's goin' to be a mother and two fathers involved in this."

"Maybe, maybe not."

Tilly nudged her cold cup of coffee with a fingernail painted silver. "Suppose you found something? Say it convinced you more than ever that he molested children? What would you do about it?"

"Go to the cops, I guess, but that's troublesome. The crimes—if they occurred—happened in Italy and I know the cops here might be reluctant."

"Good, you've thought this through," Tilly pointed out. "Even if you tell your story to detectives here they'll be slow and probably ineffective. You'll get more frustrated than ever. Since it's Leo Jones they'll also probably say you're nuts and tell Leo about you. As I see it, you'll never win this."

Harry twisted in his plastic chair.

"Now I do love a man who loves his wife," she went on. "My husband loved me that way. Never cheated. That's a rare guy and I think maybe you're one. Also, I hate killers. My work—and I know this sounds corny—is a devotion. I take killers off the streets, mean bastards like the one who gunned down my beautiful husband and diabolical ones like whoever's killin' the little girls in Italy. But, Harry, I can't help you again. I gotta go find Black Rider before the day passes. I can't spend computer time and phone calls speculatin' about your rich pervert."

Harry started a rebuttal, but Tilly gathered up her cold coffee and left the alcove. In the hallway as Harry followed her she turned to him.

"Now don't you tell a soul I helped you in the first place. My methods are unorthodox, Harry, and not too legal. It would mean my job. Also, your pal Kelton would be in the shit with us, understand?"

"You have my word," he promised.

She then gave him a direct look with something in her expression she perhaps meant to conceal. "Weston?" she added. "Fort Stockton. Yeah, it would be damned peculiar for a man with a name like that to want it changed. Had to be two fathers involved, doncha think?"

A week later Leo ran afoul of some business partners and the news broke into the local newspapers and found coverage at the television stations. Roper appeared before the cameras to explain previous explanations and to defend his client. Leo had seemingly sold some properties that he didn't legally own and then wouldn't give back millions of dollars invested by his partners. Lawsuits were filed and a few physical threats were issued. One partner, formerly an Aggie linebacker, said, "I'd like to hold him up by all that hair of his and beat his ears off." Another partner's wife checked into a hospital, mourning, as someone observed, her husband's money.

On a bright Saturday morning late in the month Harry arrived at Kelton's and April's to house sit. They were driving up to Arkansas—keeping the kids out of school for a week—to visit April's mother and to show off her new husband. Harry joined Kelton on the deck for coffee and Leo became the topic.

"How crooked you reckon he is?" Kelton asked.

It was a journalist's question, the sort Kelton often posed, but Harry had only a cryptic reply. "No billionaire gets it out of plain luck," he said.

Kelton nodded, paused, then asked, "How about your investigations?"

"I went to see Tilly again and told her about the difference in names. She says she won't help anymore."

"You know, Harry, I've been considering—just what if, I mean—what if you're right about Leo. And know what? If you're right or wrong he's real mad at you. In fact, you could be in a bit of danger."

"Yeah, Zeta said the same thing once. And the thought's occurred to me."

"Has Leo ever called or asked to see you?"

"Nope. Wanted to see me, you recall, at Jackie's party."

"C'mon, I want to show you something."

Harry followed him indoors, but on the way April intercepted them with a hand written list for Harry.

"Pay special attention to this item about the rear burners on the kitchen stove," she instructed him. "Everything else is pretty simple: where we store the extra tissue and all that. But those back burners don't light automatically, so use a match."

"I won't be cooking," Harry answered. "Where's the microwave?"

"It's the big white thing built into the cabinets. You can't miss it."

The list contained about thirty items and she delivered it with a kiss on his cheek before going off to urge the children to pack.

"In here," said Kelton, leading them into the study. At an oak filing cabinet he opened a drawer and invited Harry to look inside.

"What?" Harry asked.

"The pistol."

"That's maybe the smallest weapon I ever saw."

"It's my entire arsenal. A .22 caliber and inaccurate as hell. If I aimed at your heart at a yard distance I'd probably blow off a kneecap."

"Glad I know where you keep the firepower."

"Let's be serious, Harry, okay? If you're right about Leo or wrong about him we can assume this: he plays rough. Our group as far as he's concerned is past tense. He also may know by now that you talked with his brother, that you had lunch with Jackie, and maybe that you met with Tilly. If he knows any of it, he worries about what you're saying and what people believe of it. He's got to worry, Harry, because he'd be a fool not to. And he'll have to come after you. If he's what you say he is—and, Harry, I don't know one way or another—he'll come after you himself. If your accusations are true, he'll find you like he found Terminella, won't he? So here's my little pistol in this soft leather holster. Put it on your belt, okay?"

"Kelton, you know me. I'm the passive type. I hide behind a camera and take pictures. I can't start packing firearms."

"Put it on your belt. Keep it by your bedside while you stay here."

"It'll be here when I need it. Thanks."

April appeared to announce that everything was ready to pack in the car. She offered to go over the list, but Harry declined.

"Tell me about your mother," he asked instead.

"When she was a teenager she ran a roadhouse on the Oklahoma border. Now she smokes too much. She loves my kids. And she still thinks she's hot, so she'll probably try to seduce Kelton and take him away from me."

"My kind of chick," Harry said, grinning.

"Now here's some advice," she said. "Phone Zeta every day. If she says she's too busy and tells you not to call, phone anyway."

He gave her a goodbye hug and whispered in her ear, "Good advice. Thanks."

In the driveway April's son warned Harry to stay out of his room and not to borrow the videos, so Harry touched his heart and promised. After they drove away Harry went back to the deck with the last of the coffee, looked over the expanse of the lake, tried to think of Como, but in this rocky and arid landscape found it impossible.

After midnight once again you drive the backroads: a dark time for dark thoughts.

All over the world the nights are filled with monsters, but what do you do? You personally? Your thoughts fuse into a simple solution: I have to kill the beast.

Yet murder is a dirty business and becomes cancer, of course, that eats away at the human heart.

Murder—even for the sake of a satisfying justice—is still murder. And you wonder if Tilly, deep in her own vengeful obsession with killers on the loose, sensed that you might be a potential killer, so decided not to help you again for that reason.

Yet the professional detectives are reluctant, slow, sometimes incompetent, and sometimes bribed. Leo's money might have already bought the investigators on two continents. They never recovered the doll in Italy and their attentions seemed to bog down. An indifferent search of Leo's villa, a failure to get any DNA, a lassitude: they were at the end of a long, tiring day, and they allowed their suspect to fly off. And now Black Rider is out there, dozens like him, mad dogs and monsters, and what do our overworked detectives care for a more subtle killer in a faraway land? He is, after all, a rich man with a disgruntled friend.

You drive the backroads, headlights catching the eyes of frightened rabbits, and Kelton's warning rides with you. In your meditations you wonder how to find the monster in his sleep. You wonder if you can employ some elaborate and clever trickery, some strategy previously unknown in police annals or in the ornate plots of detective fiction? What trickery? What brilliant schemes?

Yet you know yourself well enough: you're no predator. Time has shown you that the timid camera holds you in focus. So the monster roams and searches; it finds its victims in the gathering shadows; and the truth gnaws at you, saying, if you aren't a predator, dear soul, then you're the prey, it's one or the other.

When he phoned Zeta he got her new answering machine. Amnesia, said the voice, not even hers, and he thought, how true, how true.

All his memories became Zeta: her laughter at Val's miscues, how she turned away that time to slip on her panties, how she seemed to love the talcum photos, how she gave him the last deep kiss they shared.

One afternoon he drank a six-pack of Shiner beer. Then an unusual paranoia set in: stay sober, he warned himself, Leo is going to call.

He advertised his business for sale.

It was the first week in November when a sleet storm arrived, then quickly passed. As usual a Texas cold snap lasts only a day, then the gulf humidity surges back in. For that few hours of chilly weather, though, Harry drove back to his place and picked up his windbreaker. As he tossed it in his car an ATM card fell out and he picked it up with slow realization: the Italian bank card Leo had provided for all the men that day after golf. Quick on this knowledge came a second realization: Zeta wore this windbreaker the morning she visited the waterworks. Leo hadn't followed a signal from a fake Rolex; he had followed a directional signal out of the bank card. When the Italian police inspected the Rolex and found nothing that became a persuasive argument against Harry's claims.

At his mailbox he picked up the contents—mostly advertisements -- then drove back to Kelton's lake house wondering if he could find a local expert who might confirm the presence of a directional microchip in the card, an additional proof. Adrenalin hammered through his veins, his nerves singing.

At the lake house he wore the windbreaker—was there a hint of Zeta still inside it?—and drank a beer out on the deck. Unsettled weather, the threat of something in the air, the gigantic lake grey and restless. In the kitchen he piled up thin sliced turkey for a sandwich, adding cheese, and while he nuked it in the microwave he went through the mail. And there it was: a letterhead from the State Police.

Tilly had sent him a report.

Leo Jones Weston had legally dropped his last name after a long series of juvenile offenses. Before he turned sixteen he had twice been arrested and questioned for child molestation, both cases dropped by parents of the children with no convictions. At age seventeen he had been arrested with his older brother Cooter for kidnapping. They had held a ten-year-old girl against her will for eleven hours before she had escaped. The brother served six months in prison and once again charges against Leo had been withdrawn at the request of the girl's parents. Later that year Leo had been stopped in his pickup truck with a young girl, age undetermined, who was eventually identified as a Mexican prostitute. Leo was charged with reckless driving in that case and fined. Again that year he had been accused of exposing himself at a movie theater, but before charges were complete he left the state of Texas.

Evidence. Before the age of eighteen, clearly, Leo was a potential pedophile.

At Kelton's copy machine Harry duplicated the report, replete with letterhead, leaving one copy in the oak filing cabinet and stuffing the other in his overnight bag.

He wanted to drive up Interstate 35 to Dallas and thrust it into Zeta's hands, but he hesitated.

What do you do about evil?

The terrible damning truth: little or nothing.

You repeat the mantra: it exists far away among strangers. A genocide that flares up like wildfire then burns out. A brutal police state. A killer stalking somebody else's city. If evil insinuates itself into your own family or neighborhood you usually avert your eyes. Human nature is essentially good, you tell yourself, and the aberrations are so rare that one can close his eyes, keeping them tightly shut, knowing that such mean and deliberate horrors will soon disappear. The monster will be gone in the morning light or someone else will fight it or it was a nightmare illusion, never real.

You drive these backroads unable to sleep and wanting only your sweetheart, your wife, your dearest friend, and when you see her again you'll maybe tell her that evil doesn't exist. You'll omit the obvious, that all history is bloody murder: atrocities committed out of sexual craziness, out of greed, out of religious idiocy, out of whimsy. There are no barbarians, you'll maybe tell her, and no monsters.

Yet she knows and you know. Around our violent nature swirls a mythic aura and we love it: our football, our boxing, our movies, our wars. We celebrate this truth about ourselves helplessly because the juice inside us is the blood of schizophrenics and like the toxic venom of the black widow it's far more powerful than anything required to protect ourselves, to live out our lives or to fulfill most of our ambitions. Like that little spider its chemistry is a thousand times stronger than necessary and perhaps in some deep genetic way the toxin helps us to create and imagine, perhaps it gives us some odd psychic or physical benefit, but it's also an overdose, deadly to those who come near, deadly to ourselves.

Call it testosterone.
Call it the wicked gene.
Call it paradox.

He still wanted somebody to examine that Italian bank card—he even consulted the Yellow Pages—when his cell phone rang. It was Leo.

Here it is, he told himself.

The familiar voice, rich with good cheer, said, "Harry, where the hell are you? I want you to get out on my new boat this afternoon. You and me and Olan. You got time for us?"

His thoughts tripped along and he said, "Sure. Isn't the weather still nippy?"

"Bring a jacket. We're going out on Lake Travis. Where are you, anyway?"

"As a matter of fact, I'm already on Lake Travis. I'm sitting Kelton's place while he and April are gone."

"Perfect. Has he got a dock?"

"No, his house is up on a cliff. But I can meet you at a marina. You say where."

"Maybe you could meet us at the boat. We'll be at this little private marina out Haynie Road. Know where that is?"

"I can find it," said Harry, playing the game. "Start me off with directions."

With some of the old enthusiasm in his voice Leo obliged, having Harry write down a series of turns. "We'll cruise until suppertime. I know this great new place where we can tie up and get a steak."

"It's good hearing from you, Leo," Harry lied. "Are we okay?"

"Harry, you went nuts on Lake Como, but lemme tell you, we're fine. I wanted to see you at Jackie's party, but we missed. We'll talk about things tonight after Olan leaves us, okay?"

Olan, Harry knew very well, wouldn't show up.

"When do you want me?" Harry asked, and they set a rendezvous.

Harry borrowed a heavy sweater from Kelton and put on the windbreaker. Because of the late afternoon and with the lingering cool weather the lake would be virtually empty of other boaters. A reservoir of the Colorado River as it stair-stepped into the highlands west of Austin, the lake moved between steep hills and passed many hidden coves, and Leo's proposed journey would take considerable time—en route to a restaurant, Harry knew, that was probably a fiction.

He drove about thirty miles up the lake then cut toward the water on a series of farm roads, found Haynie Road, and followed it, as instructed, to its end. The private marina was little more than a sturdy dock set on a jut of stone in the middle of nowhere, but the boat itself was a floating castle, white trimmed with chrome, with a spacious pilot's cabin, a fly bridge up top, and a mast flying the American and Texas flags.

He was there because he was afraid. Even if your best instinct is to run, he knew, sometimes you go to the cave and meet the creature head on.

Leo hailed him from the deck. His hair had grown to an exaggerated length so he looked like a miniature lion. He had a drink in his hand.

"Hey, the cabin's warm! Come aboard!"

Harry stepped up on the gunwale then down on the deck.

"Cast off that line, okay?" Leo's tone was

lighthearted and eager. "Olan can't make it. It's just the two of us!"

No surprise. Harry managed the line, stuck out a foot and shoved off as Leo started the engines.

They turned away from the dock, the hum of the engines echoing off sharply rising limestone cliffs surrounding the cove. Leo wore overalls and at the wheel looked experienced and capable, as always, chatting away.

"I haven't actually bought this baby yet," he said, raising his voice above the engines. "But I will. What I'm going to show you is the land I've bought. Since we're not going back to Como—for one damn reason or another -- I've decided to put up a lodge out here. I can use it for conferences, you know, it's all write-off."

He leased a boat for the occasion, Harry told himself. And has my car parked in one of the most remote spots on the lake. And he wore disposable clothing.

"Did I spoil Lake Como for you?" Harry ventured.

"Nah, not at all. If you want to get that topic outta the way, sure, we can do it. You were always a pal, Harry, and you've got a soft center. That's not a criticism. But you started thinkin' about little girls goin' missing, you know, and your imagination and your sympathies kicked in. We were all drinkin' too much. There were tensions. For Chrissakes, Kelton runs off with Roper's girlfriend. Jackie ups and leaves. Olan and Wade get old on us. Our fuckin' restaurant catches fire! Val blabbers on! That detective gets himself killed. Then you start blamin' everybody. Even Zeta goes nuts and says she sees me followin' her. The whole show breaks down, Harry, and my goddamned villa ain't finished, not that I mind the money, but holy shit, they should get the plaster done!"

"It was a strange time," Harry admitted.

"So we hafta get over it, correct? I got partners who wanta screw me. And Jackie to worry about. I know you got pissed off that night at Villa d'Este, but, hell, it was Olan or the goddamned waiter, wasn't it? And I know you got pissed off that I offered Zeta some work, but Jackie was gone and, shit, I needed a little consultation."

"Maybe I was out of line," Harry conceded, not meaning it.

"We all step on toes. But we gotta be resilient. This property I wanta show you is just up here another mile or so."

It figured: Leo wouldn't want to be seen on the lake for long. As they moved alongside limestone cliffs dotted with cedars and scrub oak Harry felt the certainty of something coming. Having once killed a mature male—Terminella—Leo would do this job himself, confident of success, but how exactly?

Not another boat in sight. High on the cliffs elaborate houses gazed out on the hill country, but the lake below—narrow in this stretch—couldn't be seen.

A curious dizziness came over Harry, just a momentary sense that somehow Lake Como and Lake Travis were connected through the netherworld: a subterranean connection where little bodies floated among blind predators in a whirlpool of black water. The vision passed and Leo's voice took over again.

Leo was talking about Wade and his clinic, rambling on, and Harry gathered that the disputed property between Leo and his partners might actually be Wade's. Afternoon shadows turned the surrounding water to ebony.

It occurred to Harry to ask a question that bothered him. "Leo, tell me. You never much liked Wade. Or for that matter, Olan. We've all asked ourselves why you took us on. I mean, why not a few really rich pals?"

Leo stayed at the wheel, his back to Harry. They turned with the current. Out in the lake the Colorado River moved in an undulating flow, creating eddies and more pronounced waves as it made its way toward Mansfield Dam. Harry waited for an answer.

"Why not a few rich pals?" Leo finally repeated. "Because business and pleasure don't really mix. Because those bastards aren't pals, not ever, they just wanta skin you out and you wanta do the same to them. As for our little group, hey, I was fucking all the wives and girlfriends, wasn't I? What'd you think?"

The boat seemed to shudder beneath them. Did he mean Zeta, too?

"Why not say it outright?" Leo went on. "Wade sorta knows, but doesn't want to admit it. Val's over the hill, true, but totally crazy—and crazy women, Harry, there's no fuck like 'em. Olan and Robin, they're gonna split up, so why keep things secret anymore? Now there's some prime pussy, little Robin. Jackie caught us once, you know, and maybe caught us again this last summer because I'm not completely sure why she went home. Kelton's lady, Isabella, she put out a half dozen times, and of course I sampled April before Roper agreed to bring her along this year and with luck I'll sample her again. You and Zeta are split, so what's to hide?"

"I don't believe any of this shit," Harry said.

Leo turned, his mouth tight with anger. "But I'm not lying, Harry. Would I lie to you about this?" Then a smile broke over his face. "C'mon, lighten up. I've been in love with Zeta and her body since those first photographs you sold me. I mean, hell, you put her on display, didn't you?"

That was true and it hurt, but Harry didn't reply.

"Harry, c'mon, think about it. That night you found Zeta and me in the lounge? You think we were talkin' about art? She likes to talk dirty, Harry, and you know it. Don't hold a grudge. She has more fun than you do. You're a fuckin' puritan in a lotta ways and that whole thing with the portraits when you accused everybody, shit, that proved it. Wanta know somethin' else? Robin was the best of the lot. Has that big bush and she can shake it. You shoulda tried some of that, Harry, and you woulda looked forward to your trips to Italy a hell of a lot more."

"All bullshit," Harry answered.

"Hey, be cool. Here we are. This is the spot I wanta show you."

Leo steered into a shadowed cove lined with oak and cedar, its water black, limestone rising like canyon walls all around them, and from the shore came an odor of rotting wood and the brackish puddles along a narrow beach. Leo edged the craft into shadows where the air turned suddenly cold: the breath of ghosts.

Harry prepared himself.

His hands were shaking.

"This here's a deep cove," Leo said, his back still turned to Harry as he manned the wheel. "Maybe seventy feet down. But I want you to look straight up from the port side. There's an outcrop of boulders up there. That's where I intend to build. See 'em?"

"Maybe," Harry said, keeping his eyes on Leo.

"I wanted to show you this, Harry, 'cause I really think you need to see it."

When Leo turned, Harry saw the object in his hand: a long corkscrew stretched out into a slender dagger, its curls almost straightened: the weapon used on little children, Harry knew, and on Terminella, and now meant to be used on him.

Except Harry pointed Kelton's little .22 pistol at Leo's head.

His hand failed to keep the barrel of the gun steady. He wished he had his camera so he could capture a photo of that weapon, a proof.

He wasn't meant to aim a pistol.

Split seconds remained.

Leo smiled and started to say something, but Harry didn't want to listen.

When he pulled the trigger the cove filled up with sound and became a chamber of echoes.

Leo sat down like a child falling backward, his legs stiff. His eyes flashed with astonishment then went blank.

A curiously accurate shot. The bullet went straight into the forehead. The corkscrew dagger lay on the deck and as Harry's ears stopped ringing he heard a bird's call from high on the cliffs, a single plaintive note.

He sat down on the gunwale.

Blood trickled into Leo's mane of hair.

A long period passed, so that sunlight on the cliffs overhead faded. Harry's fingers trembled and the chill of the shadowed cove entered his bones, but for some time he couldn't think. Then he got up and studied what he had done. Carefully, he turned the body and inspected the wound. To his surprise the bullet hadn't made an exit, so it was still in there, and much of the bleeding had ceased.

He showed me the weapon, he kept repeating to himself. Showed it to me and meant to use it. I had to pull the trigger. I had to.

The anchor—maybe forty pounds of it in a bell shape—lay in a coil of unattached rope in the stern. Harry found a pair of leather gloves at the wheel, put them on, then measured the anchor rope by pulling out several lengths. His estimate: about sixty feet.

He dropped the anchor over the side, paying out the rope until he could verify Leo's statement about the depth of the cove, and discovered that the anchor never reached bottom. Hauling it back up, he wrapped the body in soggy rope and tied it off around Leo's neck.

The black waters of that cove went down and down, he saw once more, and joined the glacial depths of Lake Como: the terrible darkness of lost children.

A few last moves. He took six hundred dollars from Leo's wallet. He felt like sending that peculiar murder weapon back to Benzetti in Italy via Federal Express, but tossed it over the side. Then he wrestled the body onto the gunwale—only a little blood and Leo's hair had soaked it up—and with the anchor at last in place he pushed everything over into the center of the cove.

The boat remained. He thought about where he had stood, what he had touched, and wiped everything down with his windbreaker. Then he started the engines and headed back. Turning around in the cove was awkward, but he made it, and as he steered out of its shadows relief swept over him. In the last pale streaks of sunset he headed back up the lake and at his destination, again, his ability as a pilot faltered; he banged into the dock, killed the engines, started again, backed up, and finally leapt over the side to tie off.

A last inspection. Nothing of Leo's anywhere. He took the gloves to dispose of them.

Twilight arrived quickly, the whole landscape darkening. With his windbreaker off and the night's chill coming on, he shook all over. Kelton's pistol would go back in the drawer minus a bullet. Leo's wallet and keys would disappear.

He entered the sanctuary of his car, turned on the heater and drove away. He felt absolutely no regret. And Leo had lied about Zeta, that he knew: a lie of spite and murderous anger.

In two days Kelton, April and the children returned and the next morning the newspapers announced the disappearance of Leo Jones. Leo's big SUV had been found at an obscure dock thirty miles west of the city and foul play was suspected. A business partner—the one who had previously commented he'd like to beat Leo's ears off—refused comment. Kelton read the articles, phoned his friends in the press, talked to Roper, and finally called Harry.

"What do you think?" Kelton asked.

"Oh hell, he'll show up," Harry answered.

"The police have got some sort of forensic evidence they're not talking about."

"What sort of evidence?"

"Leo's vehicle was parked by this fancy leased boat. There was some evidence that violence occurred."

"Good," Harry said. "Maybe he's at the bottom of Lake Travis."

"Roper's upset about it."

"Of course. If Leo's gone, Roper's out of a job."

"You phoned Zeta?"

"Every day. I get an answering machine. It's not even her voice."

"April says you should go see her. Appear at her door."

"Maybe in a week or so. If Leo's really gone, maybe that'll make a difference."

He waited, instead, another six days, then Zeta phoned him. By that time, clearly, Leo was gone and the newspapers carried reports of his assets and debts. Zeta asked a dozen questions for which Harry had no answers, then he said he had something to show her and wanted to come visit.

"Something to show me? What?"

"You have to see it."

"Maybe you could come up late tomorrow night," she suggested, and her words were like an elixir so that he almost laughed out loud.

"You'll have to give me directions. Remember, I don't know where you live."

"Go to the gallery and phone this number I'll give you. I only live a few blocks from there and I'll direct you."

A few short blocks from Amnesia.

He went to the Dog and Duck with Kelton for beers and burgers later that day. They talked about another case in the news: a known killer had been gunned down by police at a roadblock on the border. As it happened the fugitive was unarmed, so an investigation was underway.

"The last time I saw Tilly she told me about that guy. She called him Black Rider. He was a major priority, so she said she couldn't help me."

"Rough justice," Kelton said, sipping his beer.

"How's that?"

"It happens all the time. The police have a knack for saving the court system trouble. In my time I've heard dozens of stories."

"You mean the cops don't play fair?"

"Not usually. Only Dick Tracy played fair."

"I think Columbo played fair."

"Never," Kelton assured him.

Harry kept buying beer, trying to drink the day away, trying to reach tomorrow so he could drive to Dallas and Zeta. He had gossip for Kelton and possibly a confession, but said nothing. In the sawdust and beer smells of the bar with his old friend a feeling of warmth came over him.

Normality was out there, he knew, and he meant to find it again.

He drove to Dallas the next afternoon, doing

eighty or better with other insane drivers heading up Interstate 35, all thoughts and regrets obliterated in the competitive traffic. Back in the Oak Lawn section of the city he found the gallery again, phoned, then followed instructions to Zeta's apartment. She lived in a compound of upscale condos surrounding a garden with soft lawn sprinklers.

She met him at the door with a smile and he entered a room of familiar objects: the rug that once lay beside their bed, the matching brass lamps, the figurine. Nothing of himself. No photographs. A couple of new abstract paintings on the walls.

She offered the sofa and he slumped down with the folder in his hand, declining a drink.

"You always have a drink after a long drive. Not even a glass of wine?"

"Not right now," he said, and she took the big chair across from him. She wore a white dress shirt with jeans and her hair had gone ash blond.

"Something to show me?" she asked, glancing at the folder.

"When you read this," he said, "you don't have to say anything. It'll be the last time I'll ever bring the subject up. It's about Leo. Whose real name is Leo Jones Weston."

"Oh, Harry, please."

"Just take a look. It's getting late and you're right, I'm tired."

He gave her the folder and she opened it. Time like a palpable presence entered the silence between them as she read Tilly's report. He could see the *comballis* sailing the smooth waters of Lake Como, the ancient stone walls, the old villas and terraced vineyards surrounded by mulberry trees: centuries of gory history. Barbarossa and the fishermen warriors of Gravedona. The evil eye. The faces one tries to read.

With the document still spread across her knees Zeta looked at him. Then she started reading it again, her finger tracing over the letterhead, taking in its authority.

"So," she finally said, looking up. "I suppose you were right in what you thought."

"Maybe," he said. "We'll never know or have to know, will we?"

"What do you think happened to Leo?"

"He had a lot of enemies." She nodded in response and he added, "And he can't matter to us ever again."

They had seen a lot of the world together, moving among friends who weren't really their friends, among mirrors held up to mirrors and masks to masks, but now he forgave Zeta if she needed forgiving and took her forgiveness for himself. Did he know his own wife? Maybe not. She didn't want the brutalities too close; she wanted to escape into her aesthetic and perhaps to see him wrapped up in his own: colors, contours, shades of light and darkness, and the conversations of a gallery existence. No monsters, no more missing children, no Leo.

"Are you going to show this to anybody?" she asked.

"Just you. Then I'll tear it up because it doesn't matter."

"Good," she said with a sigh.

"I think I've sold the business," he said.

"Really? How'd we do?"

"I'll probably lose on some of the equipment, but the building looks like it'll bring four times what we paid for it."

"That's wonderful. What'll you do with yourself?"

"Take pictures. Probably move out of Austin. Right now I'm dead tired. I think I'll go get that drink and find myself a hotel. I hope we see each other tomorrow."

"Harry," she said, raising her eyes to his. "It's already getting late. Let's have a glass of wine together. Just sleep here tonight. Sleep with me."